THE MALL of CTHULHU

SEAMUS COOPER

NIGHT SHADE BOOKS
SAN FRANCISCO

First Edition

ISBN: 978-1-59780-127-0

Night Shade Books
Please visit us on the web at
http://www.nightshadebooks.com

THE MALL of CTHULHU

To my father.

PROLOGUE

1993

L aura woke up nauseous, disoriented, and covered in blood. This last fact was not immediately apparent to her, which is why she focused on Teddy, who was standing across the common room emptying a gasoline can onto the floor.

"Teddy?" she asked. Teddy? That kind of geeky kid who was Steve's roommate? The kid who wanted to study folklore? The one everybody in the dorm called "Shaggy"?

At the sound of his name, Teddy paused from his pouring and looked up. "Oh my God, Laura, are you alive? Are you okay?"

She had that feeling that she had just awoken from a really good dream. It was coming back to her. Camilla. Camilla had kissed her, had licked her lips, and had asked her, "Do you want it?"

Laura had assumed that the "it" Camilla had been referring to was the same "it" that kids in dorms all over campus were getting at exactly that moment. She had been about to say yes when everything went black.

As her mind fought through the fog of disorientation, it occurred to her that everything had actually gone red. She wondered what that meant. And now here she was, still on

1

the red velvet couch in the Omega Alpha house, but with no Camilla and with Ted pouring gas on the floor.

"Uh, I guess I'm okay. What the hell's going on? Where's Camilla?"

Ted shook the last few drops of gas out of the can, stood up and looked at Laura. "She didn't bite you, did she?"

"Uh, I don't think so. I mean, I just wish, but…"

"I'm completely fucking serious, Laura. Did she bite you?"

"I don't remember. I don't think so. What happened to her? I think we were going to… I mean hey, it's Bitsy!"

Bitsy came through the archway into the Omega house common room looking slightly different than the last time Laura had seen her. For one thing, her eyes were not their usual ice blue. They appeared to be glowing red. Also, she appeared to be covered in blood, and a long string of drool mixed with blood hung from her suddenly sharp, unusually long canine tooth. She was also roaring, a fierce, deep-throated yell that Laura would not have believed could come from someone named Bitsy.

Bitsy lunged across the room at Ted. Well, she actually appeared to be flying across the room, but Laura told herself she must still be drunk or high or whatever she'd been before she blacked out.

Teddy, displaying strength and agility Laura would not have believed an hour earlier, dropped the gas can, fell to the floor, picked up a double-headed fire axe and swung it in a strong, graceful arc above him. Bitsy, Omega Alpha rush chair, senior communications major, and vampire, was cleanly beheaded.

Laura was off the couch immediately, screaming. "Jesus, Teddy, what the fuck? What the, what the, I mean you fucking psycho, what the fuck are you doing? You just killed Bitsy! Oh my God, you've been the Ivy Ripper all the time! "

Ted looked up. "I'm not the Ivy Ripper, Laura. It's them. The Omegas. They're vampires, Laura. Vampires. Did you ever see any of these bitches in the daytime?"

"Well, no, but, Jesus, if you're going to behead everybody who takes night classes…"

"I'm telling you, Laura, all the murders come back to this house, to this—" he gestured at Bitsy's beheaded form— "thing."

"Bitsy? Bitsy is the Ivy Ripper?"

"One of them. I mean, look at this and judge for yourself." Teddy picked up Bitsy's head by its long, blonde hair and pointed at the still gaping mouth. "That's a fang. With blood dripping off it. Q. E. fucking D."

Laura took in the grisly spectacle of a wild-eyed, sweat-drenched, filthy Teddy holding a head that did indeed possess a pair of bloody fangs, and her mind completely shut down. She just stared, hoping that the acid or whatever she was obviously on would wear off quickly and she'd be able to laugh about the horror-movie bad trip she'd had. Teddy holding disembodied vampire heads. Yeah, right.

Teddy stared at her for a moment, then tossed Bitsy's head into the corner of the room. "Look," he said, "I need to burn this place to the ground now. I don't have time for the garlic in the mouth and the running water, but I am pretty sure that beheading and fire will work just as well."

Laura decided to ignore the whole vampire thing and focus on reality-based questions. "Where's Camilla?"

"Camilla was about to turn you, from the looks of things. So I, uh, gave her the Bitsy treatment. Well, no. It wasn't as clean with her. She came after me. She's in pieces in the kitchen, if you'd like to go have a look."

Once again, Laura was dumbstruck. She did not know anything except that she had no desire to go into the kitchen and see Camilla's severed head. Teddy picked up the gasoline can and splashed the rest of it onto the floor.

"Okay, I need to commit a pretty serious act of arson here, and this place is going to be a crematorium in about a minute and a half, so you need to come with me now."

Teddy grabbed Laura's hand and pulled her up. She broke free from his grip and ran from the building as Teddy flipped open Steve's Zippo with Elvis on the side (Why did Teddy have it? Where was Steve?), and the common room of the Omega Alpha house burst into flames.

Laura stood on the sidewalk as Teddy came running out, straight at her. She got ready to run, or maybe fight, because she thought she could probably take him (but then, Bitsy had probably thought the same thing), but she saw that he was sobbing.

He threw himself into her arms, tears running down his face, crying hysterically, "So much blood, Laura, there was so much blood, why was it me, why did it have to be me, why was there so much blood, all I wanted to do was study folklore and get laid, why did it have to be me, Laura, why did it have to be me?"

ONE

T ed wiped his wand.

Michelle had been very clear about this point in training. "No muck on the wands! Customers don't want to see muck on the wands! Wipe your wand every time!"

Ted had snickered and looked to the group of Queequeg's trainees around him, looking for somebody else who might be amused, somebody else to whom he might say, "That's actually a high quality piece of advice in other aspects of life as well!" but he had only found the blank stares of the artists and students ten years younger than him and the earnest, attentive stares of the immigrants looking for the bottom step of the American Dream ladder.

So he'd kept his joke to himself and tried to pay attention as Michelle went on about how you can't just leave a pitcher of steamed milk sitting there and keep reheating it—you have to get fresh milk, and if it took longer to move the customers through, well, they'd thank you when their espresso drink didn't have that weird, thrice-steamed milk taste. And he pretty much kept to himself during his shifts at Queequeg's; of course he still had enough hush money

5

from the university that he didn't need this job, at least from a financial standpoint, but once, in a former life, he had been a good student, and in this life, he still had enough desire to please the teacher that he wanted to avoid Michelle's wrath. The best way to do that was to keep your head down and your wand clean.

The customers in this particular Queequeg's location—across from the Suffolk County Courthouse in downtown Boston—were not chatty: they were on their way to the office, or to court, they were already late, maybe they were hung over from trying to drink away the emptiness of their lives last night, and they wanted their lattes five minutes ago, goddammit, and they were always on their cell phones anyway, talking to real people while barely making eye contact with their caffeine-pushing servants.

But this was, except for the ten o'clock lull, a busy location, which gave him less time to think, which was good. He'd spent a lot of time over the past ten years thinking, and it was an activity he really didn't enjoy. Because what was there to think about? The Omega house, and the blood, and the way the axe had resisted slightly when it hit their necks? Or the unfairness of the fact that he was the one who'd had to deal with the vampire problem, that there were plenty of other people, bad people, stupid people, mean people who'd been on the same campus and were now happily cranking out babies and pumping money into retirement accounts, while he, who'd never so much as been in a fight, had to become a killer and wake up screaming every night. Well, no. He didn't have to. He could have wasted a lot of time running around trying to convince other people that what he'd found out was real, and then Steve would have been turned and Laura would have been turned, and it wouldn't have been long before they came for him and either turned him or drained him. So he'd been the one with the axe and the gas can and the Zippo. And for what? To save a bunch of people who would think he was insane if he ever told them that he'd saved them?

Still, it had been a decade. Why couldn't he put anything like a life together? It's not like he could go to therapy or a support group for traumatized vampire slayers or anything, but he doubted that would help anyway.

So he pulled lattes at Queequeg's and woke up screaming every night at three, and on the nights when he couldn't go back to sleep, he made a pot of coffee he got at a somewhat stingy employee discount.

Ted checked his watch. Laura was due at ten, and it was only nine-forty. Norah Jones blared from the speaker above his head, wondering why she didn't call for the fourth time that morning. Ted was wondering why she didn't just shut the hell up. The lights above the small, uncomfortable blonde wood tables gave off a feeble glow. The two comfy chairs next to the front windows were occupied by bald, bespectacled men typing on their laptops. Everything in here was muted—the music, the décor, everything but Michelle, a six-foot-tall, pear-shaped abusive whirlwind of stress who belied the fake serenity of her surroundings.

Right now Michelle was in the back, and Ted realized he should just sit back and enjoy the fact that the ten o'clock lull had come early today.

But all he could do was watch the seconds tick by on the timers on the coffee urns. He couldn't wait, and he hated himself some more for having only one friend. Ted thought that many guys would be happy to have a beautiful woman they'd known since college in their lives, a woman to whom they could tell anything, a woman who knew the very worst thing they had ever done and loved them not in spite of it but because of it.

Actually, he knew most guys would love to have Laura in their lives, because every time he'd ever been around her and other men, he saw the envy in their eyes as they looked from the raven-haired petite professional with the killer rack to his gangly, goofy self. If they only knew.

Ted was happy to have Laura in his life. It's just that she would never be in his life like those envious guys thought she was, not unless he became a woman, and probably not even then.

Ted sighed and glanced at the urn timers again. In twelve minutes he'd have to dump the Yirgacheffe, and, two minutes later, the Columbia.

"Ted!" Jean-Marie yelled. "Large skim latte!"

"Sorry, sorry. Large skim latte comin' up." Ted hadn't even noticed a customer coming in. He grabbed the cup and had no idea what name Jean-Marie had written on the side. He couldn't even guess male or female.

He made the espresso, steamed the skim milk, and mixed them perfectly, slightly off the Queequeg's approved ratio, but perfect according to the formula he'd been secretly working on for the last few months. He looked up and saw that several more customers had come in. So much for the lull. Using both hands, he reverently placed his creation on the counter. He imagined a spotlight shining down on it and a choir of angels singing. It was possibly, he reflected, the perfect latte, the very platonic ideal of a latte, the latte against which all other lattes would forever be measured. He hoped that whoever consumed it would appreciate it, would take a few minutes to savor it and not just gulp it down on their way to court.

"Uh…" he said to the three or four customers assembled by the counter. "I'm sorry… I can't read this. I'm gonna guess Rachel? Maybe Rowena? Rodney? Richard? Something that starts with an R, or possibly a K? Large skim latte?"

A tall woman with short auburn hair and a black, sleeveless shirt came to the counter. "It's actually Rhiannon," she said.

Ted looked at the cup again. "No, I'm pretty sure your name is Rodney." He braced himself for the onslaught of abuse, but instead he got a small laugh. "See, it says it right here."

She took the cup and squinted at it. "Hmm. I think it's actually Ricki. That's at least a little more unisex than Rodney. And thank you for not saying anything about Fleetwood Mac."

"I try to avoid the subject of Fleetwood Mac at all costs."

Did her eyes just sparkle? And did it just get brighter in here, or was that just her smile? "I'd love to do the same, but my parents guaranteed me a lifetime of Fleetwood Mac jokes."

"I guess it could be worse. They could have called you 'Landslide' or 'You Make Loving Fun.' Dumbass! He just made a Fleetwood Mac joke!

Rhiannon was still smiling. She took a sip of her latte and still didn't move away from the counter. "That was actually a Fleetwood Mac joke. But I forgive you, because you have made what I think is the best latte I've ever had."

She *did* appreciate the platonic latte! And she still wasn't running off! "Hey," he said, "I don't know if you are…"

Jean-Marie interrupted him. "TED! I said medium half-caf, half-soy mochachino!"

Half-soy? Who the hell wanted half-soy? Make up your mind!

"Hey, can I get my drink sometime this week?" Ted looked at the half-soy mochachino drinker. He was indistinguishable from any of the other guys in suits who came in here—white guy, medium height, medium build, look of barely suppressed rage like he'd probably once played a contact sport and now had become a lawyer so he'd have a socially acceptable place to put his aggression.

Rhiannon was now fading back from the counter. "I'll be back tomorrow," she said, and she smiled and disappeared.

Ted smiled at this little miracle. Funky, beautiful women just didn't come in to this Queequeg's unless they were on their way to their arraignment or something, and, given the fact that she'd said she'd be back tomorrow, it seemed a safe bet that Rhiannon wasn't on trial for anything. The half-soy guy was tapping his fingers on the counter, so Ted began the process of assembling the half-caf, half-soy mochachino. Half-soy. Jesus Christ. He wondered if it was even worth trying to assemble perfect proportions for this particular drink, since nobody else was ever going to order it. Dutifully he steamed the milk-soy mixture, and the guy was practically hanging over the counter, on which he was resting his big leather man-purse. "I really have an important meeting," the guy said.

"Yes sir. I am steaming with all due speed," Ted said.

"Don't be a smartass, okay, just make the fucking drink," the guy said. Ted simply wasn't feeling macho enough to counter this with anything at all, so he poured the drink and called out, loudly, "Half-caf, half-soy mochachino! And may I suggest foregoing caffeine entirely next time!"

There were snickers from the other patrons, and the guy grabbed his drink, slung his man-purse over his shoulder, and stormed out. As he swung the man-purse off the counter, a CD case fell out of it and clattered to the floor at Ted's feet. There was no way he was calling after the guy for that, and he seriously considered just crunching it under his foot, but then Jean-Marie was calling more orders.

He made five more drinks, and he kept kicking the CD case as he shuttled from fridge to steamer, so when there was a temporary lull, he reached down and picked up the CD. He considered throwing it away, but then, without really knowing why, he tucked it into the pocket of his ocean-blue apron instead.

TWO

L aura looked up from the ATM receipts to the grainy video on her computer screen. Was that Whitey? Some old guy in a baseball cap and sunglasses withdrawing four hundred dollars in Boca Raton. Well, he might well be a fugitive gangster. Or else he was just an old guy with bad fashion sense in Florida.

She rubbed her eyes and stood up. She looked over the tops of white cubicles bathed in cold fluorescent light, over the identical heads of all her co-workers, to the one sliver of window visible from her cubicle. She could see that it was a sunny day outside, and for a brief moment, she thought she should just feign illness, go get on her bike and enjoy the sunshine, maybe in the Arboretum. Or maybe she should just quit, just say the hell with it, and see if Ted could get her a barista job where at least she would never have to think about old people at Florida ATMs again.

Suddenly, McManus' doughy, florid face was peering over the top of her cubicle. "Find something, Harker?"

Startled, Laura said, "Uh, no sir. I mean, well, more of the same."

"Well, Harker, I don't know what kind of song and dance the recruiters at your top-five law school gave you, but the real business of law enforcement is often boring as shit."

"Yes sir."

"There's no shortcut, you know. They caught Capone by combing through his books. You think that was fun?"

Laura wanted to tell him that she'd seen that movie, that she didn't need any lectures about Eliot Freaking Ness, and that this office would have caught Whitey ages ago if people inside the office hadn't tipped him off. Instead she said, "I'm sure it wasn't, sir."

"Goddamn right it wasn't. There are no shortcuts in this work. Even if you're brilliant and female and get out of paying the dues other people have to pay."

What, exactly, was she supposed to say to that? She figured McManus was trying to bait her, and, unable to think of a safe response, she said nothing.

"Well. Back to work, then."

"Yes sir." She watched as McManus walked away, then carefully pressed her hand against the slate-blue carpeting on the cubicle wall and flipped him the bird.

Sighing, Laura sat back down and looked at the clock at the bottom of the screen. Shit! It was already ten, and she still had so much more work to do. There was no way she was going to make it to Queequeg's to see Ted this morning. On the other hand, she could really use the caffeine if she was going to be staring at grainy video for eight more hours. Maybe she could get Ted to deliver.

As she dialed Ted's cell phone, Laura realized this was at least partly a passive-aggressive move. Maybe he wouldn't show up. Then she could just drink bad coffee from the lounge and she wouldn't have to see him. She felt guilty—as much as Ted needed her, which was very much indeed, and as tiresome as this got, she had certainly needed him when she had been captured by Camilla's hypnotic gaze, when she'd been powerless in the face of evil. She owed Ted not only her life, but very likely her soul as well, because if it weren't for him, she would have signed right on for the bloodsucking, and the day sleeping, and instead of being a cog in the machinery of law enforcement, she'd be an abomination, enduring the soulless eternity of the undead.

Except, sitting here in a cubicle with slate-blue fabric walls under flickering fluorescent lights, it was very hard to believe in the undead. It just seemed impossible that a world as mundane as the one she inhabited also contained unholy murderous creatures of the night. Still, there were living humans every bit as evil as the undead, horrible sociopaths who terrorized and tortured and killed people. She'd joined the FBI in hopes of chasing them down, of being a strong woman who didn't need some skinny male nerd to rescue her, of being a woman who helped make the world safe for the living.

Instead, she was looking for an old man in Florida—a pointless search for hay in a haystack—and she just didn't feel like dealing with Ted's babbling, with his neediness, with the pathetic wreck of his life that only reminded her that while she had a better paying job and some career prospects, she hadn't managed to get close to anybody else in the last ten years either. Well, how can you get close to anyone when you can't tell them about the central event of your life? How do you create a self that doesn't include the very event that made you who you are?

Ted answered his phone. "Hey there, Clarise Starling! What's up?"

"Confidential drudgery. Listen, I'm up to my neck in incredibly boring data that needs sifting through here. Any chance I could get a delivery?"

"Sure. I'm happy to get a break. The usual?"

"Ugh. You'd better give me an extra shot of espresso today. I'm gonna be here a long time, and this stuff is just so far from interesting that I'm going to need a lot of caffeine to get through it all."

"Can do."

Laura saved her work, walked through the cubicle maze hoping to avoid the eyes of McManus, her supervisor who insisted that it was suddenly urgent to pore through a year's worth of Florida ATM crap looking for Whitey, though he'd been missing for years.

At the end of the hall, Laura swiped her ID to unlock the door. Inside the elevator, she swiped her ID to get downstairs. In the lobby, she waved at Hassan the security guard, and then headed outside to wait for Ted with her coffee.

Only a few minutes later, Ted arrived with an extra-large Queequeg's cup in hand. God bless him.

"Oh, thank you so much. I really don't think I could complete my workday without this. You really have no idea how boring law enforcement is."

"Well, I know that *you* did not have a flirtatious conversation with a very hot young woman named after a Fleetwood Mac song this morning."

"Shows what you know. I stopped by Big Love's desk just this morning."

"Special agent Big Love?"

"Yeah, she sits next to Gypsy."

"Isn't that a Stevie Nicks solo song?"

"I'm pretty sure it's Fleetwood Mac."

"Who cares? Anyway, I think something's gonna happen. She lingered around the counter and gave me this heavy-lidded smile and told me she'd be back tomorrow."

"She did not give you a heavy-lidded smile. That's an exclusively post-orgasmic look."

"Well, I do make a hell of a latte." Poor poor Ted. Maybe Go Your Own Way really was flirting with him, and he'd get laid, and then he'd fall in love, and then he'd have to explain, because Ted always had to explain, he couldn't come up with a cover story, he'd come to the point where he either didn't trust her enough to tell her about the vampires, or else he did trust her enough and he'd tell her about the vampires and she would think he was nuts and he'd be devastated.

This, of course, was wildly different from what happened in Laura's relationships. Because she wasn't crazy enough to think that anybody would ever believe the part about the vampires, so there was always an important part of herself she wouldn't share, and eventually there'd be a fight, often with screaming and tears, you're so distant, you don't trust me, this isn't a real relationship, and Laura would say this is how I am, take me or leave me, and thus far, everyone had taken the latter option.

She returned to the present, and the matter of Ted's supposedly orgasm-inducing espresso drinks. "Well, I'm drinking one of your lattes right now, and I have to say I'm not even close."

"Yeah, well, you don't play for my team."

"So your lattes are so good they induce orgasm, but only in straight women. What about gay men?"

"I don't know. Okay, okay, it wasn't the latte. Maybe it was just looking into my sensitive, tormented eyes."

"Anything's possible, I guess. Anyway, thanks for bringing the coffee over. I'm going to be working late tonight and probably tomorrow, but maybe we can have Indian food on

Thursday." She actually wouldn't be working late tomorrow, but goddammit, it had been ten years. She needed to carve out a little bit of Ted-free time.

"Oh…" He looked a little crestfallen, and Laura felt guilty. "Well, okay. I'll probably have a date by tomorrow anyway." He glanced at his watch. "Oh shit. I gotta get back or Michelle is going to chew my ass, and if she were just a little more attractive, I might enjoy that, but as it is, it's just no fun at all."

"Okay. Say hi to Sara for me."

"Ha! It's Rhiannon!" And he was gone, running back to his coffee-slinging. As Laura headed inside and began the x-raying, metal-detecting, badge-showing, and badge-swiping ritual that would allow her to get back into her office, she did kind of envy Ted. Usually she felt some combination of tenderness, gratitude, worry, and annoyance, but now she added a little dollop of envy. Ted was the fuckup, the perpetual slacker who had his life ruined, and she was the achiever, the one who didn't let the trauma hold her back. And yet he was practically skipping back to his workplace, while she was definitely trudging. And neither one of them seemed able to sustain a relationship with anybody else.

Well, there was really no point in thinking like that, or in thinking at all, except about whether Whitey was dumb enough to open a bank account and access it from a strip mall in Boca Raton. She took a long sip of her latte, and while she was nowhere near orgasm, she did have to admit that Ted made a hell of a good coffee drink.

THREE

T ed approached Queequeg's and decided that the best way to avoid Michelle's wrath over his now-seventeen-minute break would be to try to sneak in the back and pretend he'd been back there arranging bags of sugar or something.

He walked through the filthy alley behind Queequeg's, squeezed past the rusting dumpster and winced at the smell, then cursed as something brown dripped from the dumpster's black plastic lid onto his apron. He opened the back door and beheld stainless steel counters, the fridge, a mop bucket, giant jugs of ammonia and giant foil bags of coffee. He threaded his way past the cleaning supplies and giant bags of coffee, and pushed the stainless-steel swinging door to the front. The door refused to swing open wide enough to allow him access to the front.

"Shit," Ted said under his breath, "I bet fucking Michelle did this, just so I'll have to pound on it and then she can come and yell at me about my seventeen minutes. Shit!" At the last word, he pressed his shoulder against the door and shoved with all his weight. It moved a crack. He shoved it again and again until there was just enough room for him to squeeze through. He had made so much noise it was going to be completely obvious he was late, but at least he'd deny Michelle the satisfaction of having him pound on the door.

He squeezed through, and immediately tripped over whatever had been blocking the door. "Fuck!" he said as he went sprawling. "Michelle, you'd bett—" He stopped as he realized that Michelle was what he had tripped over. Well, Michelle's big, long body anyway. Ted felt a sick rush of adrenaline such as he hadn't felt in a decade, and he screamed—Michelle's apron was soaked in blood, and Ted felt it, still warm, seeping through the fibers of his clothes from the floor.

His brain shut down. What was happening was clearly impossible, which meant that he was actually in bed having a nightmare, and if he could only scream loud enough, maybe he'd wake himself up. He kept screaming. He stood up and looked around. He had a second to register the fact that there were two corpses at the corner table, and that the new artful splatter pattern, red against the orangey-yellow walls, was probably their brains. Something dripped off the wall and landed with a wet splat. Ted continued to scream. A man in a suit lay in front of the counter, half of his face hanging off of his skull, and intestines drooping out of his abdomen. There was blood everywhere.

All of this took maybe a second. Ted's brain started to kick into gear again, and he was annoyed by the sound of screaming, unaware that it was coming from him. He turned and saw another guy in a suit, Mr. Half-soy, Half-caf, standing in front of him with a gun.

"Where is it? Where the fuck is it, slacker boy? Do you want to die fast or slow?"

Now, this was actually a question Ted had given a fair

amount of thought over the last ten years. Not simply the speed at which he wished to die, but whether he wanted to live at all, whether there was any point to his being alive. His grandmother had always told him that God has a purpose for every life, and he figured that his purpose was to dispatch a colony of vampires from a major research university, that God had wanted him to remove that evil from the earth He'd created, and the fact that he was still alive was pretty much of an oversight on the part of the Almighty. And it was a shame that his purpose hadn't been to be the patriarch of an enormous happy family, but most people don't get what they want.

So now a man with dark hair and a gray suit that was covered in blood was pointing a weapon at him and asking him how he wanted to die. If he'd wanted to, Ted might have been able to have a quite lengthy conversation about this issue, but something in him, the part of him that had killed multiple times in one evening ten years ago, woke up for the first time in ten years and asserted that it would rather not die at all.

Without thinking, Ted grabbed a pitcher of milk that still had steam coming from it off the cappuccino machine and tossed it in Half-caf's direction while diving under the counter. The gunshot and the scream happened almost simultaneously, and Ted was showered with broken glass and crumbs of muffins and brownies as the baked-goods counter exploded over his head.

Half-caf was still screaming, and Ted said, "I've killed a lot worse than you. I killed a fucking colony of vampires— *vampires*, man, not some pussy with a gun, *vampires!* With a fucking axe! So *Don't!*" As he said this, Ted saw himself grabbing the gigantic stainless-steel urn of Decaf Sumatra off the warmer and tossing the steaming contents over the counter onto Half-caf's prone form, *"Fuck!"* And now it was the Ethiopian Yirgacheffe, *"With!"* And good old Colombian to finish, *"Me!"*

Half-caf was still screaming and would hopefully be covered in third-degree burns. Ted turned to run away, then stopped. He grabbed a cloth and wiped the foam off the wand. He hadn't liked Michelle, but her insistence that the milk always be steamed fresh had probably just saved his life, and he wasn't going to pay her back by letting her be found with a dirty wand. He ran through the back room and out the back door, and, with no plan in mind, he ran for the harbor. He reached the fountain at Post Office Square—jets of water hitting columns of slate. A few early lunchers were already gathering on the benches that ringed the fountain, and they gaped as he ran through it, watching the blood diluting and running off him, staining little streams of water pink until they swirled down the drain. He ran again, past men and women in suits and the odd family of tourists. Finally he could see the Boston Harbor between the buildings ahead of him. He came to Long Wharf and ran past the tourists signing up for whale watches, the school kids filing into the glass-and-steel aquarium, past more tourists strolling obliviously out of the lobby of the hotel on his left, all the way to the end of the pier, where he stood, looking out at the boats going back and forth across Boston Harbor and the planes coming in low to the airport across the water. He vomited until there was nothing else left in his stomach, and then he just heaved over and over again, while strings of bilious mucous dripped down from his mouth and made iridescent streaks on the surface of the water.

He wiped his mouth on his damp, cold apron and decided

he could not continue to wear it. He reached back to untie it so he could throw it in the trash, and as he took it off, he felt the CD in the pocket. He grabbed the CD and stuffed it into the right butt pocket of his pants, then stuffed the apron into a garbage can overflowing with Dunkin' Donuts cups, and dialed Laura's number.

"What's up, Ted?" she answered, and Ted suddenly found himself unable to speak. He knew that the minute he opened his mouth, he'd start to cry. He tried whispering.

"Laur," he said. "I'm in trouble."

FOUR

L aura sat on her couch and watched the news on the flat screen TV hanging on the wall. Channel eight just couldn't get enough of the blood-spattered walls of Queequeg's, while channel twelve favored the police composite sketch of Ted which had been made from the recollections of customers. Fortunately Ted had largely let his wand do the talking in his time at Queequeg's, and so most of the customers couldn't really summon up anything too specific. They had gotten the pale skin, the goatee and the long, dirty-blond hair, but there were probably ten thousand guys in Boston who fit that description, and those identifying features could be easily disposed of. Of course, the police probably already had all his personal information off the hard drive in the computer in the Queequeg's back room, which meant that they'd probably already searched Ted's apartment, and they'd be pulling the logs of his cell phone (which, GPS chip and all, now resided at the bottom of Boston Harbor as Laura had instructed), and pretty soon her phone would ring, and at that point she'd have to either summon up her prodigious lying skills or else just give him up and be shed of him forever. (The forever that would be an eternity of blood-soaked nights if not for Ted, she reminded herself.)

But if they had the hard drive, why were they holding back Ted's name? And all the accounts listed four people dead of gunshots and said nothing about a horribly burned man with gunpowder all over his hands. Either they were holding this back (though Laura couldn't imagine any reason why they would do this, since the burn victim was the shooter, and they'd want to reassure the public that this case was closed) or somebody had come for him, probably only seconds after Ted left. And probably taken the hard drive from the computer, which meant somebody knew who Ted was, but it wasn't law enforcement. In which case perhaps he wasn't so stupid to run and call her instead of staying put and calling 911. In which case she might owe him an apology.

Then again, she was putting her law-enforcement career in jeopardy just having him in her apartment, even though he was only officially a "person of interest" rather than a suspect. And if the whole thing had happened the way Ted described it, surely the ballistics, the bloody footprints, all the physical evidence would show that the shooter was in front of the counter, and that Ted had been behind the counter the whole time. Right?

Well, a small, nasty voice from a dark corner of her mind said, That's if it happened as Ted described it, and he hadn't just snapped. For ten years he'd had nightmares, for ten years he'd been a wreck—was it possible that he'd just had a psychotic break and reenacted his killing spree of ten years ago?

No, that was ridiculous. Ted didn't have a gun. And people didn't just go on killing sprees and not remember it, except in cheesy movies when they were possessed by demons or something. Which Ted was not. Right? Well, who knew. It always seemed unlikely to Laura that everybody involved in the Omega house colony was gone. Somebody must have started that particular chapter of the Vampire Sorority, and she didn't think it was Bitsy. Was someone involved in the dark arts getting revenge on Ted? Wouldn't it be the ultimate irony if they'd used him as a puppet to kill innocent people, after he'd killed so many, uh, things that were neither innocent nor people?

Laura chided herself, tried to bring herself back into the world she'd felt so sure of at work this morning, the world of cubicles and fluorescent lights. The dark arts probably weren't real. After all, just because vampires were real, it didn't necessarily follow that werewolves and demons and the boogeyman and the tooth fairy and Santa Claus were all real. Since joining the Bureau, she'd done a lot of unauthorized poking around in files and had never found anything anywhere that even suggested the existence of anything but incredibly depraved but otherwise normal humans.

She flipped through the cable news stations, which had picked up the Queequeg's massacre story and were now going into talking-head mode. She stopped as one red-faced guy was yelling, "Queequeg's is the embodiment of godless secular liberalism! It's not surprising at all that this hippie-era, Manson Family White Album degeneracy comes home to roost at the very place that foments it!"

Laura clicked off the TV in disgust. With the TV off, she could hear Ted dry-heaving in the bathroom. The sound made her slightly nauseous, as did the thought of cleaning his puke splatters off the pristine white tile in her bathroom. He had been kind of okay for a few hours, had then vomited, had then eaten an entire large pizza from Fred Ciampa's Same Old Place, and now appeared to have finished vomiting that up. Laura knew it made her a bad person, but she was just tired of holding up his head and wiping his chin. She figured that Ted, especially with all the alcohol and drugs he'd done in the last ten years, could probably vomit on his own with the best of them.

What was she going to do? They had to go to the police. Didn't they? If the police knew about Ted, it would certainly be better to go to them before they came knocking on her door. But it had been ten hours. Laura would not be surprised if she were the only number Ted ever called from his phone, so surely the police would have called her by now if they had Ted's name. So she had to assume that the police did not have the shooter, that someone else had come for the shooter and had taken all the information that would lead the authorities to Ted. If people willing to wade into a crime scene across from a courthouse and remove a screaming burn victim and a computer in the moments before the police arrived were looking for Ted, Laura wasn't sure any place was going to be safe enough.

So maybe they should go to the police. Maybe that was the best way to keep Ted safe. Except that Ted's story fundamentally didn't make any sense. One deranged customer (or employee, Laura tried to stop herself from thinking) shooting up a Queequeg's was a believable atrocity, but the idea that there was some kind of swift-moving conspiracy behind this—well, it just didn't make any sense. Why would an organized group of whackos target Queequeg's without issuing a statement explaining themselves? And why would they strike the customers rather than the establishment? Terrorists? But a suicide bomb is a much more reliable way to take out a café full of people. No, something was wrong with Ted's story, and that meant they couldn't go to the police.

Ted emerged from the bathroom, face and hair freshly wetted down. A plush purple towel that matched the bath mat and hand towels in the bathroom was around Ted's neck, and Laura winced thinking about Ted wiping his puke with it. Well, she could always buy more towels.

"Hey—what's the word from the local news? What did the hottie on channel 29 say about me?"

"Which one?"

"Bridget Tran y Garcia, of course!"

"She really doesn't look Irish. You think she just decided to add Bridget when she got hired in Boston?"

"Who cares? She looks really hot! What did she say?"

"She said your police composite sketch made you appear devilishly handsome, and that she was aching for your touch despite, or possibly because of, the heinous act you'd just committed."

"Cool."

"Yeah, that's about as good as it's going to get, I'm afraid. So far you're just a "person of interest," but I'm sure the *Boston Mail* will have you upgraded to suspect by five a.m."

"Nothing about Half-caf?"

"No. Which means the police probably don't have or know about him. Which means he probably wasn't acting alone, which means—ugh, I hate to say this—fleeing in terror down to the harbor was probably the right thing to do."

"Man, I wish I could tape record that. Could I just write 'Ted was right' on your calendar?"

"No."

"So nobody thinks I might have been the guy who got away and was now hiding in terror?"

"Well, that's not as good a story as you flipping out because Michelle docked you for a seventeen-minute break or something. In that scenario, there's only one bad guy, and that's just much simpler and easier for everybody to get their heads around than some kind of conspiracy. Which seems weird, because these psychos almost always work alone. I can't understand why there would be any kind of organization behind this, Ted, I really can't. It doesn't look like terrorists, and it doesn't look like some fair-trade blow against Queequeg's corporate hegemony."

"Is that how you say that word?"

"What?"

"Hege... that one. I've only ever seen it written."

"I don't know, Ted, that's the way I say it, okay?"

"Okay,"

"But do you get what I'm saying? I mean, I'm mostly an ATM snoop, but I am a law-enforcement professional, and your story and the data just don't fit."

Ted looked angry. "So you think I did it?"

Maybe. Probably not. "Of course not. I'm just saying that your story rests on a conspiracy that makes no sense."

Ted's face went from angry to embarrassed, and he was now shifting from foot to foot and looking kind of guilty. "I think I might have a clue about the conspiracy."

"What?" Ted reached into his butt pocket and pulled out a CD. "What the hell is that?"

"Uh, it's a CD that fell out of Half-caf's bag that I pocketed."

"Jesus Christ! Why the hell didn't you tell me this?"

Ted's face twisted up and turned red, and Laura felt guilty for snapping at him. "Because!" he yelled through tears that turned into gut-wrenching sobs. "Because this makes the whole fucking thing my fault! Those people..." More sobbing. "They just wanted a goddamn latte, and they got their brains plastered all over the walls, and it's *my fault!* Oh God!" He fell to the floor and tried in vain to vomit, but just crouched there with his mouth open making strangled coughing sounds.

Any annoyance Laura felt fell away. He really was a pathetic creature, and it was saving her that had made him this way. Now she went to him and rubbed his back and pulled his hair away from his face. "It's not your fault, you know," she said quietly. "People leave shit in coffee shops thousands of times a day, and this is the first one I ever heard of who ever came back and shot the place up. You didn't cause this, Ted. You're a victim."

"Yeah…" Ted raised his head. "Jesus, Laur, it was so horrible. It was so horrible."

"I know. Why don't you try to get some sleep." She helped him to his feet, wiped the corner of his mouth with her plush purple towel, and brought him down the hall to her room. In spite of the clean, zen simplicity of Laura's room, Ted managed to make the place seem messy and chaotic. His rumpled, dripping form overruled the neatly made bad and transformed Laura's bedroom. She helped him over to the edge of the bed, and he lay down on it. Laura thought about asking him to remove his shoes, then thought better of it.

"Uh, Laur?" he said.

"Yeah, Ted?"

"I know this is silly, but would you mind just sitting here for a minute? I know I'm a baby, but I just don't want to be alone right now."

"You're not a baby," she said, and sat at the foot of the bed. Five minutes later he was asleep, and she took the CD and popped it into her computer.

FIVE

T ed was eighteen. He was in the library, sitting in a little carrel piled high with books for his paper on vampire legends for his folklore class, when he saw the photo of Elizabeth Stevens, alleged vampire from 1890 who'd been buried alive by fearful townspeople who blamed her for a tuberculosis outbreak. "Bitsy," he said. "Fucking Bitsy."

Suddenly he was in the Omega house, standing in a corner, wearing an ill-fitting blazer, trying to catch Steve's eye as the sorority girls swarmed around him. "There are no mirrors here," he said to Steve. "What kind of sorority house doesn't have mirrors?"

"Maybe they're all on the ceilings of the bedrooms," Steve said, leering. "I'm gonna find out!"

And two weeks later, Ted was covered in blood, swinging the axe he'd dipped in holy water at St. Swithin's a few blocks away. He kicked in a door and saw Nancy bent over Steve. Steve was screaming. It took two strokes to take Nancy's head off. The stump of her neck steamed from the holy water, and her blood covered Steve, who was still screaming.

"Oh Jesus, oh God, oh Jesus, you were right, Teddy, I'm sorry I didn't believe you, shit, she got me." And Steve began to sob. "I'm done, oh, God, Teddy, you have to save me, you have to save me."

Tears blurred Teddy's vision. "I'm sorry, Steve, I'm sorry, I'm too late, I'm too late."

"Then kill me, Teddy, please, you have to fucking kill me! Don't make me end up like them, don't make me melt in the sun, please! Please, for Christ's sake, kill me before I turn! Kill me! Make it quick!"

"I... I can't do it, Steve, I'm sorry, I..."

"Bullshit you can't! You just took Nancy's head off, you can do mine! Do it, goddammit!"

"Oh, Jesus, please, Steve, don't ask me this, don't, please, I can't..."

"Kill me, you little pussy! It's you or me! I can smell your blood, Teddy, I can hear your heartbeat, and I don't want to kill you either, but already I want to drain your body, I wanna stand over you and howl with your blood running down my chin, don't make me do that Ted, I'll go to hell. So just do it, you worthless pussy! Fucking kill me, okay? Save my soul! Do it!"

Ted reached the axe back, but it had turned into a coffee urn, and Steve had turned into Half-caf, and he threw the boiling hot coffee on him, crying and shouting, "Die!"

Ted woke up screaming, with tears running down his face. He sat bolt upright in bed, realized he wasn't in his bed, and screamed again. He looked at the clock—it read 4:18, and he realized he was at Laura's house.

He was relieved to be somewhere safe, and to be in the dark, away from the blood, the fire, and the screaming that haunted his dreams. He loved the way everything in Laura's apartment was neat and orderly and uncluttered. It was so unlike his apartment, so unlike his mind. He got out of bed and walked to the bathroom without tripping over dirty clothes or crunching DVDs under his feet or knocking over week-old, half-eaten Chinese takeout containers. He peed for a long time into a toilet bowl that was not stained brown, and he washed his hands with a tiny, un-slimy scented soap and dried his hands on a little towel instead of his pants. He realized his screaming would probably have woken Laura, so he decided to poke his head into the living room and offer her the use of her own bed for the next few hours. He certainly wasn't going back to sleep tonight.

Laura was not asleep on the couch. She was in front of her computer, which was giving off the only light in the room, and she was sipping a mug of tea. "Hey," she called back to him. "You did pretty good. I thought the nightmares usually hit at 3."

"Yeah, I got an extra hour in. Lucky me."

"So I gotta tell you, I am completely stumped."

"About what?"

"I have been looking through this CD for hours. It's mostly spreadsheets, with no labels on the columns. The files are called things like 'Spreadsheet 1,' or 'Spreadsheet 24.' I mean, I guess it's possible this guy was keeping Whitey's books or something, but you really would have to know exactly what you were looking at to make any sense of this. I mean, somewhere there must be information on what the column headings are and what these files correspond to, but this is pretty useless stuff without that information."

Ted pulled a chair over next to the computer. "And that's it?" he said.

"Well, that and a couple of save files for some computer game."

"What games?" Ted guessed they all involved a psychopathic shooting spree.

"Uh, let's see. 'Age of Mythology'; 'Roller Coaster Tycoon'; 'Virtuality.' Ever heard of any of them?"

"Yeah. Age of Mythology is one of those strategy games, Roller Coaster Tycoon is pretty self-explanatory, and Virtuality is a game where you can create a virtual person, or a whole group of virtual people, and then put them in a house, get them a job, take them out, stuff like this. You can go online and put your people into the Virtuality world, and they can interact with other virtuals."

Laura looked at Ted blankly. "Why exactly the hell would anybody want to do that? Do you get to like have sex, or go on shooting sprees or something?"

"Nah. The software won't let you do anything like that on screen. I guess you could talk about sex or something. But you definitely can't kill anybody."

"So what's the point? I mean, I get why all these fat dorks want to be buff adventurers and stuff, but why would you want to play a game that's just as mundane as your real life?"

"Got me. It seems especially weird if you're a psychotic killer holding Whitey's accounts on a CD."

"Yeah. Well, look, I'm going to make a copy of the CD and take it to work, and don't worry, I'm not going to say where I got it, but I'll just ask one of the data guys who has a crush on me to look at the spreadsheets and see if he can at least figure out what they are supposed to be."

"Does this data guy know his crush is a non-starter?"

"This might come as a shock, but the FBI is not exactly the safest workplace in which to come out."

"So you're using the guy's poor doomed crush to get him to do favors for you."

"Pretty much, yeah. You got a problem? Because, if you'd

rather I didn't engage in that unethical behavior, I could start being strictly ethical, which would of course involve turning the CD over to Boston Police before I have anybody look at it and also telling them the whereabouts of a certain person of interest."

"Okay, okay, geez, you don't have to bite my head off." Ted hadn't missed Laura's annoyance, her "I'm your long-suffering friend" vibe that had been growing ever since she'd been transferred to Boston and he'd moved up here to be close to her. "You're not really going to turn me in, are you?"

"Agh, no, Ted, I owe you my life, and that's why I'm putting my entire career on the line here, but it does kind of stress me out, you know, I mean, I don't know if you've really thought about what the consequences might be, but I do this stuff for a living. I know exactly what could happen to me if we get found out, and I'm not really comfortable withholding evidence in a murder investigation, so I'm a little on edge."

"Plus, you can't get your favorite latte today," Ted offered, hoping to lighten her up a little bit.

Laura cracked a smile, which felt like a victory. "Tell me about it! I have to drink that sludge from the lounge!"

"You'd think Ashcroft could spring for a cappuccino machine for the hardworking government employees on the front lines of the war on terror."

"Yeah, ask him the next time you talk to him, willya?"

"I'm on it."

"Okay, listen. You need to cut your hair and shave the goatee today. I have disposable razors in the medicine cabinet. Do not use my regular razor. Otherwise, watch some TV, do not under any circumstances leave the apartment, and most importantly, absolutely no porn on my computer."

"Geez! I'm going to be here alone for nine hours! What am I supposed to do? They're gonna miss me over at chubbymilf. com!"

"Okay, I have no idea what the hell you just said, but I'm sure it was disgusting. No porn!"

"Okay, okay."

Laura showered and got herself looking professional, and Ted examined her cereal selection. An array of bran-based products displayed in identical glass and steel canisters from the Container Store lined the back of the kitchen counter. Grape Nuts was the closest thing he could find to something edible. He wondered briefly if Laura suffered from constipation and reminded himself to check the medicine cabinet later. Hey, he was supposed to go in there and get a disposable razor anyway! If he happened to see some stool softener while he was there, well, that would just give him something to tease her about!

Which, upon reflection, would be a terrible idea while she was in "my entire career's on the line" mode. Laura left, and Ted waited a respectful ten minutes before cruising for pornography on her computer.

For some reason, tight-bodied lesbians in the throes of simulated passion weren't doing it for him today, so Ted closed the laptop and went to cut his hair and shave his beard.

Great, Ted thought once he'd finished and thrown away all his discarded hair. He'd accomplished his task for the day, and it wasn't even nine o'clock yet. What the hell was he going to do with the rest of the day? He needed to be not thinking. Where did Laura keep her booze? He opened cabinets in the kitchen, and found only orderly stacks of dishes and alphabetized spices and dry goods. "Come on,

Laur, where's the booze? Don't you even have any cooking sherry or anything?" Finally, in desperation, he opened the freezer. He seemed to remember Kendra, that attorney Laura dated briefly, pulling some kind of horrible-flavored vodka out of there when he was here last summer....

And, of course, it was still there, and probably hadn't been touched at all since Ted was here, it was sort of two-thirds full, as Ted imagined most bottles of frozen fruit-flavored vodka were in yuppie freezers all over America.

He reached for the bottle, yelling at his inner Jiminy Cricket to shut up, yes, he was going to drink the whole fucking bottle and then probably puke it up, but so what? He was a raw nerve, he was probably having some kind of post-traumatic stress, he needed it... he knocked a pint of Chunky Monkey out of the freezer, and it bounced painfully off the top of his foot before hitting the floor. He looked at the ice cream on the floor and the bottle of lingonberry vodka (What the hell was a lingonberry, anyway?) in his hand, and stood there until the freezing cold bottle started to hurt his hand. He put it back into the freezer and closed the door and leaned down to pick up the ice cream.

"I reserve the right to get absolutely shitfaced on that horrible shit any time I fucking want, okay?" he said testily to Laura's empty apartment. He picked up the ice cream. "Hmm, I wonder if this would be good with Grape Nuts on it..."

While he ate, he decided he'd have a try at the original CD while Laura's IT buddy looked over the copy down at the federal building. He looked briefly at the spreadsheets and found they made no more sense to him than they had to Laura. He tried to look at Half-caf's Age of Mythology and Roller Coaster Tycoon files, but he couldn't open them without the software. But Virtuality was web-based. Once you bought a subscription, you just logged in. Maybe he could make himself useful and find something out today. Maybe at least view a profile or something, find out something about Half-caf. But then if there really was some kind of conspiracy behind Half-caf's rampage, then there were other people still out there looking for Ted and the lost CD, and they would probably be lurking in the Virtuality world waiting to see if anybody would log in with Half-caf's account so they could trace the connection back and get the CD. So he couldn't use Laura's internet, or they might trace it all the way back here. What he needed was a wireless hotspot. Such as he happened to know was at the Queequeg's down the street.

But that would mean leaving the apartment, risking arrest, risking death. Ted chewed on that for a moment. Eventually he talked himself into thinking it would be no big deal. Boston Police didn't have the resources to have every Queequeg's in Boston under surveillance, and anyway he looked completely different, and Rhiannon and Half-caf were probably the only people alive who could positively ID him, and Half-caf might well be dead. Besides, he wasn't going to cower in here all day. Goddammit, he was Ted, the scourge of vampires, Ted, who had faced down a gunslinging killer while armed only with a pitcher of steamed milk.

He was also Ted whose clothes were still bloodstained, and that would certainly draw unwanted attention to him if he left the house. Well, Laura's ex, Kendra, had been a rather beefy 5'10"; maybe she'd left some clothes here he could use. She almost certainly had. What was that joke Laura always told about lesbian second dates involving a U-Haul? It must have been based in something, because at the back of the closet, Ted found a pair of sweatpants that would reach up to Laura's head, and an extra-large Boston Breakers-replica jersey.

He tucked Laura's laptop under his arm and walked down the stairs from her third-floor apartment. He turned onto the tree-lined street and his courage took a nose dive. A tattooed couple walked by hand-in-hand. The guy was wearing a Cannibal Corpse shirt—surely they were into blood and gore and had probably studied Ted's composite picture so they could have it tattooed on themselves somewhere. A woman jogged by pushing a stroller. Ted had never seen anybody actually jogging with a jogging stroller. Was she a cop? Was that a real baby? He knew it was stupid. But it felt real anyway.

Laura lived as far from a Queequeg's as probably anyone in Boston. It took Ted ten agonizing minutes before he saw the familiar, if no longer comforting, blue sign at the end of the street. He was glad that this particular Queequeg's was on the corner of Centre and St. John—this saved him having to walk on Centre Street, with its stores and restaurants and nosy pedestrians. He approached from the St. John Street side and saw a large American car, the kind that only cops and old people drive, parked across Centre Street from Queequeg's. The two guys sitting in it were wearing sunglasses and appeared to be under forty. Undercover cops? It couldn't be. Could it? Even if it was, they wouldn't be able to ID him. But for all Ted knew, they might be taking pictures of everyone who walked in, and that was too big of a chance to take.

Ted ducked into the alley behind Queequeg's, hoping he could still tap into the wireless signal back here. He saw nothing but the metal fire doors of the businesses and the dumpsters that held their trash. There weren't even any windows back here. Ted opened the plastic flap on the Queequeg's dumpster, tossed Laura's computer inside, climbed in and shut the lid.

He tried not to think about what he was sitting on, and reminded himself that stale coffee gave off this ammonia smell that was a lot like piss, so it was probably just old coffee, though there was a sour note that was almost surely some milk that had gone off. And there couldn't be any rats in here, could there? He powered up the computer and looked around in the blue light emitted by the screen. He saw nothing but black garbage bags that looked kind of cool with blue light reflecting unevenly on their folds and creases.

He popped the CD in and logged on to the internet using the Queequeg's wireless connection. Once at the Virtuality site, he double-clicked on the file on the CD. "Uploading settings" the screen told him, and two full minutes later, just as Ted was about to give up on this whole adventure and devote the rest of the afternoon to trying to get the piss and puke smell off of himself and, more importantly, Laura's computer, the screen changed. "Welcome back, Nyarlathotep," the screen said. Ted thought that Half-caf's user ID seemed familiar.

"Play as which avatar?" the screen asked, then presented him with only one name: "Randolph Carter." This sounded familiar too. Ted clicked on the checkbox, and the screen changed again. "Welcome back to Virtuality! Proceed to Miskatonic U. expansion area?"

"Sure," Ted said.

Soon Randolph Carter was strolling, in his jumpy, not entirely naturalistic stride, through the leafy campus of Miskatonic U. He knew that name. Where did he know it from? Was it even important?

Ted looked in Randolph Carter's inventory and found

a dorm room key with "Innsmouth 212" stamped on the side... He proceeded to a green quad with knots of students sitting at the foot of trees and four guys tossing a Frisbee. He imagined what Laura would think of guys sitting immobile in dark rooms pretending to play Frisbee out in the sunshine. The red brick walls of the buildings were covered with some kind of climbing plant that looked like a strangely sinister version of ivy. He wondered if it was supposed to look like that or if the Virtuality programmers had just blown off making believable ivy. He walked up to five buildings before he finally found Innsmouth Hall. His key opened the front door, and he walked down a long hallway. A staircase led down, and a sign with a downward-pointing arrow said "Subterranean Passage to Howard Phillips Hall." He suddenly realized where he knew all these names from.

"Yog-Sothoth on a bike," he opined to the garbage bag next to him. "This guy's a friggin' Cthulhu geek." Like most of his friends, Ted had spent a great deal of time in the eighth grade reading the horror fiction of Howard Phillips Lovecraft, and every name in Half-caf's virtual world referred to a Lovecraft story. Ted remembered what it was like to be a fourteen-year-old who played role-playing games, read comic books, and obsessed about Lovecraft. Only later had he realized that all the energy he spent on these things was fueled by a desperate, all-consuming horniness. He had often wondered what would have become of him if Kate DeAngeli hadn't decided in the twelfth grade that Ted's interest in horror and fantasy was a close enough match to her own interest in goth culture that she was willing to date and, more importantly, blow him. Perhaps if his horniness had never found a proper outlet, he would have turned into the kind of guy who shoots up coffee shops.

He found another stairway going up and went up to the second floor. The door opposite the staircase read "222," and he watched as his blocky, robotic avatar, Randolph Carter, walked down the hall to his dorm room. As Randolph Carter turned the key and entered room 212, Ted felt his heart pounding just as it might have if he'd been pretending to be someone else and sneaking into their room in real life. He had to remind himself that he was crouched in a Queequeg's dumpster, and that there was no Miskatonic U. Even still, he was reluctant to switch to the first-person view so that he could see what was on Randolph Carter's desk. It was just comforting to look at Randolph Carter's back in that over-the-shoulder, third-person view. That way he'd see if somebody was sneaking up behind him to clock him over the head.

Which, of course, would not have any effect on Ted's real self here in the dumpster.

He looked around the room. The walls were plain white with only one decoration—a maroon pennant with "Miskatonic U." in white letters. The pennant hung over a cheap metal bedframe with a thin mattress and white sheets. There was a desk that looked too cheap even for IKEA, where Ted always bought his own barebones furnishings, in front of a gothic-arched window. Ted marveled that Half-caf had actually managed to create a virtual dorm room even more cheap and dull than most real dorm rooms. What the hell was the point?

Finally, confident that he wouldn't be caught, Ted clicked on the point-of-view toggle and moved his cursor over the stuff on Randolph Carter's desk: a notebook, a pen, a photo of Anna Paquin as Rogue, and a map of Providence, Rhode Island. Ted picked up the map and examined it, but it appeared to be a normal map. Well, Ted actually wasn't familiar enough with Providence geography to know if there was anything unusual about the map. He poked around the menu and found a way to save the map as a jpeg file on Laura's desktop.

He clicked on a notebook that said "Class Notes"—scrawled on the first page was: "The return of the Old Ones can be secured by using the thirty-seventh incantation in one of the places of power." Ted rolled his eyes and clicked on the next-page arrow. "Diana is hottt!" Next. "Temple is not the Place of Power. Place of Power is adjacent."

Ted clicked on next, and the notebook closed. He clicked on pens and pencils and a ruler and got only a dialogue box asking him if he wanted to write. He clicked on the computer, and a box popped up that said, "In-game computer games and email available at Platinum Level membership. Upgrade now?" Ted clicked "no" and shook his head in disbelief. The geeks who played this game were, in a way, his people (or at least they belonged to the tribe he had belonged to before he'd taken an axe to his roommate and a passel of sexy vampires and set a sorority house on fire), but even he was mystified that people would actually pay extra so that they could sit in front of a computer screen and watch a character they'd created sit in front of a computer screen and play games. It was even stupider than the Frisbee thing. He wondered if the in-game avatars could create their own avatars in a virtual version of Virtuality available only to platinum level members. It really could go on indefinitely. "Curiouser and curiouser," Ted said to the bag of trash next to him.

He clicked on the desk drawers—they were all empty, except for one which held a book with Arabic writing on the cover. Just as he was about to click on it to examine it, a dialogue box popped up. "Conflict alert!" it said. "Randolph Carter, you have been struck on the back of the head! 121 Vitality points remain! You need food!"

"Son of a bitch!" Ted said. Someone actually had cold-cocked him! He toggled back to third-person view and saw Randolph Carter rubbing the back of his head while a tall blonde woman with enormous breasts stood there with a length of pipe in her hand.

The back of Ted's shirt suddenly felt wet, and, without even thinking, he reached up and rubbed the back of his head to check for a wound. He realized this was absurd, and he moved the laptop up to head level and saw that something white was dribbling out of a hole in the garbage bag that he'd been using as a pillow. Ecch.

Crouched in a dumpster, Ted felt uniquely qualified to talk trash to his attacker.

Is that all you got, Colonel Mustard? The lead pipe? he typed.

No firearms allowed in Virtuality, Ted. Ted felt his skin go cold. He wanted to run—not in the virtual world, but the real one.

No, he typed, *my name is Randolph Carter.*

Bullshit, Ted. We know everything about you. Well, Ted thought, that's a bit of a lofty claim. What's my favorite porn site? Who did I have a doomed crush on for all of seventh grade? How many vampires have I killed? Hell, even Ted himself didn't know the answer to that one.

Still, if they knew his name, it was more than likely that they'd gotten it off the Queequeg's hard drive, which meant that he was probably talking to one of the people who had pulled Half-caf out, which meant that Half-caf really was part of a conspiracy and not just a lone whack job.

Ted knew he should fold up the laptop and just run, but goddammit, these were the people who'd shot up his place of employment. He called on his inner action hero and decided to try to brazen it out.

Then you know that people who fuck with me get burned, he said.

What we have planned for you will make second-degree burns seem like a vacation, Blondie said.

Oooh, are you gonna sic the Old Ones on me?

Mock the Old Ones at your peril, Ted. Soon you will be begging for the sweet mercy of death, and it will be withheld from you, and your soul will suffer in a nameless, formless agony…

Blah blah blah. I know, I know, and the geometry is all wrong, and the horror is so nameless and indescribable that it will drive me mad, mad I say. You are really a bunch of pathetic dorks, aren't you?

Do continue to joke, Ted. I shall be the one laughing while you scream for the sweet mercy of death.

Listen. First of all, you are obviously some fat guy in a comic book store pretending to be a blonde with huge tits, which is just pathetic. I have no idea why you'd want to shoot up a coffee shop, except that probably being a forty-year-old virgin makes you snap. But I am so far from afraid of you. This, of course, was a lie, as Ted was jittery and sweaty and terrified, but the beauty of the internet was that nobody had to know that. *You bunch of pathetic gnomes are nothing compared to what I've already killed. I've got money and nothing better to do, and I am going to hunt every last one of you pathetic fuckers down and pour scalding hot coffee on your nuts.* He realized that his use of the word "nuts" might have given his threat an unintentional comedic note, but it was too late to retract it. Darn!

Thank you for talking so long, Ted. Now we know which Queequeg's you're in.

Ted's stomach lurched. Somehow they'd traced him here. Of course, they didn't know he was in the dumpster. Still, it might not be a great idea to stay here, and he didn't want another Queequeg's to get shot up, so he decided to give his Amazonian adversary a final taunt.

Shows what you know. I'm across the street. Catch me if you can, bitch! With that, Ted snapped the laptop shut. Gingerly, he opened the lid of the dumpster. Seeing that the alley was empty, he sprinted to the end of it. He looked up and down the street and saw no cars coming. He cut through back yards, hastily crossed two streets, and eventually found himself at an entrance to Franklin Park. He disappeared into the wooded section, running down one hill and up another until he found a clump of dense bushes. He burrowed inside and looked out. For an hour he twitched at every sound, but then a profound boredom overtook him. He thought about opening the laptop and playing some minesweeper or something, but then he remembered that he was hiding from very bad people who told him they'd have him begging for death—correction, for the sweet mercy of death, and he thought maybe being bored might not be so bad. After two hours, he heard running footsteps approaching. He tensed up and prepared to run. He realized he hadn't even picked up a stick to use as a weapon and thought he might have to swing Laura's laptop. She'd be pissed if he broke her computer over some guy's head, even if he did it to save his life. Fortunately, it wasn't a would-be assassin, but rather, a brown dog, who looked at him quizzically, squatted, and deposited a sizeable mound of shit about five feet away from him. He heard a man's voice calling, "Cooper!" and the dog trotted off, leaving both his shit and Ted behind.

After that, Ted didn't see or hear anybody for hours.

Six

Laura marked a section of ATM surveillance tape as potentially significant, saved, then put her computer to sleep and began the tedious process of swiping her ID card to get out of the building, then swiping her T pass to get home. She remembered that she had left Ted with nothing to eat but a variety of high-fiber cereals, so she figured she should stop off at the Indian restaurant with the shockingly surly staff and the shockingly good food. She grabbed a chilled bottle of Riesling at the liquor store next door. She normally couldn't stand those Kool-Aid wines, but back when Ted had been in his wine phase, he'd convinced her that it was the perfect pairing with rich, spicy food.

She trudged up the three flights to her apartment loaded down with wine, samosas, and saag paneer, turned the key in her front door and said, "Ted! Dinner!"

Nobody answered. She heard a click in the rear of the apartment, dropped her burdens, and drew her sidearm. "Ted?" she said again. "Ted, are you asleep? TED!"

No answer, but the click now became a rattle which seemed to be coming from her bedroom. Laura mastered her fear and began systematically clearing the apartment. She did a quick sweep of the kitchen and living room, pointing her gun behind the couch and the chairs. Nothing. She kicked open the bathroom door and swept the shower curtain open with her left hand while holding her gun steady with her right. Empty.

The rattling sound had stopped, but now that she was confident that no one was lurking behind her, she could turn her attention to her bedroom. Heart pounding, she stalked down the hall. She swung around, crouched in her doorway, and found herself pointing her gun at Ted, who was climbing in the window.

"Whoa!" he said. "It was just one site, I swear! Okay, two! Jesus, you really take this porn thing seriously!"

Laura laid her gun down on the floor and found that the hand that had been able to hold the gun so steady suddenly couldn't stop shaking. "You fucking asshole!" she yelled at Ted. "What the—Jesus Christ, what were you doing out of the apartment? You could have been killed! And you could have been killed by me! You are such a fucking idiot!"

Ted finished clambering in and looked sheepish. "I'm really sorry. But I've been hiding in the park all day, and I think I found out something really important."

"I dropped the saag paneer! I dropped a fifteen dollar bottle of wine! And you smell like a fucking dumpster! Ugh! Oh, please tell me that's not my computer under your arm. And please tell me that dried milky substance on it is, in fact, milk, because otherwise I'm going to have to puke and kill you, not necessarily in that order."

Ted explained how he had sneaked out to the local Queequeg's dumpster to use their wireless internet so he could check out the game files.

"Yeah, my data guy just told me what I already knew, which was that the spreadsheets are indecipherable. He said the fact that all the numbers were so low was kind of strange—nothing appeared to be above the low thousands—but maybe the units were hundreds or something…"

"I don't know about the spreadsheets, but I… the Virtuality file… I got…"

Ted's eyes were shining, and he looked actually happy as he flipped the computer open. Laura wondered where the puking wretch from this morning had gone. "Okay, so the guy's avatar—the character he plays with is Randolph Carter. Who attends Miskatonic U. Who lives in the Innsmouth House dorm! Which is right next to Howard Phillips Hall!" He looked at Laura like she was supposed to get the significance of all this.

"Uhhh…"

"Lovecraft?"

"What the hell is that—is that one of your porn sites?"

"No, no no! H. P. Lovecraft? Writer?"

Laura looked blank. "Hey, can we talk and eat? I'm starving, and that saag paneer isn't getting any hotter."

Ted's face, already lit up, got one shade brighter. "Oh, thank you! Indian food! I have to tell you, the whole bachelor fridge and bran cereal thing you have going on here is just really not working."

"Yeah, well, they feed you really well in jail."

"Point taken. But why all the bran? I mean, is there some kind of a problem with your plumbing that needs to…"

"My plumbing is not up for discussion. Come out to the kitchen and help me dish this stuff up."

They went to the kitchen, where all the food had survived its drop very nicely. Ted picked up the bottle of Riesling that had rolled under the table and gave Laura a big hug, which was such a rare experience that she didn't really know how to react. Tentatively, she hugged him back and then felt instantly awkward, not to mention disgusted, since he still smelled of the dumpster.

"Okay, I want to hear everything, but you have to change your clothes. You're not very appetizing smelling like that."

"Okay, okay! Kendra leave anything else here?"

"Well, let's just say it's nothing I want to see you wearing right now," Laura said, smiling. Ted retreated to her bedroom and emerged a minute later wearing her ratty old New York Liberty t-shirt and a pair of workout shorts that were enormous on her but made Ted look like he was playing basketball in the 1970's. She couldn't help smiling.

They ate and drank in silence for a moment, and Laura felt slightly guilty as she saw how ravenous Ted was. Eventually, Ted was able to get out, through the adrenaline fogging his brain and the saag paneer clogging his mouth, that he'd taken the CD to Queequeg's and logged on to some video game from a file on the CD, and that he—or rather the computer person he'd been pretending to be—had been attacked by a busty blonde who'd called him by name, thus confirming that Hal-caf hadn't been working alone and that his associates had probably taken the Queequeg's hard drive. The fact that Laura hadn't been called by the police today had led her to believe that someone other than the police had the hard drive, and this pretty well sealed it. She didn't think assault by virtual centerfold was in the Boston Police playbook.

Everything in the area of the game where Ted had been "attacked" related to Lovecraft, who was apparently some kind of horror writer from the twenties who wrote a lot about gigantic octopus-headed creatures from other dimensions that he called "The Old Ones" and their nameless horrible horror, and bad geometry. Or something like that.

"So, your shooter couldn't get a date in high school. What's your point?"

"Hey, I represent that remark! There are a lot of hours to fill up pondering why the popular girls don't like you, and for some of us, a rich fantasy life augmented by fantastic fiction and yes—role playing games—there, I said it, helped us through this difficult period. You know, it's really just like why you played field hockey."

"First of all, I played soccer, and second of all, popular girls liked me."

"Yeah, but did they *like you* like you? How many did you nail?"

"Lesbians don't *nail*, okay? That verb implies the use of an implement that..."

"Ducking the question. So you were 0-for-high-school, is what you're saying."

"Yes, fine. Anyway, why is the fact that these people are your fellow dorks important?"

"Because it's *real*. That's the only reason they'd shoot up the Queequeg's. They can play this game and pretend they're dorks, and coordinate this thing nationwide or maybe even worldwide on the internet. Anybody who stumbled onto anything would just think these guys were Lovecraft fans, but they are really Cthulhu cultists! For real!"

"What the hell's a Cthulhu cultist?"

"Well, in one of these stories, it's a bunch of degenerate sailors and the like—you can tell they're evil because they're not white—I know, I know, somehow the racist part sailed right over my head when I was fourteen—anyway, they are trying to open portholes to other dimensions to bring about the return of these creatures so horrible to contemplate..."

"That contemplation of their horror would drive you

instantly mad, I get it."

"Right!"

"And this is real."

"Yes!"

"That's nuts."

"True! Also, there's no such thing as vampires. You could look it up."

"Ted, there are so many holes in your theory. First of all, what is anybody's motivation for bringing nameless horror to the Earth? Second, if they do all their planning in what is essentially a public space, why would they need to shoot up a Queequeg's to get it back?"

"I don't know. Maybe you can't get in to Randolph Carter's room without a key. Or maybe they found information from the *Necronomicon* and encoded it in the spreadsheets."

"What the hell's the *Necronomicon?*"

"Ugh, it's the book that unlocks the secrets of the dead. It was written by the mad Arab, somebody."

"The mad Arab?"

"I can't remember. Al somebody. Listen, these stories are from the twenties. They're not exactly PC. But Randolph Carter had a book written in Arabic tucked into a desk drawer!"

"I'm not buying."

"Well, I am. Which is why I'm going to Providence tomorrow."

This stopped Laura short. Ted was leaving town? Ted was doing something active? He'd followed her to Washington, to New York, and then to Boston, clinging to her like a remora. And now he was the shark all the sudden? It didn't feel right.

"I'm all for you getting out of town, but what's in

Providence?"

"Well, Randolph Carter had a map of Providence in his dorm room. I actually downloaded it to your computer, so we can look at it if you want..." Ted opened the laptop and Laura reached out and snapped it shut.

"You downloaded a file from a hostile web site?"

"Well, it's not a hostile site, I mean, it's just that some hostile people use it, and—"

"And you downloaded a file from this site where hostile people hang out and you were about to open it on my computer."

"Well, yeah. I thought we could look at it and compare it to a real map of Providence, you know, see if there are any clues..."

"Did it ever occur to you that there might be a virus or something on this file?"

"Uh. No. I mean..."

"Do not open it. In fact, give me this." Laura reached out and grabbed her computer away from Ted. "Okay, so besides the killer Trojan horse virus map, what else makes you think you should go to Providence?"

Well, some people believe that the *Necronomicon* was real and that Lovecraft had it and hid it somewhere in Providence before his death. Other people think he donated it to Brown, but of course their libraries insist there is no such thing as the *Necronomicon*."

"Which only proves to these nutballs that Brown University is part of the conspiracy, right?"

"Exactly! Because if they did really have it, they'd deny it! So, I figure they're in Providence looking for the *Necronomicon* somewhere. I'll get a bus down there or something and see what's up."

Laura felt something strange when Ted said this. It took her a minute to realize she was kind of hurt. All this time dreaming of Ted being out of her hair, and now he was just taking off. He'd only be fifty miles away, but still. Who was going to look out for him? And didn't he feel like he needed her anymore? And if he wasn't weighing her down, what would she use for an excuse for not having a real social life?

After dinner, Ted settled in to watch some reality show that Laura found too stupid to even use to kill time. So she sat down to plan the Providence Operation. Because Ted was nuts, of course, and this was way more likely to be an organized crime thing than some kind of cult killing, but what if he wasn't? Certainly if somebody had told her at the beginning of freshman year of college—or when she was a first-year student, she reminded herself, remembering how she had ripped into anyone who dared to call her anything containing the word "man" when she was eighteen—that there was a colony of vampires, and that the incredibly hot sorority girl she had a crush on was several hundred years old, she would have said they were nuts.

And besides, even a fruitless chase after the cult of C-somethingorother was more exciting than looking for Whitey at the ATM, which looked like a project that was going to drag on pretty much indefinitely, as they had a fresh tip to check out a strip mall ATM in Naples now, and the videos were being uploaded and would probably be ready for analysis tomorrow. Ugh.

So she decided to play a little thought game. Let's assume these people are really in Providence, and that they are incredibly powerful badasses. It wouldn't hurt anything to assume this as she did her planning. (And, some part of her brain whispered, It would keep Ted safe, because she had to keep her Ted safe.) First of all, Ted getting on a bus and going to Providence alone wasn't going to work. He hadn't been seen in his completely clean-shaven persona yet, except by some rats in the Queequeg's dumpster, but she didn't like the idea of him in an enclosed space like that for an hour. And maybe the authorities and whoever else was after Ted would be watching South Station and its adjacent bus depot.

"Hey!" Ted called from the couch. "Wanna watch *Massachusetts Marriage?* Twenty people in a gigantic house on Martha's Vineyard, and nobody knows who's straight or gay, but there will be at least five weddings at the end!"

"Can't talk. Working." Laura turned back to the computer, then turned back to Ted. "You made that up, right? That's not a real show, is it?"

"I swear to God!"

"I had a summer like that, except it was Nantucket, and nobody got married."

"No shit?"

"Well, there were only five of us, but one girl told me we could fool around, but we couldn't go out, because that would make her a lesbian."

"Whoa. Okay, drunk girls are making out on TV—I need to pay attention to this."

Laura turned back to the screen and her operational planning. She felt an excellent brain buzz coming on—the kind she thought she'd get running investigations at the FBI. Her mind felt electric instead of foggy as she thought out all the angles. If she were an evil conspirator searching for Ted, what would she do?

Okay. He'd need an apartment, but he couldn't rent the apartment, because then he'd have to put his social security number into circulation, and they had to assume that the Cazulu people had that from the hard drive at Queequeg's. So she'd get her bar ring (a big cubic zirconia engagement ring she'd bought for twenty bucks that helped her ward off male suitors when she was in a non-lesbian bar) and say she needed a place for her and her fiancé.

This was a good plan, but now she reached the problematic part. She was sure that she couldn't keep Ted from going to Providence, and going there would make him marginally safer from the Boston Police and FBI and whoever else was looking for him. But if the Cawhatever cult was real, and they really were in Providence, then they'd be looking for Ted while he was looking for them. And it just seemed very unlikely that Ted would be able to poke around so discreetly that no one would know he was poking around. So she would have to supervise any serious surveillance on the weekends. In the meantime, she needed to give him something to do that seemed like real work but would actually keep him out of harm's way.

She needed to do some research. She went to the kitchen, grabbed a container of Clorox wipes from under the sink, and wiped down the outside of her computer. Then she opened it and gingerly wiped down the keyboard. She replaced the Clorox wipes under the sink and found her screen-cleaning wipes in the top drawer of the desk. She wiped the screen clean and stuck her face up close to the computer to make sure the stench was completely gone.

"Did you just sniff your computer?" Ted called out. Laura gritted her teeth and fought back the tirade about how somebody had to make sure all the toxic filth was off of it.

Ted had said something about a temple, so Laura searched

for Jewish houses of worship in Providence and found ten different temples scattered all over the city. If she put him on surveillance of each temple for a day, that would buy her two work weeks of Ted doing probably pointless stakeouts. During that time, she might be able to figure out whether it was worth going down there and doing any real investigating.

"Oh my God, you have to watch this! This girl Nadine has already made out with two women and a man, and it's only day 2! She's such a ho!"

Laura didn't even respond, because she didn't have the energy to lecture Ted about his outmoded patriarchal judgments of female sexuality. She printed the map of Providence with the locations of the temples circled and typed up detailed instructions for Ted about inconspicuous surveillance. She knew she was risking offending him, but she felt like she had to be really basic, so she included instructions such as "Do not ask anybody anything while you're doing surveillance."

She flipped her laptop closed and found that, though she'd been up for over thirty-six hours, she was too hyper to sleep. Ted was asleep on the couch in front of the *Ten O'clock News*. Laura sat down to watch, and reflected that Bridget Tran y Garcia was pretty hot, and the next thing she knew it was five a.m.

Laura explained the plan to Ted and called in sick. She then dug out a needle and an old hoop earring and explained to Ted that he needed his ear pierced.

"No way! It's gonna hurt!"

"Don't be a baby. You got shot at, and now you're whining about getting your ear pierced."

"Yeah, well, he didn't shoot at me with needles, okay?"

"I don't care. You need stuff to distract people from your face. You wear a big earring, people will see that and not pay attention to your identifying features that can't be removed."

"Gah, okay, be quick! I hate this!"

Five minutes later, Ted was successfully pierced. Bald and clean-shaven with a gold hoop earring, he looked like a gangly Mr. Clean. Laura changed into exercise clothes, walked down the stairs and started up her Nissan Altima. She drove the five blocks to the Glen Road entrance of Franklin Park and parked her car in what she judged to be the most inconspicuous spot.

She got out of the car, popped her headphones on, and ran the tree-lined path up the hill, around by the high school football stadium, past the basketball and tennis courts and the back entrance to the zoo, and through the dirt path through the woods, and then back up the Hundred Steps, always her favorite place to end a run, even though she almost always had to stop running and start staggering by about step sixty. When she got back to her car she was covered in sweat but felt more awake and alert than anyone carrying as big of a sleep debt as hers should feel.

She got behind the wheel and said, "Ted? Are you in here?"

"Yes, and I'm already cramped up, and my testicles aren't used to this kind of compression. I think I'm gonna be sterile by the time we get to Providence. Isn't this kind of excessive?" he said. "I mean, we couldn't have just left the house normally?"

"Listen. You think there is a far-reaching conspiracy, and that these people want to kill you. We know for a fact that the latter part is true. So if the first part is true, we have to be extra careful. We can't be seen together at all, at least not within a mile of the Queequeg's where they knew you were yesterday."

"So you really think I'm on to something?"

"I think you're nuts, but I'm going to run this operation as if you're not nuts. Whether these people are supernatural cultists or just gangsters, we proceed extra carefully so we can keep you safe."

Ted was silent for a moment. "That's sweet!" he said, and Laura suddenly felt embarrassed. Fortunately, any maternal tenderness she felt toward Ted quickly evaporated when he said, "But wouldn't I be safer with a seat belt on? I'm just saying. In addition to my testicular discomfort, I'm gonna have such a knot in my back by the time we get to Providence that I won't be a very effective investigator, especially given…" Laura turned up NPR and tried to drown him out.

Once they arrived in Providence, Laura drove up the hill to Brown University and pulled the car over. "I'm going to go walk down the street to the admissions office to ask for some information for my niece who's coming to visit. Wait five minutes and get out of the car. Spend a couple of hours ogling Brown girls or something—"

"Are we near RISD?" Ted called out from the floor. "Because while I certainly have nothing against the Ivy League cuties, I think I'm more in an art school mood today."

"Knock yourself out. Walk down to the river and ogle the secretaries having lunch if you want."

"Hmmm… professional façade, wild, untamed interior? I like the way you think!"

"Christ, Ted, that's the way *you* think. All I meant was that I don't really give a shit what you do for the next four hours as long as you stay inconspicuous. So listen. Right now we are at the corner of Prospect and College streets. Okay?"

"Got it."

"What's the corner?"

Ted paused. "Prospector something?"

Laura gritted her teeth. "Prospect and College. Say it back to me."

"Prospect and College."

"Good. Now if you walk down the hill on College, you'll come to a coffee shop on the left before you come to the river. Got that? If you get to the river, you've gone too far."

"Got it."

"Just be in the coffee shop at 4. Hopefully I'll be able to give you the key to the apartment I'm renting for me and my fiancé."

"Okay, honey! Have a good day apartment hunting, sweetie!"

"Fuck you, sweetums!" Laura trilled in return. When she returned from the admissions office, Ted was gone.

She went and met the real estate agent, a woman named Aline who was wearing a rhinestone pin in the shape of a house with the word "Sold!" written in fake rubies across it. Aline took her first to a building with peeling paint and split banisters that looked like it might be condemned, then to a building where the blue vinyl siding was separating from the exterior walls and the interior doors appeared to be made of cardboard, and finally to a utilitarian gray box of a building containing six tiny, spartan studio apartments. It was not a nice place by any means, but it was the Taj Mahal compared to the other places she had seen.

"So as you can see it's a little snug, but it's easy walking distance to Brown and downtown, and of course the mall. The State House—didn't you say you'd be working at the

State House?"

"Yes."

"That's great. You can walk to work in twenty minutes, or drive in five. And hopefully you and your fella can put some money away while you're here so you can afford a better wedding."

Laura pasted a smile onto her face. "That sounds great. I haven't even dared to tell him what the dress cost."

"Honey, take my advice. Don't. Don't tell him what anything costs. What he doesn't know won't hurt you." Aline grinned conspiratorially at Laura, who gave a giggle that she hoped was the appropriate response for one of these "we sure do put one over on the boys" conversations that her real self would never have.

She went back to Aline's office, signed a check and the rental agreement and got the keys. She spent the next hour procuring a futon with sheets and a blanket and a prepaid cell phone for Ted's use. She dumped all the stuff in the apartment and went to the coffee shop to meet Ted.

He was in line right in front of her and surprised her by not waving and smiling and blowing their cover. As Laura added milk and Splenda to her coffee and Ted fumbled with the half-and-half, she laid the key and Aline's card with the apartment address on the counter by the stirrer sticks and Ted palmed it like a pro. She took her coffee to go and looked back at Ted sitting alone at the table. As she walked back to the car, she felt a terrible sadness and longing to go back and be with Ted. She wondered if this was how parents felt when they left their kids playing in the block corner in preschool and went off to work for the first time.

It was dark as she drove back to Boston, and she tried listening to NPR, but she couldn't focus. She found herself worrying about Ted. She resisted the urge to call him until she got half an hour away, and he didn't answer. Her heart started pounding, and she wondered if she should turn around at the next exit. She told herself she was being silly, that she'd try him again in ten minutes, and she was reaching for her phone to call him again when it started ringing. She saw it was Ted and felt a surge of relief.

"Hey," he said. "Sorry I missed your call, but I kinda had my hands full, if you know what I mean. You think you could have furnished some tissues here?"

"Aaagh! I just wanted to check and make sure you were okay, but obviously you're well enough to be disgusting. Good night."

"Good night. Oh, and, um. Thank you. For everything."

"You're welcome," she said, and hung up the phone.

SEVEN

T ed woke up disoriented, then realized he was in his new apartment in Providence. He shuffled to the bathroom, his footsteps echoing loudly through the nearly empty apartment, peed for a really surprising length of time, and went into the kitchen nook. The peeling brown linoleum on the floor felt disgustingly moist on Ted's feet. He opened the fridge and found it empty and smelling slightly musty. Okay. He had to get out of here.

He padded back to the futon and found the instructions Laura had written out for him. She really did think he was an idiot. "Drink only enough caffeine to stay alert—you don't want to pee too much," she'd written, followed by, "Bring a container to pee into if you think you can do it discreetly. Getting arrested for indecent exposure would compromise your investigation. ☺" The smiley face was doubly annoying because it was so un-Laura and seemed to be saying, "I am completely serious but I think you'll take my condescension better if I present it in a semi-joking way."

And, anyway, temple surveillance sounded boring as shit. Laura had obviously spent too much time in a cubicle doing the boring scutwork of law enforcement. Well, she had to do what her superiors said, but Ted sure didn't. He wasn't going to lurk around watching kids go to Hebrew school while a pack of deranged killers who were, at least in their minds, in league with supernatural forces of evil, roamed the streets free. No. The hell with that. He was going looking for the *Necronomicon.*

Or at least looking for the people looking for the *Necronomicon.* The first stop was the library at Brown. He went back to the bathroom and examined himself in the mirror.

He was unshaven, he hadn't brushed his teeth, his head was looking slightly stubbly, and he was wearing clothes he'd slept in. "Perfect day to impersonate a grad student," Ted said to his reflection. He grabbed the stack of cash Laura had left so that he could go to the mall later and get himself a new wardrobe, pocketed his key, and left the house.

Ted walked down the street in the direction he thought he remembered Brown being in. He knew he was on the right track when his surroundings turned from working-class Italian to broke-upper-class college student and the bakeries and corner markets turned into used CD stores and coffee shops. Finally he reached the Brown campus.

It was a beautiful spring day. Ted enjoyed the smell of the air and the slightly cold breeze on his face. He found a campus map and located the bookstore and the Rockefeller Library and wandered slowly across the campus. The streets, sidewalks, and greens were full of students, and there was infectious joy about the end of winter in the air. All of the students were rushing the season—they'd shed their parkas and sweatshirts and were strolling around in shorts and short-sleeved shirts and even, right across the street, a tank top, though it couldn't be sixty degrees yet. Ted just took in the parade of undergraduate girls. Legs were visible, arms were visible, breasts were concealed by only one or two layers, and, thanks to the wind, nipples were, for the most part, erect. It was springtime, and everything seemed beautiful, and for the first time in ten years, Ted had something important to do. For the first time since Half-caf had shot up the Queequeg's, and probably for the first time since the fire, Ted had the fully formed thought that he was glad he wasn't dead.

He exited the gate on Prospect Street and realized Laura had parked right across from the Rockefeller Library yesterday.

The Rockefeller Library was a giant concrete cube with long, skinny windows. Ted wondered briefly who had decided that this was the default architecture for college libraries. He personally thought they should be more gothic and creepy and full of little nooks of knowledge.

He walked up the steps and read the sign on the door. "Anyone Entering Brown University Libraries MUST Have Valid Brown ID or Affiliated Photo ID." Well, that killed his "wander around the library looking for the *Necronomicon*" plan. He peeked through the glass door, then slapped his forehead like he'd forgotten something, and walked down the hill to the same independent coffee shop where he and Laura had performed the James Bond-style covert key exchange yesterday. He was never setting foot in a Queequeg's again if he could help it. He ordered a large Sumatra which was served to him in a pint glass, and he took it to the bar in front of the window, sat on a stool and thought. He'd seen the usual bored student checking IDs at the entrance to the library. He didn't have the expertise to break in any other way, so he'd have to get past the ID checker. He really wanted to call Laura and ask for her expert opinion on how to infiltrate a college library, but then he'd have to explain how he was actively pursuing evil instead of peeing into a Snapple bottle outside of Temple Emmanuel. He looked around and briefly considered trying to steal somebody's card—the guy at the entrance to the library wasn't even looking to see if pictures matched faces—but unless he got very lucky, he'd have to spend days lurking around hoping somebody would drop or forget their ID, and that was going to be way too boring.

Lacking any better plan, he had to brazen it out with the "forgot my ID" ploy. He could try it on every student drone's shift until he got away with it. But first, he'd need some more stuff to make himself look credible. He gulped down the end of the coffee, hoped that it wouldn't be too hard to find a public bathroom in forty-five minutes or so, and went to the bookstore.

He purchased a backpack, then walked up and down the sidewalk until he saw a bus coming up the street. He ran across the street in front of the bus, dropping the bag in a way he hoped looked accidental as he ran. The bus driver blew his horn, gave Ted the finger, and gleefully ran over the backpack. Once he'd retrieved the backpack and dusted it off, Ted decided it looked weathered enough to be credible. He returned to the bookstore and bought enough notebooks and pens to give the bag a convincing heft.

From the bookstore, he proceeded to the library. He walked through the door and faced the ID checker—a pale guy with a mop of brown hair and stubbly cheeks. Ted made a big show of looking into his pockets, then swung his backpack around and rooted through it, opening the Velcro pockets. He hoped his "I'm surprised, flustered, and angry by my inability to locate my ID" act was convincing.

"Aw, geez, I'm sorry," Ted said, "I must've left my ID

at home. Do you think you could let me in anyway? It's a twenty-minute walk back there, and I have class in an hour...."

Ted's heart pounded during the long seconds while the ID checker looked up from his fat textbook, sized Ted up, and decided he probably was exactly what he was pretending to be, rather than some pervert who wanted to masturbate in the women's studies stacks or something. "Okay," the guy said. "Sign in." He shoved a white binder with tattered photocopied pages bearing illegible signatures at Ted. Ted signed his own name in a completely undecipherable scrawl and strode through the turnstiles.

He walked around the library for a few minutes. The directory next to the elevator said nothing about rare books, so, walking past the hideous glass globes that illuminated the stairwell, Ted walked to the basement and began a systematic search of the library. The smell of books was heavy in the air, and the quiet seemed to surround him. All he could hear was the clacking of fingers on keyboards, and the occasional page turning. He hoped that nobody monitoring the security cameras was finding him very interesting.

When he saw the Absolute Quiet room, Ted fought back the urge to run in there and fart really loud. He imagined an instruction from Laura: "Avoid audible flatulence in situations where quiet is necessary. ☺"

After ten more minutes, Ted had walked every easily accessible inch of the Rockefeller Library. He'd found neither *Necronomicon* nor Cthulhu cultists, unless they were in here doing an excellent impersonation of grad students.

Feeling dejected, Ted trudged out of the library.

Exiting the library, Ted decided to turn left on Prospect Street. He walked around a bunch of utility workers tearing up the street in front of the List Art Building, another rectangular concrete fortress that seemed to be a rejected college library design. Glancing to his left as he continued up the street, he saw a white building marked Hay Library. He pushed the heavy wooden door open and found himself in a marble entryway with a portrait of someone he assumed was Hay gazing benevolently down on him. To his right was a small room with a bunch of papers in display cases. A small sign read "Items from the Lovecraft Collection." Of course! The *Necronomicon* wasn't in the Rockefeller Library at all! It was here! Maybe.

Ted examined the papers in the cases. There was a letter from Lovecraft in New York denouncing all of the Mongrel Races he encountered there. Nice! There was a typescript of "The Call of Cthulhu." The rest were all letters and essays and certainly not the *Necronomicon*. But if it was anywhere in Brown University, it was in this building.

Ted decided to wander around. Through doors at the end of the hallway he could see the librarians behind a counter. It would certainly be no good to wander up and ask for the *Necronomicon,* so Ted decided to poke around. He walked up carpeted steps and found himself in another hallway under the gazes of a variety of portraits. He gingerly opened a couple of wooden doors with brass handles and saw people working behind desks. He walked up another flight of steps and found more doors and more hardworking librarians.

Well, if the *Necronomicon,* certainly the crown jewel of the Lovecraft collection (if it existed), had been stolen, it was unlikely they'd put other stuff from the collection on display. It was also unlikely that he'd be able to wander more or less freely through a building that had recently had a priceless text stolen from it. Then again, would they have been able to tighten up security after the theft of a book they claimed they didn't have?

Ted left the Hay Library and turned on to brick-sidewalked, tree-lined Prospect Street and walked aimlessly. Glancing to his right, he saw a wooden colonial house with a small wooden sign on the corner. "Samuel B. Mumford House," it read. Lovecraft had, according to a label in the display in the Hay Library, lived in the Samuel B. Mumford House at the end of his life.

Pulse quickening, Ted walked around the back of the house, trying to pretend he was just a grad student out for a stroll. There were no cars in the gravel driveway, but there was a garbage can. Still feigning a casual attitude, Ted opened the lid of the garbage can and found what appeared to be ordinary household garbage. A recycling bin next to it held a few issues of the *New Yorker* and *Vanity Fair*. Somehow Ted doubted that these periodicals were favorites of Cthulhu cultists. Still, it could be that they were occupying the Mumford House and posing as regular people while ripping it apart searching for the *Necronomicon*. There was nothing else to do but break in.

Ted gingerly removed the contents from the recycling bin and turned it upside down. Standing on it, he gently pushed upward on one of the windows, silently thankful that old colonial houses like this didn't have screens or storm windows.

The window seemed to be stuck or else locked. Ted spread his fingers on the glass and tried to give the window a more forceful push upward. This time it did open, but just about half an inch. As Ted was getting ready to slide his fingers under the bottom of the window, an alarm began to scream.

Panicking, Ted ran blindly from the house down Prospect

Street, then turned right hoping to get downtown and cower by the river or slip into the crowds at the mall or anything to just get the hell away from this neighborhood where the police were probably already looking for him for breaking and entering and/or murder. Stupid, stupid! He cursed himself for trying to do Laura's job and fucking it up so thoroughly. He'd be lucky to get home alive.

Ted was so busy cursing himself that he didn't realize he'd stumbled through the protective tape and into the Ocean State Power work site he'd passed earlier. He decided to brazen it out and keep running down the hill. Unfortunately, he soon found his path blocked. He stopped short and looked at the roadblock. The guard was a forty-year-old white guy who was remarkable only for the absence of the gut that most guys his age, and, indeed, most of the guys on this job site carried around.

"Can you not read?" Mr. Average said. He was obviously annoyed, but this strange diction and relatively low volume was not the obscenity-laced tirade Ted was expecting. "Where could you possibly be going in such a hurry?"

A part of Ted, the part that tended to speak in Laura's voice, knew he should just step around this guy and not draw any attention to himself, but another, louder part resented this guy questioning him like he was the high school principal instead of a guy digging up the road.

"Well, I hate to keep your wife waiting," Ted said, smiling.

The guy's face reddened and he got right in Ted's face. "I suggest," he said through clenched teeth, "that you walk away from this work area. You have disrespected me, and I cannot brook such disrespect. Uniform or not, if you are not gone from my sight in ten seconds, I shall take you into the back of the Ocean State Power van and perform such unspeakable acts of torture upon your person that you will beg me for the sweet mercy of death."

Ted froze. How many people on earth would use the phrase "beg for the sweet mercy of death"? He was standing here like an idiot having a face-to-face argument with the guy who'd impersonated a busty blonde in Virtuality and threatened Ted's life, nay, his very soul.

Ted quickly turned and ran, throwing "And you wonder why your wife wants a piece on the side. Freak!" over his shoulder. He ran until he found some steps down to the sidewalk that ran along the side of the river. He came to a bridge and clambered up the crisscrossing supports and hunched in the shade twelve feet above the walkway. For ten minutes he did nothing but watch the walkway beneath him. Eventually he convinced himself that the coast was clear, and he climbed down and took a circuitous route home. Once he was inside his apartment, he called Laura.

"Hey!" she said. "Find something at Temple Emmanuel?"

"Laura, I found them!"

"They're at Temple Emmanuel?"

"Ah, no, not exactly. They're, uh, tearing up College Street."

"They're tearing up College Street? How?"

"Well, they've got Ocean State Power trucks."

Laura sighed. "And what exactly makes you think they're evil cultists?"

"I, um, actually spoke to one."

"You *spoke* to one? Jesus, did you even look at the instructions I wrote you?"

"Well, I got hung up on the part about peeing in a plastic jug."

"I did not say a plastic jug! That would make way too much

noise! Anyway, you… You know, your life could very well be in danger, and you just go toddling into even more danger! Do you *want* to die, Ted?"

Ted was ashamed. "No," he said quietly.

"Then you have to let me help you. Now. Why did you speak to this guy?"

"Well, I got distracted because I was running away from… uh."

"Running away from uh? What the hell is that? What were you running from?"

"I set off the alarm when I tried to break into Lovecraft's house."

Silence came on the line, stretched out, and made itself at home, not leaving for a full minute. Finally Laura spoke.

"And what did this power guy say that made you believe he's in league with the unholy?"

"Well, after I implied that I was late to an adulterous liaison with his wife, he told me he was going to make me beg for the sweet mercy of death."

"Yeah? And?"

"That's exactly what the virtual centerfold with the lead pipe said to me in Randolph Carter's room! Do you think there are two people in New England who would say 'beg for the sweet mercy of death'?"

Silence came back, but this time it was banished after only ten seconds.

"I guess I hate to admit this, but probably not. Unless that's like some line from one of your tentacle stories that everybody quotes or something."

"You think most power company employees quote Lovecraft when somebody says they're tapping their wife?"

"Tapping? What the hell is that?"

"You know, gettin' busy. Gettin' some. Hittin' it. Tappin' as in tappin' that ass!"

"Tapping? I guarantee that's a frat-boy coinage. Woman as keg. Jesus. Every time I think you guys can't stoop any lower, you surprise me."

"Yeah, okay men are pigs. I know I only did one year of college, but I had that down by my first semester. You're ducking my question."

"Alright. I admit it seems unlikely that a power company employee would defend his wife's honor with quotes from old horror fiction."

"Exactly! So they must be looking for the *Necronomicon* there."

"What street did you say they were on?

"College. In front of some concrete monstrosity of a building. Something art center."

Ted heard the clacking of keys in the background. "Okay. Is it the List Art Center?"

"Yeah."

"That is the original location of the Samuel B. Mumford House, which was Lovecraft's final home. They moved the Samuel B. Mumford House around the corner in 1959."

"I was right! Because if Lovecraft buried the *Necronomicon* under his house, that means it's under the List Art Center now! So they really are Cthulhu cultists!"

"Well, this does make it a little more likely that the people you saw digging up the street are actually looking for the *Necronomicon*. Up in the air is the question of whether this book which, by the way, everybody insists Lovecraft made up, actually exists."

"Still! I did some top-notch investigating!"

"Yeah, well, Sherlock, let me ask you a question. Was it

the Samuel B. Mumford House where you performed your botched break-in?"

"Yes!"

"Well, according to the site I'm looking at now, there's a plaque on the front that says 'Moved To This Location in 1959.' Did you see the plaque, Ted?"

"Well, there was something under the name of the house, but I didn't actually read it."

There was a percussive sound on the line. "That, Ted, was the sound of me slapping my own forehead."

"Yeah, yeah, read the signs next time, I got it. So what's our next move?"

"Let me think about that and get back to you. Oh. I gotta go. Talk to you later!"

Ted had a list of temples to check at home, but he wasn't even sure what he was supposed to be looking for there. A temple that was adjacent to a Place of Power. What the hell was a Place of Power, and would he know one if he saw it? Probably not. Back in Washington, he'd briefly had a girlfriend who was into all kinds of new age crap, and now Ted was wishing he hadn't been so good at tuning her out whenever she started talking about stuff like that, because "Place of Power" sounded like it was right out of the crystal-using, psychic-healing, spirit-channeling world that Ted had always found annoying.

Feeling dispirited, Ted decided to get some lunch. He wandered into a sandwich shop that seemed frozen in 1972. Not only were all the wooden chairs and tables at least thirty years old, but the names and prices of the sandwiches were scrawled on a chalkboard behind the counter in barely legible Deadhead script. Baffled by both the names and the penmanship, Ted stood in front of the counter with his mouth hanging open. From behind the counter, a young man bellowed, "You here to read or eat?"

"Do they pay you extra to be a dick, or is that a service you offer for free?" Ted said.

The sandwich guy looked momentarily nonplussed, and Ted decided to press his advantage. "What's the matter? You can dish it out but you can't take it? Is this like the thing here? You abuse the customers and they meekly take it because it's part of the charm? Is that the gimmick? Do you know how to make a Reuben, or do I have to call it "Friend of the Devil" or "Jerry's Folly" or something?"

Still reeling, sandwich guy called down the counter, "One Robert!" and said to Ted, "Seven-fifty."

Smirking, Ted paid too much for his sandwich and went over to the pickle barrel and removed a big dill pickle with a pair of tongs. Two minutes later, he was eating an exquisite Reuben and pondering his next move.

Should he go home and get the list of temples? He didn't feel a whole lot of enthusiasm for that. He was starting to get depressed again. The one thing he'd done right was figuring out that the Ocean State Power guy was a Cthulhu cultist. Or was connected to the people who removed Half-caf's body from the bloody Queequeg's. Maybe. Anyway, he talked like those people. And although Ted's confrontation with the Ocean State Power guy had allowed him to figure things out, it also pretty much guaranteed that he wouldn't be able to wander over there and observe them inconspicuously. So in finding his only lead, he'd destroyed his ability to follow up on it. Moron.

Suddenly, Ted slapped himself on the forehead. "Just remember you're a vegetarian?" his adversary behind the counter called out.

"Forgot to use a condom with your mom last night," Ted said. What had actually happened was that Ted remembered the long, skinny windows on one side of the Rockefeller Library faced directly onto the work site. It would actually be easy for him to watch these guys dig for the *Necronomicon* without being observed. That is, provided he could get into the library with no ID again.

He uncorked an oily, vinegary corned beef and pickle belch and set off for the library. Fortunately, a new student drone was on duty checking IDs. Ted gave the same sob story about forgetting his ID, and signed in as Howard Phelps. He managed to find an unoccupied carrel next to a window on the third floor. He grabbed a book—*Patterns of Animal Disease*—from a nearby shelf and opened it to a random page. He opened a notebook and grabbed a pen and pretended to be taking notes on the book while staring out the window. He hoped that anybody glancing casually at him would think he was just a procrastinating student taking a break from his research to stare out the window.

The crew was still at work, and Ted quickly found that watching a power company crew at work was not really that much more interesting than page 246 of *Patterns of Animal Disease*. After three hours of watching guys scurry around in a hole in the ground, he'd actually begun to turn pages in the book, because apparently some viral infection in emus in New South Wales in 1952 was pretty significant, and he wanted to find out why.

Ted kept half an eye on the goings-on in the street. After another hour, darkness began to descend, and Ted had to pee and felt hungry. He wasn't sure, but he guessed Laura's surveillance manual would advise against peeing in a cup in a college library. Not that he had a cup handy anyway.

He was just about ready to give in to the demands of his bladder when something happened down in the street. All at once, the entire crew stopped moving. All except one guy who came scurrying from the direction of the List Art Center with something large under his arm. He began to pull out the object to show everyone, when the guy Ted had threatened to cuckold earlier, Mr. Average, made a gesture that clearly meant "get that thing into the truck, you idiot!"

The guy holding the buried treasure climbed into the van, and the entire crew began to pack up. Mr. Average rooted around in the back of the truck, pulled out a length of pipe, and turned his gaze right on the window where Ted was sitting. He held up the pipe and smiled.

Ted suddenly felt very cold, and his urge to pee got even worse. Could Mr. Average possibly have noticed his surveillance? Was he alluding to his virtual assault on Ted by holding up the pipe? Or had Ted just imagined the whole thing? His instinct was to cower under his carrel, but the hell with that. Slamming his book closed and forever abandoning the mystery of the Great Emu Plague, Ted ran from the library and into the street. As he turned the corner, the van was starting up and pulling away. Mr. Average did not appear to be waiting to brain Ted with a length of pipe. Ted wrote down the license number and the number on the side of the van as well as the number on the "How's My Driving?" sticker. The van pulled away down the street, and without a car or even a bike, Ted knew he couldn't possibly follow. And with Mr. Average in a pipe-swingin' mood, he wasn't sure he wanted to. Still, he could harass them.

He called the "How's My Driving" number and said, "Yeah, I was just crossing College Street legally in a crosswalk and was nearly struck by van 4C24. Yes. My name? Charles Dexter

Ward. Right." He'd used another name out of Lovecraft, hoping that if this call ever bore fruit, the guys in the van would at least know someone was on to them.

His next call was to Ocean State Power customer service. "This is August Derleth at the List Art Center?"

"Can you spell your last name for me, sir?" an unmistakably Indian voice asked.

Ted spelled it, gave the street address, and said, "Your crew that was digging here seems to have done some damage to the south wall of our basement."

"I'm sorry, sir, I have no record of any of our crews working in that area today."

"Well, we have a record of it—a crack in the wall and plaster dust all over the place. It was van 4C24."

He heard keys clacking. "I'm sorry, sir. My information shows that van 4C24 is currently undergoing maintenance."

"I see. Well, this is clearly a matter for Providence Police, then. Thank you for your assistance."

"Wait, sir—" the guy in Bangalore said as Ted hung up. Well, that ought to rattle their cage. He thought about calling the police but decided to go pee and then call Laura instead.

Laura sounded hassled when she answered. "Listen, I told you I was going to call you back, but—"

"They've got it, Laura."

"Who's got what?"

"The cultists. I was surveilling them from the library where they couldn't see me, well, at least I thought they couldn't see me, but anyway, I saw them pull something out of the ground and pack up and drive off."

"So maybe they found that rat that chewed through the cables."

"When I called Ocean State Power, they told me that van

was out of service. This has to be it. What do we do?"

"The first thing we do is calm down. Now this thing is written in, what, ancient Sumerian or something?"

"I guess probably Arabic, since the author was—"

"The mad Arab. I remember. Okay. So it's unlikely that they're going to be able to put the information they have to use right away. So the best thing we can do is to keep going about this systematically. You have to check out the temples. When I come down, I'll poke around at Ocean State Power."

"I called in a complaint that they'd almost run me down with the van, and also that they'd damaged the basement of the List Art Center."

"Hey, that's great work, Ted!" Against his will, Ted felt a surge of pride. "That will give me the cover I need to nose around and ask questions. You've done a great job today. Now go home and rest up for some temple surveillance tomorrow."

"Yes, Boss."

There was nothing to do back at the apartment but sleep, so Ted treated himself to a large portion of Pad Thai and followed it up with an ice cream he ate while watching girls. Alarmed by his own stink, he bought himself some soap and a Miskatonic U. t-shirt. At nine o'clock, he returned to the apartment, collapsed onto the futon and slept until seven the next morning.

When he awoke, Ted took his bar of soap into the shower, washed off the dirt of a day's surveillance and realized he didn't have a towel. He pulled on his new Miskatonic U. t-shirt, sniffed his boxers and decided that he'd be going commando today, and pulled on his pants.

He got coffee and spent a few minutes looking over the

temple map. Temple Beth-El was the closest, so he figured he'd start there. Once he made his way to Temple Beth-El, he looked for what was adjacent to it. Across the street was a park, which gave him a nice place to do surveillance and which could, he supposed, be a place of power.

Ted watched the temple for hours from a park bench with no shade. The skin on his face began to feel hot and tight, and he realized he'd been out in the sun all morning with no sunblock. He also realized that, being bald for the first time in his life, he might get to know the joy of the sunburned scalp.

He was hot, sunburned, and hungry, and not only was nothing out of the ordinary happening at Temple Beth-El, it actually appeared that nothing at all was happening there. Not a single person had come in or gone out in the three hours Ted had been watching.

"Screw this," he said. His Miskatonic U. shirt now had big sweat stains in the armpits, and his only other shirt was a sweat-soaked ball on the floor of his apartment. Well, he could rule out Beth-El and its adjacent parks as being the places mentioned on Randolph Carter's desk. Maybe that was enough work for one day.

He decided he was done for the day—it was time to go to the mall and get some clothes. He walked down to the mall, and his feet began to complain pretty seriously. He decided the shoe store should be his first stop. He knew this was the right decision the second he walked into the mall. Entering from the street, it wasn't clear to him exactly how huge the mall was, but once he walked in, he realized that, even with the tasteful beige and maroon industrial carpeting cushioning every floor, he'd definitely need new shoes just to get around the damn thing. It was gargantuan—like the big brother of every mall he'd ever been in. The mall was laid out like an "L", and here, in the long part of the L, three levels of stores ringed a cavernous atrium where, in front of the ferris wheel and next to the fountain, a band was tuning up. The short part of the L was, according to the map he stood in front of, home to the food court. Next to the map, there was a brass-and-glass information kiosk announcing various sales and special events. Taped to the kiosk was a neon green poster that said: "If you like Evanescence and Avril, you NEED to see Cherrified!" He didn't know if he should feel worse for the band playing a mall gig on a Wednesday afternoon, or the shoppers who were soon to have something that sounded like Evanescence and Avril Lavigne inflicted on them.

After about two bars of Cherrified's first song, Ted sided with the shoppers. Including himself. He quickly followed the comparatively appealing sound of dance pop into Old Navy, then hit the Gap and, finally, Banana Republic. ("In case I get a date," Ted said to himself as he strolled in to the most expensive of the Gap family of stores.) Finally, Laura's money was all spent, Ted was loaded down with a total of seven outfits, one for each day of the week, and Cherrified had, thankfully, stopped playing.

He checked his pockets and found two ones and a dollar seventy-two in change. It was only then that he realized he had no food and no means to pay for any. He'd have to call Laura for an infusion, but it would probably be sometime tomorrow before she could get him any cash. In the meantime, he decided that a big dose of caffeine would be the best bet for keeping his hunger pangs away for a few hours. Though it made him sweaty and panicky, he walked what he gauged was a quarter-mile to the Queequeg's on level three and purchased a medium latte. Unable to bear the idea of actually sitting in the Queequeg's, he found a bench next to the railing and in front of one of the free-standing vendor "pushcarts" that dotted the walkways of the mall. He collapsed on the bench and sipped his hot, sweet drink and thought about nothing and was content.

Until Cherrified came on for their second set. They had not saved their best material for the second set, and Ted groaned aloud. The pushcart vendor, a short, young woman with jet-black hair with one magenta stripe and piercings in her ears, eyebrows, nose, and tongue (and where else, Ted wondered), said something, but Ted's brain was so busy exploring the piercings he couldn't see and theorizing about the effect they might have that he didn't process what she said.

"I'm sorry?" he said.

"I said, I hear you. This band sucks so bad I can't believe it. This is their third afternoon here, and they're not getting any better."

"Wow. You ought to be able to get hazard pay or something. Can you get time and a half for this?"

"I wish," she said. "The worst part, I mean the part that really makes me nuts is that these awful songs are now stuck in my brain. I walked out of here last night singing one of them under my breath. I was pissed."

"I hate it when that happens."

"Yeah. So, you got any interest in some new body jewelry?" Ted was puzzled, and then realized that the pushcart bore a sign that said "Rings and Things." He also realized he was being flirted with, and he liked that. Of course, this girl thought he was the anorexic Mr. Clean instead of Ted, but then again, maybe he wasn't Ted anymore. Teddy died in a sorority fire, and miserable, broken Ted took his place, and maybe miserable broken Ted died in Queequeg's, and somebody new—who?—had taken his place. So maybe if it wasn't the real Ted this pierced girl liked, that was okay, because maybe he wasn't really the real *him* anymore. Maybe there was no real him—just a bunch of synapses that responded to whatever bizarre stimuli came his way.

"You know, I would love something, but I—well, it's a long and not very interesting story"—and Ted felt something funny in his guts and realized it was that he didn't like lying to this girl, even a lie as benign as that one—"but I kind of found myself without any clothes, and so I had to spend every single cent on clothes, and now I can't even afford dinner, let alone a new earring. This latte is my appetite suppressant."

The pierced one said, "Well, I'll buy you dinner if you let me wear one of your new shirts."

Did she mean what he thought she meant? Like when exactly did she want to put the shirt on? *After?*

Before he could answer, something weird caught the corner of Ted's eye. Mr. Average, no longer in his Ocean State Power uniform, now wearing a navy blue polo shirt and khakis, was strolling along the mall corridor. Ted had to hand it to the guy—if he were any more nondescript he'd be completely invisible. Mr. Average was carrying two obviously heavy bags from Ye Olde New England Candlery. That certainly didn't seem to fit the profile of a guy who tortured people until they begged for the sweet mercy of death. Then again, it was kind of cute that he was getting in touch with his softer side.

Ted was torn. If he stayed here, his night might get a lot better, but if he didn't follow this guy, his whole mission down here might go to hell. And, for that matter, if he followed this guy and got caught, he really might end up begging for the sweet mercy of death. And who the hell wanted to do that?

And yet, if he was right about the whole Cthulhu Cult Conspiracy, he couldn't just sit by and hope somebody else dealt with it. He'd have to take action. As much as he hated it, he decided to actually do his job, or whatever this stupid, crazy, pointless thing was, and possibly blow his chance with this completely adorable body-jewelry retailer. He blurted out some damage control. "I don't even know your name—"

"Cayenne."

"Like the pepper?"

"I was originally one of five Jennifers in my class."

"Uh, Cayenne, that is such a fantastic offer, and I really want to take you up on it, but I am—I actually have to run away right now, but I'm not running away from you, and I'll be back tomorrow, and I hope you can extend your offer because it really sounds fantastic and also I'm probably going to be completely famished by this time tomorrow."

Cayenne looked unconvinced. "Well, I don't know your name…"

Neither do I, Ted thought, then said, "Jonathan," before he could even think. Mr. Average was about to disappear around a corner, and Ted grabbed his bags and started to run to catch up to a comfortable following distance. He realized he should probably ditch the bags, but then what would he wear?

He ran until he reached what he hoped was an inconspicuous distance. When Ted reached the mall's exit, probably half a mile from the end of the mall from where he had entered, Mr. Average looked back. Ted quickly ducked into a lingerie store, and by the time he'd fought off the three saleswomen who had descended on him when he entered, Mr. Average was gone.

He walked out of the door and tried not to look like he was

looking around. This end of the mall was on a dirty, deserted street with the highway running overhead, and it seemed a million miles from the gleaming, high-traffic entrance Ted had used. He stood alone on the narrow street for twenty seconds before a dilapidated pickup truck came rumbling by. Looking around, he could see boarded-up buildings and empty lots, and, directly opposite him, rising almost to the level of the highway above, a giant, filthy stone building that had once been white. It was narrow and four stories tall, with gigantic columns that had probably once made it impressive. The windows and doors were boarded up and/or padlocked, and signs saying "No Trespassing—Police Take Notice" competed with graffiti that was either illegible or said things like "Fuck 5th Street Crew Wannabes."

And then, scrawled next to something that looked like "Case96," Ted saw something spray painted on the bottom of a gigantic column that might have been "Yog-Sothoth." Or possibly "Yo Sheila" or "Yes O'Toole." Graffiti was really hard to read.

Ted decided to walk around to the front of the building to see if there was an obvious place where Mr. Average might have gone in. He was keenly aware of how ridiculous he looked, and of every crinkle of his large paper shopping bags with the plastic handles that dug into his hands, but he couldn't just leave all his purchases on the street. As much as it's possible to creep when laden down with rustling shopping bags, Ted crept around through a weedy, trash-strewn lot to the front of the building.

When he got there, Ted got input from two senses that told him that he wasn't crazy, he wasn't lost in a fantasy—this was all too real, and all his suspicions were correct. A strange scent was drifting out of the building: a bayberry spice candle from Ye Olde New England Candlery. And above the door, two words and a symbol were visible through the layers of grime.

He decided it would be prudent to walk away quickly and call Laura from a safe place, and as he headed home, Ted wondered if any place was safe.

EIGHT

L aura was buzzing on the horrible employee lounge coffee. It felt like the coffee might be eating a hole in her stomach, but she headed down to the lounge for another cup anyway. She had no idea if she was going to be able to continue doing this stultifying work she'd been doing for a week now. She understood that she was paying dues, but she was impatient and bored and so eager to be doing something real that she found her mind wandering to the Providence Operation all the time, even though that might or might not be something real.

Before she got more than two cubicles away from her own, her phone vibrated in her pocket. She checked—it was Ted, and she surprised herself by feeling neither annoyance or resignation, but excitement. Maybe he found something!

"Hey Ted, what's up?"

"It's all real, Laura, it's all real, and I'm scared shitless but also kind of excited, but I don't know what to do next!"

"Back up, back up. What happened?"

He told her how he'd followed Mr. Average out of Ye Olde New England Candlery, and how he'd seen "Yog-Sothoth", or else "Yo Sheila" spray-painted on the building next door.

"And then I smelled a scented candle coming from inside

the building!"

"So the guy's looking for a filthy thrill, and he took a date there to do it among the pigeon poop."

"You know, if you'd seen this place, I think you'd understand that that's actually more far-fetched than my theory. But anyway, guess what the abandoned building was!"

"I don't know."

"Guess!"

"I don't know. A comic book store?"

"A four-story comic book store? No, It was a temple, Laura. An abandoned *Masonic* temple. The mall is the place of power! It's adjacent to the temple! Remember what it said in the notebook? They are trying to bring the Old Ones back to life right in the middle of the Providence Towne Centre Mall!"

"What the hell is a place of power, anyway? Is that from your pal's racist horror fiction?"

"Okay, he was dead long before my birth, so he's not my pal, and it's not in his fiction, at least not that I remember. Do you remember when I went out with Moonstone?"

"Moonstone? Was she the one with the crystals and the incense and stuff?"

"Yeah. I used to think about how hot her sister was whenever she started talking about New Age stuff, so this might be a little—"

"You used to think about her hot sister? Jesus, you are a disgusting human being."

"Yeah, yeah, I'm male, we knew this already. Moving on, what I think I remember about places of power are that they're places where the, like, boundaries between dimensions are thin, or something like that."

"The boundaries between dimensions."

"Well, yeah! If you're trying to call nameless horror forth

from another dimension, maybe you need to go where the walls are thin!"

"That's nuts."

"I know. I mean, I even think that's weird and crazy, but these guys appear to believe it. I mean, in these stories, there are always a bunch of evil conspirators trying to bring the Old Ones back. I can't imagine anything else you'd possibly be trying to do with a Necronomicon in a place of power."

"Okay. I'll google places of power and see what I get. Where are you?"

"I'm home, or whatever, in this apartment."

"Were you followed?"

"No. I took a really roundabout way home, and I was checking the whole time. You'd be proud of me—I'm totally paranoid!"

"Let me think about our next move and call you in tonight." Laura suddenly didn't need any more caffeine. She decided she'd take a few minutes to look for places of power and then do some illicit digging through the Bureau's electronic files for stuff about Cthulhu. Maybe if any of it was real, there would be some kind of clue somewhere in the Bureau's database. Of course, she'd leave her footprints all over the system, and if McManus ever decided to check up on her, he'd see exactly what files she'd been calling up, but she'd worry about that when it happened.

First she clicked on her internet browser. She typed "Places of Power" into a search engine and spent the next fifteen minutes clicking around looking for information. What she found, on a variety of new-age blogs and huckster websites, was a remarkably consistent picture of what places of power were, and Ted, with just his horror-fiction background and some half-remembered at his disposal, had pretty well nailed it. All the sites claimed that there were places where the barriers to other dimensions were especially thin, and that people always responded to such places, whether they realized it or not, by building things like Eiffel Towers and Washington Monuments and Stonehenges near them. A badly translated lecture by some Czech guru or something said: "Humanity feels the pull of places of power, and, therefore, will build structures of important in such places. So clock towers, town squares, monuments, all these things are cited where they are situated because of the energy powerful of the location felt by planners and builders of the monumental structures, especially popular works."

Ted had said the place of power was adjacent to the Temple. Laura supposed it made sense that planners and builders were sensing the energy of the place of power and sited the mall where it was situated due to the energy powerful. She smiled. It wasn't Stonehenge, but nobody could deny that the Providence Towne Centre was an important symbol of what its builders revered.

Laura thought for a moment. It might be time to start taking this whole thing more seriously. She'd been relying on Ted's second-hand Lovecraft knowledge for background information, but if she was taking him seriously at last, she had to find out some more information on her own. She typed Cthulhu into the search box and got millions of results. Someone had posted "The Call of Cthulhu" online, so Laura read it. It was pretty much as Ted had described it—bad geometry and horror so indescribable that it defied description.

Having finished with the primary source, she spent a few minutes looking through Lovecraft fan sites, ads for "What Would Cthulhu Do?" t-shirts, Lovecraft related porn, (of course) and the rantings of a few cranks who claimed that some combination of the Rand Corporation, the Trilateral Commission, the Illuminati and the international Jewish Banking conspiracy were hiding the Necronomicon and/or using it to control world events. It was pretty telling, though, that none of the millions of Cthulhu-related pages Laura could call up said anything about a conspiracy to bring the Old Ones back. Even the loonies who believed that a cabal of Jews was controlling the world with a Necronomicon pilfered from the Knights Templar had nothing to say about an active conspiracy to bring the Old Ones back.

Glancing around her cubicle to make sure no one was approaching, she accessed the FBI's internal network and searched for Cthulhu. No records found. She tried Randolph Carter and found a guy from Louisiana who was wanted for mail fraud. Lovecraft—no records. Yog-Sothoth. Nothing. Necronomicon: Level Z clearance required to access these records. Password?

Shit. Level Z? What the hell was that? She'd never even heard of Level Z clearance. Her own clearance was A-14. Well, whatever a Level Z file was, she wasn't going to be seen putting bad passwords into it. But why would this file even exist? Maybe it was the code name of an operation. Or maybe Ted was actually on to something.

Laura cleared her browser's history, gathered up her stuff, and swiped out. She'd made precious little progress on Whitey's withdrawals today. She hoped McManus wouldn't notice that either. Would anyone notice? The word around the office was that everybody knew this project was bullshit, that D.C. had just shoveled this bunch of shit their way to punish the Boston office for embarrassing the bureau nationally by having at least two agents in bed with Whitey.

Laura thought about the best way to help Ted keep an eye on the mall. If he was lurking around all the time, he'd eventually attract the attention of mall security, which was a bad thing for a fugitive from justice to do. She left the building and called the management office of the Providence Towne Centre.

The mall had two pushcart retail kiosks available. One thousand dollars would reserve one for the Harker corporation for a month. Laura read her Amex number out to the guy and hung up. A thousand bucks was a lot to invest in a surveillance operation, but she supposed it was cheap as far as saving the world went.

After work, Laura called Ted and told him that she'd put a deposit down on a month's rental of a pushcart at the Providence Towne Centre so that Ted would have an excuse to be in the mall looking bored all the time. She promised to find something unappealing for him to pretend to sell and have it overnighted to the apartment.

"So I looked up places of power," she said.

"Yeah?"

"Yeah. So it turns out you were right. They're places where cosmic energy currents run, or barriers between dimensions are semi-permeable, or so the people peddling crystal healing claim."

"I knew it! So they're going to summon forth the Old Ones right there in the mall!"

"Well, it certainly looks like they might at least try. So, uh, what happens if they succeed? Is there any more detail than what I read in 'The Call of Cthulhu?'"

"You read Lovecraft? That's really sweet!"

"It was for the investigation. Anyway, does your white supremacist pal have any more stories about what happens if they come back?"

"He wasn't a... well, I guess maybe... well, he wasn't active in any organizations. That I know of. But anyway, if they come back? Bad, bad shit. They are namelessly incomprehensibly evil, and I guess they cause untold horror, death, and misery."

"Got it. It's kinda convenient that so much of this stuff is unknowably indescribable, isn't it? I mean, it really saves him from having to imagine something and then describe it. So basically we have no idea what to look for."

"Well, I think we'll know if it happens. And it'll be really really bad."

"Okay. I can't... I mean, I really can't believe I'm saying this, but I think you have to call this in to the Bureau. If it's real, it's more than the two of us can handle, and it might be good to get some of the Bureau's resources behind it. You have to find a payphone, look carefully to make sure there aren't security cameras or an ATM with a camera or anything nearby, and call them up. Tell them about the temple, and tell them you know that the mall is the target. But don't mention anything about Cthulhu. Just tell them you think there's a terrorist cell meeting in the temple and that they are going to hit the mall. That'll at least get them to check out the temple."

"Okay. I'll do it."

"Great."

"Can I ask you something, though?"

"Okay."

"Are you just humoring me? Or are you just really bored at work? Or do you actually believe me? I mean, I don't know what pushcart rental costs, but it couldn't be cheap..."

"A thousand bucks a month. They'd better make a move

within the next thirty days, because I won't be able to afford to save the world for two months in a row. Anyway… there's something else."

"Yeah? What?"

"Well, I poked around in the computer system today. There was nothing for most of the bizarre words you've been throwing my way, but there was a file for Necronomicon."

"What did it say?"

"I couldn't get into it. It's a Level Z clearance. I don't know if anybody in my office could even get into it. I've never even heard of a Level Z clearance. I thought it stopped at E-1, and everybody with an E-1 clearance is in DC."

"But… what's that mean?"

"I really have no idea, but I suspect it means there's something big going on, or somebody really important knows about it. Maybe I'm wrong, and it's just a code word for a sting operation on mail-order brides for comic store owners or something. In which case I'm probably telling you to waste the FBI's time, but if this is something real, I just feel like it's actually more cautious to do something at this point than it is to do nothing."

Ted was silent for a moment. "It means a lot to me, you know. You believing me. Even in a kind of half-assed way."

"Well, you were right before, and it was pretty important. So maybe you're like the proverbial stopped clock." She smiled, and she hoped Ted could hear it through the phone.

Ted laughed. "Okay, so since I'm on a roll, let me tell you about the girl I met today. Ted prattled on about some overly-pierced pushcart vendor he had a crush on, and Laura signed off. She had a hard time sleeping. She wondered if Ted should get a gun.

The following morning, after the usual card swiping

routine, Laura sat down at her desk, clicked on her email, and groaned when she saw McManus' name in her inbox.

"Harker: my office as soon as you read this," the email said, and Laura felt that sour-stomached, trip to the principal's office dread (she had, despite the type-A nature of her last ten years, actually been sent to the principal's office twice in her life: once in second grade for kicking Steve Raymond in the groin in a heated kickball dispute, and once in seventh grade because Christian Zur had copied off of her math test.). Shit. He had checked up on her, the one day she was doing something she wasn't supposed to. How was she going to answer the questions about searching for Cthulhu? And how many extra hours of ATM tape would she have to go through to atone for not doing enough yesterday? Her mind raced, trying to think of a credible lie. She came up with something about how a friend gave her this story about a cult to read, and she was just curious, wanted to see if it had any basis in reality. Thin, but it was all she had.

She looked at the email again, and the dread quickly gave way to hatred for McManus, which was more fun and more manageable.

"Would it kill you to put a verb in that sentence? Christ," she muttered, deciding to play this in the "I'm really busy right now why are you annoying me" way versus the "Oops, you caught me," way, and hoping that it would make a difference.

She did not hover in McManus' doorway but walked purposefully toward his desk. He sat there, doughy red face even redder than usual, gut straining at the buttons of his shirt. "You need to see me?" Laura said.

McManus looked up. He appeared to be clenching his teeth.

"Harker." McManus paused, and Laura could see, even

through layers of jowl, his jaw muscles on the side of his head pulse in and out several times before he spoke again. "...I don't have any idea how you managed to work this, especially without going through me, but I got word from DC today that your transfer has been approved."

Laura searched her mind. She hadn't put in for a transfer, and if she had, it would have had to go through McManus. What the hell was going on?

"Uh, sir, I, uh, I'm sorry, but I'm a little confused."

"Yeah. I'm confused too. In my day, we had to pay dues before we ever got any kind of assignment worth doing. But I'm just an old white guy, some kind of dinosaur, and apparently the old rules don't apply to young women, or something. I suppose I should count myself lucky you didn't file some bullshit hostile environment claim or something, so at least you didn't take me down on your way up." He paused and glared at her like nothing would make him happier than jumping across the desk and clocking her. "Well, it's the twenty-first century. I guess we had our shot at running things, and now you get to take over. So go celebrate. You've got your wish. You're going to counter-terrorism."

"But, sir, I..." she wanted to say she'd never put in for the transfer, but then she might not get to go to counter-terrorism, and whatever they were working on over there, it had to be a hell of a lot better than what she was doing here.

"I mean, don't get me wrong. You're a good agent, you work hard, and God knows I'd give my left nut not to have to do this Whitey ATM bullshit anymore, so I don't blame you, and I don't even blame you for going around me, because if you thought I'd stand in your way, you were right, so at least they got a smart one. But I've got twelve guys in this office every bit as smart and competent as you, with more seniority, but no ovaries. That's all. Oh, yeah, they want you up there right away."

"Thank you, sir!" Laura said, turning around and all but skipping out of the office. She'd fantasized for ages about telling McManus off, and, in the end, the best thing she could possibly do to piss him off was to smile and thank him for the transfer. Ha!

Feeling happier than she could remember, Laura went back to her desk, decided she could clean it up later, and took a pad of paper and a pen to the elevator. Heart pounding with excitement, Laura pushed the button for the tenth floor.

Once she reached the tenth floor, she was disappointed to see that it looked exactly like the eighth floor—a cluster of drab cubicles in the center of the room, offices with glass doors ringing the outside wall, offices with wooden doors to show you who was really important, and a couple of conference rooms. Laura noticed that counter-terror had much newer conference room furniture than organized crime. She wondered if they just moved the stuff down as it got older, until the mail fraud guys down on four got milk crates and old doors.

Agents were bustling around, and nobody seemed to notice her. She walked tentatively over to one of the offices with a wooden door. The door was ajar, but Laura gave a knock she hoped was confident and respectful at the same time.

"Come in!"

Laura walked into the room and found herself facing a middle-aged Asian man. According to the nameplate on his desk, he was Mr. Nguyen. Normally she would have begun with "Mr. Nguyen, I'm Laura Harker," but she realized to her embarrassment that she wasn't really sure how to say

Nguyen, which threw her off her stride, so she found herself saying, "Uh, Mr., Uh, good morning, sir, I'm Laura Harker? I was told to report here?"

"Yeah. I just got the paperwork last night. Your transfer came in from DC. You must have some pretty powerful friends."

"Honestly I don't, unless you count my friend who works in the coffee shop, heh-heh." Mr. Nguyen looked at her blankly, and rather than interpreting this as, "I understand that you have made a joke that is completely unfunny," Laura thought he meant he didn't understand that she'd made a joke.

"Because, you know, everybody needs their coffee, right? He could slip them decaf, and the city would come to a halt!" Mr. Nguyen continued to look blankly at her. "Pretty powerful…" Laura trailed off.

There were five agonizing seconds of silence, during which time Mr. Nguyen didn't blink. "Well, be that as it may, you're here now, and I'm always happy to get additional personnel up here, so I'm glad you're here. And I happen to have an assignment for you."

Yes! An assignment! Cool!

"I'm afraid it's kind of a rookie hazing thing—that is to say, I know you're not a rookie after—" he glanced at his computer screen—"three years with the bureau, but you're new up here, so I'm afraid I have to give you this.

"We got an anonymous call about somebody trying to hit the Providence Towne Centre Mall. Now, as you probably know, malls are our softest targets, and frankly our worst nightmare, because if they start hitting malls, the economy's going to tank in a way that will put 9/11 to shame."

"Not to mention the loss of life," Laura said, then realized she should have shut up. Too much adrenaline, and she was having trouble controlling her mouth. That was supposed to be Ted's problem.

Mr. Nguyen looked at her for five seconds, then said, "Goes without saying. So, anyway, we got this anonymous tip about people hitting a mall, and it said they were using an abandoned building next door for planning. So I'm taking three guys off the playoffs and sending them shopping. And, I'm sending a panel van down there with some surveillance equipment to watch the building next door. You know how to run a listening rig?"

Laura considered lying, but instead said, "No, but I did see *The Conversation*."

Once again she got the look, and Mr. Nguyen said, "Great movie. Well, Agent Killilea's a great tech, he can make sure it's all running okay and you can just sit there with the headphones on."

"Yes sir."

"I hope you showered this morning, because you probably won't for a couple of days. It's not going to be glamorous, but try to remember two things. The first is that although the overwhelming majority of these tips turn out to be complete bullshit, there is always the possibility, however remote, that it's not bullshit, and that by doing this boring, unglamorous, ultimately thankless job, you're going to save hundreds or thousands of lives."

Laura felt a little swell of pride. Now *this* was why she got into law enforcement.

"And if that's not sufficient motivation, picture yourself in DC with fifty cameras in your face answering questions from some pole-up-the-ass senator about why you didn't prevent this horrible attack. Get the picture?"

"Yes sir."

"Good. You'll find Killilea in the third cubicle on the right. Get to it."

"Yes sir." The spring was back in Laura's step. The chase was on! And even though nobody knew it, nobody could know it, she was responsible for this assignment. Which meant that if it turned out to be a bust, she'd be suffering more than anyone, sweaty and constipated in the back of the van, but if it was for real, she'd be an honest-to-God law enforcement hero. Pretty damn cool.

She really wanted to call Ted and tell him the good news, but Killilea had to brief her for what seemed like hours but was only forty-five minutes, and when they gave her an hour to get home, get changed, and get back, she stole time in her apartment as she pulled on comfortable stakeout clothes and called Ted.

"Hey, boss!" he said.

"Ted, guess what? Ugh, no, you know, no bra is eighteen hour, no matter what they say—"

"You called to tell me that?"

"No, no no. I'm multi-tasking because I'm in a hurry. But I got transferred, I don't know how or why, but I'm not gonna argue, and I'm staking out a certain place adjacent to a certain place of power! Today!"

"Thank God. Because I woke up at four, totally freaking out about how I'm going to get killed, how this thing is way bigger than we thought it was, how I was over my head, I'm a crappy secret agent."

"Well, with a couple of notable exceptions, you've done great so far."

"I know, I know! Hey, what the hell are these things you bought for me to sell at the pushcart?"

"Two gross of cell phone covers for a model Nokia no

longer makes. They were very cheap, and I don't want you distracted from your real work by having any actual customers."

"Cool!"

"Alright, I gotta go. I gotta turn my phone off while I'm doing the surveillance, but I'll call you when I can. Be careful—you're on your own for a few hours."

"I got it!"

NINE

When the FedEx guy—white, red-faced and grumpy, had arrived at Ted's apartment, he'd had a moment of panic until he realized that the guy was most likely delivering the cell phone covers and not here to kill him for trying to prevent the summoning of the Old Ones. Sure enough, Ted signed for the package and the FedEx guy went on his surly but peaceful way. Carrying his wares, Ted trudged down to the Providence Towne Centre. He was trying to think more like an undercover agent, and right now he was thinking that lugging a couple of big, clear plastic bags full of crap down the street was not the greatest way to stay inconspicuous.

Once at the mall, Ted wandered around looking for the management office, because he had no idea where his unpushable pushcart was located. Eventually he saw a narrow, linoleum-tiled hallway tucked in between the Wilsons Leather and Natural Wonders. He walked back until he came to a white metal door that said, in plain black letters, "Mall Office."

Ted opened the door and found himself in a small, white room, lit by fluorescents in the drop ceiling. In the center of the room was a nondescript brown desk, and behind the desk was a middle-aged black man in a blue suit.

"Uh, hi, I'm Jonathan, uh, Salem? The lady at the Harker company sent me down here to sell stuff at a pushcart?"

The guy extended his hand and said, "John Thomas." Ted shook his hand and used all the energy at his disposal to suppress a fit of giggles that was fighting its way to his mouth. "Yes. I currently have two cart vacancies. Your employer didn't express a preference, so I guess it's up to you. I've got one outside Industrial Dessert Company, and one outside Ye Olde New England Candlery."

Near where Cayenne worked! Score! Also, up there on the third level, he could keep watch on more of the mall than he could on the first level. Ted tried to quiet the part of his brain that said he'd need at least four other people to really watch the mall effectively.

"Uh, well, I like the candle smell better than the smell of the food at Industrial Dessert, so I guess I'll take that one."

"Are you sure? That first-floor location sees a lot of foot traffic."

"But not enough to keep the cart in business, huh?"

"No, they were doing great—I just got too many complaints from family diners that they had to explain to little Jimmy what a novelty condom cart was, like little Jimmy doesn't know that from sneaking down and watching Cinemax on Friday night, but whatever. I don't see how they could object to their precious angels seeing some cell phone covers."

"All the same, I think I'd rather have the candle one."

"Okay. You know where it is?"

"Yeah."

"You got signage?"

"Sorry?"

"Signage? You know, a sign?"

"Oh. They didn't provide me with one."

"Well, I'll let you open today, but tomorrow you have to have one up. Here's a sheet with the approved fonts, sizes, materials, and manufacturers. Make sure they get one here soon. All the carts have to have signage."

"Okay. Signage. Got it."

The mall manager rose and shook Ted's hand, and Ted walked back from the spartan office to the relative opulence of the mall. He took the first escalator up and walked for a full five minutes until he came to the empty pushcart.

He threw his bags down and looked at the Rings and Things cart. The stool was empty. No sign of Cayenne.

Well, that was fine anyway. He wasn't here to flirt. He was here to surveil. Or whatever. Look. Watch. Keep the mall under surveillance. He hoped the FBI was watching. He did feel good knowing that Laura was around somewhere, even if he didn't know where. He wasn't alone.

He was ravenously hungry, though. Laura had been so excited and had gotten off the phone so quickly that he'd forgotten to ask about another cash infusion. He really didn't know how he was going to get any money. His merchandise was specially designed not to sell, and anyway, as he looked at the cart, he realized that he was supposed to provide his own cash register. Which he didn't have. While he hoped the FBI was watching carefully enough to prevent any attempt to call forth the Old Ones, he also hoped the FBI didn't look too closely at him, because if they were at all observant, they'd notice that he was only somebody who was pretending to work at a pushcart.

Ted moved the stool to the end of the cart closest to Cayenne's cart and tried to remember to look alert. But what was he looking for, anyway? He'd only recognize one of the cultists. Would they walk in here with a gigantic leather-bound book and a bunch of bayberry spice candles and draw a big old chalk circle on the floor and invoke their evil masters? Or would they just mumble something under their breaths and rip open a hole in the fabric of reality, bringing gigantic octopus-headed evil deities through to romp through Providence?

Ted suddenly felt like his stomach was clenching around a block of ice as he pondered what it would really look like to have the Old Ones loosed upon the earth. Would it really be the end of the world? Would the Old Ones prefer to rule over a barren wasteland with bad geometry, or would they be happy to have insignificant human gnats doing their bidding? Would seeing them drive everybody completely insane? Ted figured the best-case scenario if the cultists succeeded was that these giant monsters would go on a Godzilla-style rampage and kill tens or even hundreds of thousands of people before the US military took them down. And the worst-case scenario was that life on Earth would be transformed into an unfathomable nightmare forever. Ugh.

Ted looked at the old people in their white walking shoes strolling by, at the hot young moms pushing strollers, at the teens obviously skipping school, and he envied them their ignorance. They went to bed every night thinking vampires were just something from the movies, and that horrific alien Gods were just figures out of overwritten horror fiction. They had no idea that everything they cared about or valued was teetering along like a unicycle-riding clown on a tightrope.

Well, this was a depressing line of thought. Ted tried to call back the heroic adventurer he'd believed himself to be, the one who was active in the face of danger, the one who was going to win. He suspected that guy wouldn't come back until he'd eaten something.

He went back to putting the old cell phone covers up on the little shelves. Just as he was deciding where to put the last of the Hulk movie tie-in cell phone covers, Ted saw Cayenne walking toward her post with a gigantic cup and a small bag from Queequeg's. "Hey! Cayenne!" Ted called.

Cayenne looked up and smiled. "Hey, Jonathan. You weren't kidding about coming back, huh?"

"Yeah." He tried to think of something else to say. Because I am hunting devotees of horrifying deities? Because you're hot? Because I am pursuing a career in obsolete merchandise sales?

"So." She said. "Did you ever get any food?"

Ted smiled. "You know, I didn't. I'm having some difficulty accessing my money right at the moment…"

"All your assets tied up in obsolete cell phone skins?"

"Something like that. So, no, I haven't eaten anything since lunch yesterday. I think I'm going to have a mystical experience."

"Well, do you wanna eat my muffin?"

Ted stared at Cayenne for far longer than he should have. Finally he realized she was holding out the small bag from Queequeg's and actually offering him a baked good. "Oh wow, that is really sweet. Are you sure? I mean, I don't want to poach your mid-morning snack."

"I had breakfast. Go ahead."

Ted opened the bag, saw the famous Queequeg's double-chocolate muffin, and had a brief flash of exploding glass and crumbs when Half-caf had shot up the baked goods just a few days and an entire lifetime ago. He felt a brief upswell of nausea as he remembered the gore everywhere, the intestines, the brains, the blood. With a great effort, he turned off the movie of the shooting, banished the horrible images from his mind ("If you're going to wake me up screaming every night, you can at least have the courtesy to leave me alone during the day," he told them.), and took a bite of the muffin.

Suddenly his mouth was filled with saliva, and he thought his brain might explode with pleasure as he ate the most delicious thing he had ever tasted. He looked up seconds later and realized that Cayenne was looking at him slack-jawed, and that stuffing his face like that might not have been the best impress-the-strange-but-hot-girl move.

"Wow." She said. "You really were hungry."

"Yeah," Ted said, crumbs dribbling from his mouth. He could feel himself blushing.

"So," Cayenne said. "What brings you to an exciting career in pushcart sales?"

Shit! Ted had no cover story at all! How could he be so stupid? What could he possibly say? He tried to stall. "I will tell you, but how about you first."

"Are you sure you want to hear it? It's actually a really sad and weird story."

"Are you sure you want to tell me? I mean, I didn't mean to get personal…"

"Well, see, that's hard, because when you have some horrible thing happen, then everything relates back to that, and so even the most innocuous question gets personal."

Ted didn't know exactly what to feel. He felt that Cayenne might be a kindred spirit, somebody as traumatized as him. On the other hand, she barely knew him and was verging into what was probably going to be oversharing territory. His crazy-o-meter was beeping, and he was afraid the full crazy klaxon alarm would sound in his mind if he let her keep talking, so he had to steer the conversation to more innocuous territory.

"Okay, okay, let's save that stuff for later, then. Tell me about a childhood injury."

She told him about a tire swing and a broken arm, and just as Ted was getting ready to tell the story of when he'd been pushed off a slide and bitten a hole in his cheek, a pack of teens approached Cayenne's cart and peppered her with questions. Ted took the opportunity to look around the mall, and he realized he should've been doing this all along. He felt a little bit guilty about being a crappy secret agent, especially with the fate of the Earth, or at least Providence, hanging in the balance.

So he looked around and tried to take in everything he could see about the atrium end of the mall. Two white-haired, white-sneakered matrons were making a circuit of the mall. Were they really geriatric fitness walkers, or were they just unlikely cultists? He reminded himself to watch them. Nobody else looked too out of the ordinary, but, of course, to judge by Mr. Average, the cultists didn't look too out of the ordinary. There were two guys in sunglasses wandering around down in front of the video game store. They were carrying big shopping bags that were obviously way too light to be stuffed with purchases. They wore jackets that looked a little too bulky even for the mid-spring temperature outside, much less for the seventy-one climate-controlled degrees in the mall. He hoped they were FBI guys, and he hoped they were being so obvious so they could act as deterrents to people hoping to rend the space-time fabric. The other options were that they were cultists preparing to provide covering fire when the ritual went down, or that they were FBI agents trying and failing to be inconspicuous.

He continued to eye the mall and realized that it was going to be impossible to weed out the cultists from the normal people. The fact that the cultists in the power truck had all been white guys in their thirties didn't mean he could rule out the Black, Asian, and Latino shoppers in the mall. And he couldn't assume that everybody white was in on it. Because, for one thing, that would implicate Cayenne, but also it would just make his job impossible. So, okay. He created a profile in his mind—a thirty-something white guy with a quick temper. That fit both Half-caf and Mr. Average, and he'd just have to assume that's what they were all like until he got new information.

The teens had dispersed from Cayenne's cart, and Ted tried to remember what they'd been talking about. But then one of the teens was actually at his cart. "No way! I've been looking all over for this! I got my mom's ghetto hand-me-down phone, and—well, look"—the kid—a white boy dressed in Celtics warmup gear that looked like it was sized for an actual member of the Celtics and not the five-and-a-half-foot kid in front of him—reached into the folds of his pants and pulled out a phone bearing a pink and blue skin. "Now how I'm supposed to make a call with this? You know? I'm gettin' digits from girls, I can't put it in my phone! How's that gonna look? 'Hang on, baby, let me just get out my pink and blue phone'—how much, yo?"

Ted had thought it so unlikely that any of his merchandise would sell that he hadn't even begun to think of a price. "Uh, five bucks. Three for ten."

"All right! Here you go, my man!" The kid hit Ted's hand with a twenty and walked away with six manly phone skins. "I know mad kids with this phone! You're gonna be popular!" the kid said, and he practically skipped away.

Cayenne was smiling at him. "Well, I had no idea you had such a brilliant business plan."

"Yeah," Ted said as he stuffed the twenty into his pocket, "neither did I."

"Hey—I'm gonna go get a sandwich. You want one?"

"Sure," Ted said, and reached in his pocket for his newly-acquired cash.

"It's on me," she said. "Just watch the cart and make sure nobody steals my inventory, willya?"

"Absolutely."

Cayenne returned with a chicken Caesar wrap and a Greek salad wrap. They ate in silence, mostly because Ted was still ravenous. He worked very hard not to shove food indiscriminately into his mouth.

The afternoon got busy for Cayenne, so their conversation never really got back on track. Ted saw the guys he hoped were FBI strolling not-quite-nonchalantly along the perimeter of the mall in a regular pattern: clockwise on one, counterclockwise on two, clockwise again on three. The senior citizens disappeared. Ted counted five angry-looking white guys in his field of vision, then ruled out the three who were obviously with wives and/or children because, despite how he'd taunted Mr. Average, he doubted either of the cultists he'd already met were marriage material, and he couldn't imagine anybody being stupid enough to bring their kids along on their attempt to rend the very fabric of reality.

He sold six more cell phone skins to two other absurdly grateful teens. He had forty dollars in his pocket! One angry-looking white guy—big, muscular, with short, dark brown hair—made an apparently pointless circuit of the mall. He wasn't holding any shopping bags, and he wasn't even pretending to glance into storefronts. He was just walking around. Ted hoped the FBI guys were noticing this, but the angry white guy was going clockwise on three while they were going clockwise on one, so he was pretty much directly on top of them, ensuring that he wouldn't be noticed. Ted felt his heart start to hammer as the guy walked toward him. He certainly looked like he was walking purposefully now, and whatever his purpose was in approaching Ted, it really couldn't be good. Ted looked around frantically for escape routes. He was still between the guy and the nearest exit, so he could probably run for it, but that would pretty much eliminate the possibility of his remaining an invisible vendor and might even get him shot if there were other FBI agents watching the mall who were getting bored and jumpy.

The guy got closer and closer. Ted looked around—he had nothing he could even hope to use as a weapon, and his hand-to-hand fighting skills were poor, especially when matched up with a guy as big as this one. In the midst of his panicked fight-or-flight response, Ted had a moment of sick clarity. "This is how my story ends," he thought, and followed this quickly with, "At least I got rid of the vampires." He was glad he wouldn't be around to see the Old Ones take over, but he wished he'd told Laura he loved her.

Finally the guy got right up in Ted's face. He smiled, but it looked far more like a threat display than an expression of happiness.

"My phone," he said, through gritted teeth. "It's obsolete. How much for a skin?"

Ted's mouth was so dry that it took a minute for him to creak out, "Five bucks. Three for ten."

The guy seemed to take that in for a second. Ted could see the muscles on the side of the guy's face pulsing as he clenched his jaw. "Seems like a high price for something obsolete. I saw them at Ocean State Odd Lots for two."

"Well, high overhead here at the mall, what can I tell you. I don't actually set the prices, I just…" before Ted could finish, the guy shoved five bucks in his hand and grabbed a new cell phone skin.

He turned to walk away, then turned back to Ted. "Where's your cash register?" he asked.

Ted felt himself sweating, but tried to brazen it out. "Oh shit! I am so fired!" he said, smiling. The guy turned and walked to the temple side of the mall and exited. Ted took four deep breaths. He just knew that guy was one of them. The question is whether the guy knew who *he* was. Ted hadn't actually seen his cell phone, so he had no idea if the guy was really just buying a skin or if he was just checking Ted out. Or maybe he was one of the other guys who'd been digging up College Street in Ocean State Power uniforms

Should he follow him? No. Leave that to the professionals. He knew Laura said not to call, but maybe she'd take a text message. "I saw one. Headed 4 Temple," he sent. His phone told him the message had been sent successfully, but three minutes passed, and he didn't get a reply. He felt sick and woozy, and he realized he'd only had a muffin and a Greek salad wrap to eat in the last thirty hours.

Cayenne was finishing up with a twenty-something guy whose bare, chiseled arms were covered in tattoos. She was smiling and laughing at something the guy said, and Ted felt jealous. He looked at his own skinny, un-chiseled arms and wondered if he should maybe join a gym. As soon as the guy walked away, he walked over. "Hey, I'm gonna close up for the day. It turns out that I have some money now. Can I take you to dinner at one of the Providence Towne Centre's fine family dining establishments?"

Cayenne looked at him for a moment, then broke into a smile. "I'd like that," she said.

TEN

Laura sat in the back of a panel truck bearing a sign for Demarco Catering. Sadly, the inside of the van had never seen wedding food, though the vinegary smell stinging Laura's nostrils made her believe that someone had left a half-eaten piece of fruit in here somewhere. The smell of rotting fruit mixed with the smells of mold and machine oil to make sitting here a real olfactory treat, and had made it very difficult for her to choke down her own turkey sandwich. Her legs were cramped up, and her head hurt from having headphones on. She'd been listening to pigeons flap and rats scurry about inside the temple for nearly eight hours, and her initial excitement at being in on something exciting had given way to boredom, which had given way to despair that anything interesting was happening here at all. Maybe she'd been right, and Ted had just seen an angry, kinky guy who wanted to fuck his girlfriend in a filthy place going into the temple. With bayberry spice candles, though? That hardly fit the kink profile.

Two feet away from her, Killilea, a fit, fortyish man with black hair graying at the temples, listened to the temple on headphones and watched the monitors of the infrared equipment and the feeds from the mall security cameras.

His hands were busy with what looked like a pretty elaborate knitting project. "Keeps me from going insane from boredom," he'd said when Laura looked surprised at the appearance of the yarn and needles in his lap. He'd been extraordinarily kind to Laura when orienting her to the equipment and procedures, showing none of that impatience with her ignorance that so many veterans would have shown in his place. He reminded Laura of her ninth grade English teacher, a kind, patient guy who'd broken his nose attempting to breakdance at the Spring Fling dance.

She was just about to remove the headphones and ask Killilea if she could walk around the mall for five minutes when he tapped her on the shoulder. She looked over and saw him looking intently at the screen, the forgotten knitting project lying on the floor of the van. "We got one," he said. "Camera three."

Laura looked at the grainy, black-and-white image on the screen and saw a guy look in both directions before reaching behind a sheet of plywood that covered a window and swinging it out. It appeared to be on hinges, which at least suggested that somebody came here regularly.

Laura's heart began to pound as she heard the guy's footsteps echoing through the empty temple. She wished they had cameras in there instead of just on top of the mall so she could see what was happening. She tried to imagine as she heard footfalls and the occasional curse.

"Camera two!" Killilea called out, and Laura could hear the excitement in his voice as somebody else climbed into another hinged plywood window. "Hot shit, something's actually happening here! Make doubly sure that you're recording—" he reached over to Laura's station "—press this button to make a redundant copy on the hard drive. Did I tell you that already?"

"Yeah, but I forgot," Laura said.

"Camera three again! Camera two!"

The audio landscape became a confused blur as more and more pairs of feet echoed through the ruined temple. Laura heard something give a sick, splintering crack and wondered if it was a bone. She felt a shiver travel up the back of her spine at the thought.

Finally all the footsteps stopped. She pictured them, standing in a circle amid a pile of skulls and bones, ready to do their demonic work. "Okay, turning on the infrared— there's our little sewing circle!" Laura looked over to the screen displaying images from the heat-sensing camera mounted in the cake on the roof of the van and saw a bunch of seated red figures in a green background. One guy stood up, and the heat from his body had turned the chair he'd been sitting on orange on the screen. It looked like a standard folding chair and not a throne made of skulls or anything. Laura chided herself for getting carried away and tried to remember that there was probably nothing more paranormal than a secret circle jerk going on here.

She heard the crack and hiss of matches being lit and watched on the screen as little red lights appeared among the figures.

"Brothers," the standing man (at least Laura assumed it was the standing man) said. "Our time is at hand. The book has been recovered. The transliteration is going slowly, as only two of us have volunteered to pollute their brains by learning the mongrel tongue the book is written in, but we believe the ultimate incantation will be ready within a few days. And then, at last, we, the rightful heirs of America and the world, will rule, first among humans at the feet of the old gods, kings of all the mongrel races!"

"Oh fuck," Killilea said. "Not the angry white people again. I hate the angry white people."

"Why? I mean, aside from the whole terrorism thing?"

"Because the angry white people make a mess for us. We have to shut them down, but DC doesn't want to hear that the angry white people are a terrorist threat, because too many of the angry white people voted for the current administration. So it's hard to get resources, and nobody ever gets commendations, stuff like that. If these guys were Arabs, we'd have the entire US Army at our disposal. With the angry white people, we'll be lucky if we get to keep the van."

Laura had missed something while Killilea was talking, but she didn't want to back up the recording, because now the entire group was standing in a circle. *"Yog-Sothoth, flshrauv, Yog-Sothoth, sil'iah, menduru, Yog-Sothoth, r'laugggggg,"* the men chanted, and suddenly, in the center of the circle, there was a spot of deep blue.

"Whoa, what the hell is that?" Killilea said. "Did they just open a box of dry ice or something? That's fucking cold!"

"I didn't hear anything that sounded like a box opening," Laura said, "just the chanting."

"Weird. Wonder if the equipment is malfunctioning."

"Behold!" said the voice in Laura's ear. "The gateway begins to open! With just a few adjustments to the incantation, and the additional reality-rending force of the place of power, our mission will be complete! Behold! Gaze on the realm of Great Cthulhu! Bring forth Brother Leonard!"

Two of the guys in the circle walked away and came back bearing a coffin-sized box. It was blue.

"Brother Leonard! His commitment to the cause was total, and in Great Cthulhu's realm, his burns shall be healed and his suffering shall end!"

Laura heard a muffled scream coupled with the muffled sound of someone beating something. She glanced over to the screen and saw the cold blue box suddenly develop a green stripe as it seemed to expand. "Oh Jesus," Laura said. "They've got somebody in the box." And Laura had a very good idea who that somebody might be—a Cthulhu cultist covered in burns whose appearance anywhere—especially in a burn unit that might treat what must be mind-destroying pain—would lead to questions. He was a liability, and even though she knew what he did, and believed he deserved whatever he was about to get, Laura felt herself getting sick at the knowledge that she was about to watch him get murdered.

But she didn't watch him get murdered. At least, not in any way she could understand. Two green figures bore the screaming box toward the center of the circle and heaved it into the deep blue spot, and it disappeared.

"What the fuck was that?" Killilea shouted. He started frantically twiddling knobs on the monitor. "Did you see that? The box just disappeared! Boxes don't just disappear! Do they? What the hell?"

"I… uh…." And now Laura felt sick anyway. Because Ted had been right all along, and because she'd just seen a man die, or his soul consigned to eternal torment, or something, and because nobody was ever going to believe this was a threat. A bunch of guys standing around chanting and doing magic tricks just wouldn't pack the same credibility as somebody with a van full of fertilizer.

Killilea continued to adjust the monitor and began to back up the recording. Laura took out a USB cable and downloaded the audio into her laptop as a backup. On the monitor, they saw the party breaking up as one guest at a time headed for the exits. Killilea continued to fiddle with knobs. He called into the radio to the two agents stationed inside the mall. "This is control. We're hot out here, and we've got ants fleeing the anthill. Watch for white guys coming in alone. Okay—east entrance, white guy, maybe six feet, white shirt. Northeast entrance, white guy, gray hoodie, maybe five eight. Stick on those two." Half of the cultists fanned out into the streets surrounding the temple, while the other half headed into various mall entrances.

Killilea kept messing with the equipment and turned to Laura just after she'd disconnected the USB cable from the deck. "Okay, ready for some real secret agent stuff? Watch for an opening on camera three," he said, "then get out there and follow one of these guys and see if you can get a plate number, a description, anything. Boston's going to bust our asses about this anyway, but I'd love to be able to hand them something more concrete than this fucking magic trick... Okay, guy in a baseball cap just walked into the mall. Go follow him."

Laura's cramped legs complained mightily as she asked them to move quickly, and she stumbled as she clambered out of the back of the van. She could just barely hear Killilea's voice as she closed the door: "Boston, I have a secure transmission. Here it comes..."

Laura's heart was pounding as she strode toward the mall entrance. She called Ted to try and enlist his help on this mission. She cursed him colorfully as the call went to voice mail. What the hell was his problem?

As she got into the mall, Laura fought that part of her mind that was announcing that she really had to pee, and there was a bathroom right over there. If she wanted physical comfort, she could still be poring over videos of white guys who weren't Whitey.

She walked down the corridor and into the main atrium and couldn't pick up her target among the crowds of shoppers, diners, and ferris wheel riders. She estimated that there were twelve white men with baseball caps in the crowd. Which one was her target? She looked around at pushcarts, but she didn't even know which one might be Ted's. Most of them were closed metal shutters rolled up over their merchandise, though one or two people who were definitely not Ted were closing up their carts. She waded into the crowd. As she continued to look, she noticed that one of the baseball-cap wearers was alone and moving more purposefully than your average mall shopper. He was not distracted by any of the merchandise on display and did not even glance at the window display as he passed Victoria's Secret. It wasn't anything close to a positive ID, but it was the best she had to go on right now. She was Laura Summa Cum Laude Harker, goddammit, and she'd never taken an incomplete, and she wasn't about to start that now.

Her target headed into Mexico Maria's without even glancing at the menu on display next to the door, and Laura counted to five, then walked in. The hostess, a blonde woman in a long black skirt and a peasant blouse that bared her shoulders said, "Welcome to Mexico Maria's! Party of... one?"

"Actually, I'm meeting somebody. I just need to take a circuit and see if they're here," Laura said as she blew by the podium.

"Lot of that going around," she heard the hostess mutter in disgust. Laura scanned the dining room and saw her target exiting the restaurant on the street side. She pretended to continue to scan the crowd, and then she did a double take as she saw... Ted? With a woman? A really hot woman? Who could possibly be a lesbian? Who was in tears? She had a flash of annoyance—she'd spent the entire day cramped up in a gross van largely because Ted had convinced her that this was real, that it was important, that they had a job to do. And now he was kicking back with a pitcher of margaritas and a woman whose hotness was marred by excessive piercings, but who was at least the right gender to be attractive to Laura. It crossed Laura's mind to go and grab Ted, to tell him the chase was on, that he had to help out here, that this was his goddamn assignment, but then she thought if Ted was actually getting somewhere here, she didn't want to spoil it.

It was only as she crossed the threshold of the restaurant and hit the street that Laura realized she'd just put Ted's mental and/or sexual health ahead of the fate of the entire Earth, which is what was at stake here if Ted was right. Weird. Her target hopped into a cab, and Laura memorized the medallion number: J1701. It wasn't much, but she wasn't going back empty-handed, and the guy was clearly a cultist, because who the hell cuts through an entire mall and a restaurant just to go get a taxi?

Speaking of which, she was feeling very conspicuous standing here looking stupid on the street. She walked down the block and re-entered the mall through the Industrial Dessert Company, where she told the black-attired host that she was meeting somebody, could she just wander around the cavernous restaurant and look for them? "Well, can you describe the person? It's been a slow night, I might remember."

Laura looked at the guy and said, "I'd really prefer to look around," and made a beeline for the bathroom.

Once she'd made the decision to pee, her bladder decided the matter was urgent, and she barely made it to the stall before unleashing a torrent of urine. The relief she felt as the last drops dribbled out was, she thought, a physical pleasure comparable to an orgasm. For just a few seconds, she felt relaxed, content, and confident that everything was going to be fine.

This feeling didn't even last through the hand wash, though. These Cthulhu guys really were up to something horrible, and, judging by what they did to Brother Leonard, they had the ability to do horrible things, and Laura wasn't sure they could be stopped.

Laura's dread multiplied when she climbed back into the van and saw Killilea's face. "I got a hack number!" she said.

Killilea looked at her blankly. "Well, I don't know who's going to follow up on it, because Boston's not interested."

"What do you mean?"

"I mean, I just got off the phone with Nguyen"—he said it like "nyen," Laura noted, though somebody else had said "win," and still another had said "new-yen"—"and he said exactly what I thought he would say about the Angry White People."

"What did he say about that guy disappearing?"

"He said, 'while the video is impressive, the Bureau's position is that people meeting secretly to perform magic tricks do not constitute the same threat to national security that transnational terrorist networks do.'"

"Well, shit. Something's going on. People don't just disappear like that."

"Nguyen's of the opinion that there may have been dry ice and a secret trap door involved. He said the video is inconsistent with a murder, and in any case that's Providence PD turf, so he won't even get us a warrant. He might pass the tape on to Providence PD, but there's really nothing solid enough to indicate that a crime was committed, and if we don't believe they made a guy disappear, then we also don't believe they can make a mall disappear, so we're back up to Boston and hoping that nothing worse happens during the Celtics playoffs than a first-round loss."

"Well, fuck. So we have to wait for these guys to pull their presto change-o trick on the whole mall? We just get to sit here and watch it happen?"

"Well, actually, there is another shift coming in half an hour, so they may get to watch it happen, but yeah, pretty much."

Laura sat in silence. There had to be a way. There had to be somebody who would take this seriously. Or, if there wasn't, there had to be a way that they could stop it. Yeah. Maybe. Or maybe it would be up to Ted.

That thought led Laura for the first time to contemplate the idea that the bad guys might win here. She wondered what that would be like. Would she die, or live in a world of horror so unimaginable that she couldn't even imagine it? Or, as had happened ten years before, would Ted actually, improbably, save the day? She knew that her life and her afterlife had once hinged on Ted's ability to act decisively, to do something improbably heroic and horrific, and this should have been comforting, but back then she hadn't known how much was riding on Ted's skinny frame.

She wanted a drink.

ELEVEN

Ted and Cayenne had finished their first basket of tortilla chips and were two-thirds of the way through their first pitcher of margaritas. They were awaiting burritos grandes and a soft taco platter. They had already covered most of the events of the day and their thoughts on mall culture when Cayenne said, "Okay, well, I guess I'm buzzed enough to tell you why I work here, but you have to swear to tell me why you work here."

Ted thought about this. There was really no way Cayenne was in on this whole Cthulhu plot—was there? Well, he had a choice to make—assume the worst, just to be safe, and shut down what looked like it might become something wonderful, something better than he'd had in a long time, or trust her, and risk that she'd run screaming when she heard the truth like they all did, or, worse yet, that she was in on the plot to get Providence stomped by the Old Ones, and she would kill him. But if that were true, she'd kill him anyway. Bleh. He took a long drink from his margarita glass, then instantly regretted it.

"Gah! Brain freeze!"

"Ooh, I hate that."

"Agh!" Ted rubbed the spot above his right eye—"Feels

like somebody's jabbing an ice pick behind my eye." He saw Cayenne looking expectantly at him, then realized she was waiting for his answer. *What's it gonna be, boy, yes or no?* a female voice in his head said, and he wondered briefly what song that was from before he answered. "Okay. I will absolutely tell you the truth about how I came to be an obsolete cell phone skin salesman, and one who is shockingly successful, as it turns out, but I think we're going to need another pitcher."

"Deal." Ted's burrito grande and Cayenne's soft taco platter arrived, and they asked for another pitcher.

"You know, you get, like, beef, chicken, and fish tacos here," Cayenne said, "and if I'd had one less drink, I could probably come up with a pretty good tuna taco joke, instead of just the idea that I should make a tuna taco joke."

"Hmmm—how about, 'I'll give you some of my burrito grande if you let me eat your tuna taco?'"

Cayenne looked at Ted for a long moment, and then laughed. "It's not bad, except that burrito means 'little ass.' Which really makes 'burrito grande' kind of an oxymoron, right? Big little ass?"

"Isn't that where Custer died?"

"Nah, I think that was Little Big Ass."

"Right." They chewed in silence, and Ted wondered if he'd really said that stupid tuna taco thing. Jesus, he was turning into a cheeseball in his old age.

"So," Cayenne said after making significant inroads on the steak and chicken tacos, "the reason I work in the mall is just because I was bored, and I had nothing else to do, and I spent a lot of time sitting at home by myself taking drugs, and that got boring, and pretty much everything I used to do got boring, and so I figured, well, in high school I was way too cool to work in retail in the mall, because I was alternative, or something, so I figured, well, I've tried pretty much everything else, and so I might as well try this. And it turns out to be an okay way to kill eight hours without having to think about… everything."

Ted knew enough about not wanting to think about… everything to know that this was the point at which he did not ask exactly what everything was. "I know what that's like," he said.

There was more chewing, and Cayenne took a long drink of margarita and said, "Ow! Fucking brain freeze!" and then started to cry. "Well, shit, so I'm crying already, so here goes, I guess, so my dad murdered my mom and my brother murdered my dad, and I found my mom's body and watched my brother blow my dad's head off, and I talked him out of turning the gun on himself, which seemed like the right thing to do at the time, but he's not a big guy, he's had a hard time in jail, and he won't even speak to me, so basically that's it, I'm an orphan and my brother won't speak to me and I've seen more violence than I should have had to see, and there was a lot of insurance money that I was able to spend on a lot of drugs. But, like I said, nothing dulls the mind like spending eight hours in the mall."

Cayenne wiped the tears off her face and blew her nose. "So there you go. I'm damaged goods. What about you?"

Ted paused. This was it. He owed her the truth after that, even though telling her the truth would probably be a dealbreaker. Oh well.

"Well, you're not going to believe me, and you're going to think I'm insane—"

"Shit, Jonathan, I'm insane too, obviously."

"I don't mean mood disorder insane. I mean thought

disorder insane, as in tinfoil hat kind of insane. But oh well, here you go. This part you can look up: ten years ago at a certain Ivy League University in Wilmington, Delaware, there was a terrible sorority fire. At least eight people died. You can search the archives of every paper online and find the stories.

"But, well, what they don't tell you is that that house burned down because it was full of vampires, and that I was responsible. I ran out of the house covered in blood and reeking of gasoline, and I am not in jail, which ought to also be evidence that I'm not completely nuts. I got a big payoff from the University and did a lot of drugs and followed my friend who I saved around the East Coast while she had a life.

"And I should say that my friend is a lesbian, just so you don't think I'm involved in some kind of long-term relationship, though I'm guessing you're probably losing interest with every word. Anyway, I was working in a Queequeg's for pretty much the same reason as you're working here, and my place of employment got shot up, and, to make a long, improbable story short, I got away and found out that the same people who shot up the Queequeg's are planning something big at this mall, and, as doomed an idea as this is, I am actually trying to prevent it."

Ted looked up for the first time since he started speaking. Cayenne was looking at him with her mouth open.

"So," she said, "are the people trying to attack the mall vampires too?"

Ted looked at her. "Are you fucking with me? Is there like a Buffy joke coming or something? I mean, I don't want to get hostile or defensive or anything, but I know how insane this sounds, and I know this ends with you avoiding me, and I just—"

"I'm not fucking with you. I mean, I... okay, I have a pretty hard time believing you, but, I mean...." She was crying again—"I can tell that something awful happened to you. I think it's like this club where we can recognize the other members. Anyway, so, I don't know if I believe you about the vampires or anything, but I believe that you're haunted like I'm haunted, and that's enough for me to not want to tell you to fuck off. And, yeah, I have a hard time believing in vampires, but I had a pretty hard time believing that my daddy who used to sing to me... well, you know. What happened in my family is shit that happens on TV shows. It doesn't happen to people like me. It can't. Except that it did. So I guess ever since I found my mom's bloody body, I've had a pretty hard time saying definitively that anything is impossible."

Without thinking, Ted reached across the table and grabbed Cayenne's hand. He didn't say anything, Cayenne didn't say anything, and they just looked at each other. It was the single nicest moment Ted could remember.

And it was broken up far too soon by the return of the waitress, who said, with forced perkiness, "Are you folks all set? Need another drink?"

"Just the check, whenever you have a minute," Cayenne said, and before the sentence was fully out of her mouth, the waitress had slapped the pleather check-holder down on the table.

"You have a great night," she called back over her shoulder. I already have, Ted thought, and then he thought it would probably be good if he actually said that, but if he said it now, it would sound stilted.

Suddenly, out of the corner of his eye, he saw something—

somebody that looked an awful lot like Laura running out the front door. Shit! Was the operation actually happening? In the time they'd been in Mexico Maria's, Ted, despite having told a very truncated version of the story, had completely forgotten the urgency of his mission, the fact that he'd sent Laura this urgent text message just a few hours ago, the fact that the fate of the entire world might be hinging on what went on in his mind.

He suddenly felt bad. He'd been feeling so good in the last few days, like he'd found his purpose, like he was a supernatural asskicker, but it turned out he was just the same old slacker-loser he always was.

"Hey," Cayenne said, "what's the matter? You look funny all the sudden."

"Well, I guess if you've only just noticed that I look funny, I'm doing pretty well."

She smiled. "You know what I mean. You just thought of something that made you sad."

"Well," Ted said, then paused. Things had gone way better than he had any right to hope for, and he couldn't say I just ruined this great intimacy by thinking about how I have to protect the earth from octopus-headed beings from another dimension, oh, yeah, and I'm thinking of another woman besides, even if she is my lesbian friend and not anything else... And, incredibly, he found something else to say that wasn't even a lie, really.

"I guess I was just thinking that this evening seems to be moving towards a logical conclusion, I mean, I don't want to be presumptuous, but I just feel like..."

"We're gonna do it. Keep talking."

"I just.... I really like you a lot, I mean I don't want to creep you out, but I feel this connection to you that I don't know if

I've ever felt with anyone, and I just think I've had too many margaritas to really be at my best in that department, and I really don't want to disappoint you and have you break it off, so even though I really really want to, I also don't want to because I want to make sure you stick around."

Cayenne looked at him. "You know, for a guy who slays the undead, you're really awfully sweet."

"Hey, I only did that once," Ted said, and smiled. He paid the check, and they walked outside.

"Will you at least walk me home?" Cayenne asked. "I might need protection if there are any vampires lurking around."

"Okay, now you're busting my balls."

"Yeah, but I want you to walk me home anyway."

They walked the five blocks to Cayenne's apartment in silence, holding hands. The night was cool, and Cayenne's hand felt warm and soft in Ted's. They stumbled into the street and managed to just barely keep a hold on each other's hand as they walked with a parked Mini Cooper between them. At Cayenne's door, they kissed long and slow, and the feeling of her tongue stud against his tongue gave Ted all kinds of ideas.

"See you tomorrow," she said, and Ted floated down the sidewalk. Two blocks from Cayenne's apartment, he felt a vibrating in his pants. It took him an unusually long time to realize that this was his phone. He fumbled in his pocket and dug the phone out.

"Hello?"

"Jesus, Ted, this is the fifth time I've called you. Where are you? Are you scoring?"

"Do you think I would have picked up the phone if I were?"

"Hey, I like to think I'm a priority call."

"Nobody's that high a priority. Anyway, no, I'm walking home."

"Good. I'll see you in a few minutes. I'm crashing in this apartment I'm renting for you, because I'm way too exhausted and pissed off to drive home tonight."

"What happened?"

"I'll tell you everything when you get home. I hope you've walked off some of your margarita buzz, because we actually have some work to do."

"So that *was* you in the restaurant!"

"Yeah. Talk to you soon."

When Ted reached the apartment, a haggard-looking Laura told him everything about sitting in a foul-smelling van, about Brother Leonard disappearing, about the Angry White People and Boston's disappointing response.

"That's actually really interesting," Ted said. "I mean, first of all, if they're trying to raise Cthulhu, then they sent that guy to the lost city of R'lyeh…"

"Is that a place where his burns will be healed?"

"Well, according to the stories, it's a nightmare of desolation and non-Euclidean geometry."

"Right, I remember that. "

"Yeah, the characters are always ranting about how the geometry doesn't work or something—they see parallel lines intersecting and it drives them mad, mad I say. I mean, I never got the impression from anything I read that it was a place you'd want to send one of your buddies, and since we are as gnats in the sight of the Old Ones, I kinda doubt there's going to be any healing involved."

"Well, I suppose that would explain the screams of horror I heard."

"Yeah. Spooky."

"Yeah, it creeped me out. But what's up with the race thing? I thought white supremacists were always psychotic Christians."

"That actually makes complete sense to me. In the stories, it's always the degenerate mixed-blood sailors who are involved in this stuff, but that was in the twenties. It's a different world now. All these angry white guys see the writing on the wall—you know, their light-brown-skinned, Spanish-speaking great-grandchildren won't even understand what being white even means. I mean, I noticed it in the mall—the teens cruise around in these multiracial packs, white, black, Asian, whatever. So by the time those kids have kids, they won't have any white pride or identity or whatever. So, you know, as a white guy, our day is pretty much coming to an end. So if it's the angry white guys who are the priests of Cthulhu or whatever, then they'll be sure to have some power in the new, Old God-centered world, and you know what Kissinger said about power."

"No, but I can guess. But, uh, I thought humans were insignificant gnats to these things—how are the angry white guys going to have any power?"

"No idea. Maybe the book actually gives them some control over them. Or maybe they're willing to risk the end of the world because living in a world where white people aren't on top amounts to the same thing as far as they're concerned."

Laura paused and thought. "So what are we going to do? What can we do?"

"I don't know," Ted said. "How long do you think you'll have the van?"

"Killilea says two days max. And we're—shit, Ted, I have

no idea! I don't know if there's anything to do besides arm ourselves and try to take as many of them out as we can when they start their ceremony in the mall."

"Shooting spree in the mall? Are you kidding?"

Laura looked slightly hurt. "Well, no. I mean, it's a last option, obviously, but if we're talking about saving the world…"

Ted's face was reddening. "Are you a good enough shot to avoid hitting that mom with the stroller on level three? Well, you probably are, but I'm sure as hell not. And I got away with a killing spree once—I don't think it would happen again."

"Goddammit, Ted, if they get away with this, it won't matter whether you're in jail or not! I… I mean, I don't have to tell you that doing the right thing is hard. We might have to spend the rest of our lives in jail to make sure the world is safe. That sucks for us, but maybe we're not the most important thing in the world!"

"No. Goddammit, no. I did that once. It can't keep coming down to me. It just can't. I was—fuck!" He was starting to cry. "I didn't know how horrible it was going to be last time, Laura, I just had to do it, and I'm not strong enough, I'm not brave enough, I can't… There's shit that happened that I've never told you, that I can't even bear to think about, the stuff that makes me wake up screaming, the stuff… I killed Steve, Laura. Did you know that? He cried and begged me to kill him right after they turned him and I cut his head off. It took two strokes, and I can still feel the axe kicking back in my hand when I hit his spine. It… it ruined me. You… I know you're impatient with me, that you don't get how I could still be so fucked up because you were there too, but you don't know what it's like! I was the one who had to swing the axe! I had…" Tears were streaming down his face.

"I really liked Steve, and I… oh God! And I can't do it again, Laura I can't, I don't care if the world ends—if it all comes down to me again, if I'm all that stands between the world and Armageddon, it's just going to have to end. I've just done too much killing. I can't keep killing, I just can't."

Laura looked at him for a minute like she was going to yell at him, and then her face relaxed. "You know what? Let's just get some sleep. Maybe we'll think of something in the morning. They said they needed a couple of days to get the whole incantation right, so we can probably take a few hours off here and just get some sleep. We'll think more clearly when we've slept. And when we're not still half-buzzed on margaritas."

"She's really nice. She might be able to help."

"In the morning. Talk in the morning. Sleep now."

And so Ted found himself in bed with Laura, which was a circumstance he'd spent probably four years dreaming of before finally admitting to himself that it was impossible. He thought of Cayenne and was asleep in forty-seven seconds.

TWELVE

L aura woke up early as the sun poured in the curtainless windows of Ted's apartment. She felt great—she'd slept like a log, the sun was shining, it was a nice spring day… and then she remembered everything. That the cultists knew how to open portholes to other dimensions, and were planning to do it in the mall, that they'd almost certainly succeed, and that, if they were right, it was going to be the end of the world as we know it.

Laura did not feel fine. She felt vaguely nauseous. And then she contemplated crawling back into the van for twelve hours. Well, fuck it. Killilea had made it pretty clear that Boston wasn't interested, DC wasn't interested, this was just a magic club to them. Well, she'd at least go poke around the temple and see if she could find something—anything that might convince Boston to devote some resources to this problem, enough men to take these guys out when they came in and started chanting.

Of course, this would be putting her career in jeopardy, since their warrant only covered electronic surveillance, and she'd be defying her supervisors, but what the hell. She had to do it—there was too much at stake. Was this how Ted felt when he was grabbing the fire axe the night he saved her soul? He'd never told her much about it—in fact, she'd had no idea he'd killed Steve, or how it felt to behead somebody (though she'd always had a morbid curiosity about that part). All he'd ever really told her was that he'd done two shots of tequila before he'd gone in there. But somehow he'd found the courage to focus on what was really important, and he was right—he'd done heavy lifting that she could only imagine, and it just wasn't fair to make sure it all came down to him again. She'd give him a gun to take them out if it came to that, but she needed to step up and take care of business. Ted had done it for her ten years ago, and Laura felt very strongly that it was her turn to do the same.

Her cell phone chirped, and Ted gave a groan of complaint from the bed. "Harker," she said. It was Killilea, who told her that he'd fought like hell, but the van had to go back tonight, so if they were going to find anything, they had to do it today.

Apparently the taxi whose number she'd recorded had dropped the guy at a Dunkin' Donuts, one of the cars they had a plate on had turned out to be stolen, and the third one was a rental, paid with a credit card issued to a Howard Phelps Lovecraft. The card issued to H. P. Lovecraft had a P. O. Box billing address, and the box had been rented by a guy named William Castle. Killilea gave Laura William Castle's home address and told her that they did not have a warrant, and that this investigation would be closed down by midnight anyway, so under no circumstances was she to go snooping around the house of this guy who'd left the temple after the magic trick last night.

Laura replied that she'd see Killilea in the van as soon as she was finished not doing any snooping.

"Be careful. You don't know what psychotic paranoids have

in their houses, but it's probably nothing good, and we won't be able to use anything you'd find there anyway."

"Got it," Laura said, hanging up the phone.

A haggard-looking Ted was propped up on an elbow in bed. "Jesus, do you have to save the world before six in the freaking morning? Can you see that it's—"

"Hey," Laura said. "I… I want to tell you something."

"Is it 'turn over and go back to sleep'?"

"No, Ted, I'm being serious. I… I mean, you were right. I never knew how awful it was, I mean I figured it was awful, but I didn't know, and I just… well, thank you."

There was a pause. "You're welcome," Ted said.

"Okay. So it's not all going to come down to you this time, because at least you have me. But you need to get up. We've got a name and an address."

"Ugh. So? We know where to find these guys. What's the use of knowing where they live if your bosses don't believe they're up to anything?"

"I don't know. Maybe they'll have something essential to their task in the house, and we can steal it. Maybe there will be some kind of information that tells us more specifically what they're up to and how we can stop it. In any case, it feels better than doing nothing."

"I dunno—another couple of hours of sleep might feel even better. I had way too many margaritas last night."

"Boo hoo. You had to have dinner with some hottie while I sat in the back of a van and got constipated."

"Do you really think she's hot? I think she's pretty fantastic. I told her about the vampires, and about Queequeg's, and— boy, you do have a plumbing problem, don't you? Maybe you should see somebody about that…"

Laura took a deep breath, counted to ten, and tried to

unclench her jaw. When she was confident she could say something in a calm tone of voice, she opened her mouth. "You told her about Queequeg's?" Suddenly she was yelling. Apparently she wasn't ready to be calm after all. *"You told her?"*

"Yeah. So?"

"Ted, you are a moron! Aagh, that was so stupid, even for you! So you are a fugitive wanted for questioning in connection with a multiple murder, and you just told that to somebody you just met? That's great! The cops will be waiting at your cart this morning!"

"No they won't! I trust her! She believes me!"

"Honest to God, I don't know how you could be through everything you've been through and still manage to be so naïve. You can believe that people are trying to unleash supernatural forces, but the idea that a woman might be scared of the truth about you never even fucking occurs to you! Even though it's happened every single time! You tell somebody you're a fearless vampire killer and that you weren't really the guy who shot up that coffee shop, and she nods and smiles because she's terrified, and you think it's true love! You've just completely compromised your end of this! Jesus! I mean use your head for once!"

"Nothing's compromised! You weren't there! She believed me!"

"Christ. Well, I was there, briefly, but it doesn't matter. This always happens, Ted, you throw your trust away on these women, and usually it's just your heart that gets broken, but this time it's going to be—we don't know if an extra person in the mall is going to make the difference. You might have put the whole fucking world at risk!"

"I'm going to be in the mall, first of all…"

"You'll be there five minutes before Providence police take you away in cuffs, Ted."

"Bullshit!"

"It's not bullshit. It's the way any rational woman would respond to—"

"No—it's the way you would respond. Just because you don't trust anybody doesn't mean she's like you. And it damn sure doesn't mean I should be like you. Maybe I want to at least try to get close to somebody. Maybe I don't want to drive away every woman who's interested in me."

Laura was so angry she thought her head might explode. "You—you know what, fuck you. I have carried you for ten years, wiped your nose every time you had a bad dream, and okay, I owe you that, I owe you at least that much, but that doesn't mean it's been easy. I don't have the nightmares, okay, but I don't get to have a normal life either, okay? So, yeah, I don't have anybody else, because how am I going to explain why I have to take care of you? How am I even going to have time to get close to anybody? So don't throw that shit in my face, because it's your fucking fault! Okay? *Okay?*"

Tears were forming in Ted's eyes. "Get the hell out of my apartment," he said.

"It's *my* apartment. But I'm leaving anyway. Don't go to the mall. I'm not bailing you out this time."

Ted didn't say anything. He just looked at her as she left, and Laura felt like she'd kicked a puppy.

As she drove to William Castle's house, Laura kept punching the seat next to her. Fuck Ted and his fucking stupidity. Ruining the whole thing. Being right about her not trusting anybody. Well, she was right too—he had no idea what a burden he'd been—but as she replayed her three failed relationships from the last ten years... (Three! Jesus

Christ—all those hormones and all that alcohol at college, and she'd only managed one in her three years of post-fire college. What the hell?) Perhaps Ted had a point about her not trusting anybody. Shit.

He also had a point about how a visit to William Castle's house would be pointless, but she was going to do this right anyway. Well, to do it right would be to get a warrant and knock on the door, but failing that, she was going to do a systematic search. She called 411 and got William Castle's home phone number. She blocked her number with *67 and called. She could hear the phone ringing inside the house, and no one answered.

She waited five minutes, then went to the door and rang the bell, preparing to whip out her badge and question him if he answered the door. She had no idea if it would be a good thing or a bad thing to announce that the FBI was aware of what was going on at the mall, but if William Castle got the idea that the might of the United States Government was working against him, it might cause him to at least postpone the mall operation. He'd never have to know that Laura was pretty much the only US Government employee who gave a shit about what was happening at the mall.

But William Castle did not come to the door. Laura checked the house and found no evidence of a security system. Which of course made it that much less likely she'd find anything of interest here, but she had to check. It was ridiculously easy to break in once she'd ascertained that nobody was home. The guy had an unlocked window right behind the gas grill on the back porch. He was practically asking for it. Laura slid on latex gloves, opened the window and crawled into what was supposed to be a pantry that held nothing but a few lonely cans of franks and beans. Moving as quickly and efficiently as she could, she examined the rest of the house and found nothing at all interesting. Linoleum that needed replacing on the kitchen floor. A fridge covered in dirty handprints containing a Coors Light longneck and a package of Fenway Franks, an old, filthy sofa parked in front of a thirty-six-inch television. No art on the walls. A few Lovecraft books were the only books in evidence, but that hardly counted as a lead. Some racist pamphlets sat atop the toilet with the filthy, brownish-yellow bowl, but that was protected free speech, and if Laura hadn't been so constipated, she would have been tempted to wipe her ass with them. She booted up the computer and poked through the hard drive. There was, of course, some pornography, but nothing more unusual than you'd probably find on the hard drive of every man with internet access, so they wouldn't even be able to nail the guy on kiddie porn charges. She quickly glanced at his documents file and saw a file titled "necro.pdf." Probably pornographic fiction about the guy's corpse fetish, but it was enough to make her want the entire documents file. She inserted her flash drive into the USB port and felt a surge of adrenaline as she heard a car door. She dragged his documents file onto the flash drive icon and saw the dialogue box pop up. "Copying file 1 of 562," it said, "30 seconds remaining."

She heard the rattle of keys outside the front door. "Copying file 124 of 562," the computer said. Should she pull the flash drive and run? The front door opened, making her choice for her. Finally the copying finished. She put one hand on her gun and, with the other, she yanked the flash drive from the side of the computer and stuck it into her pocket.

"What the fuck?" William Castle shouted. Great. He was at least a foot taller than Laura and probably twice her weight, and clearly shot steroids and pumped iron for a hobby. Fantastic.

Before William Castle could figure out exactly what the fuck, Laura drew her weapon and aimed it at his head.

"Sorry, Mr. Jimenez, but your ex-wife really needed a look at your financials, so I—"

Castle's face reddened. "Jimenez? I'm a member of the pure white race! Do I look like some kind of greasy—"

"You're going to look like a stain on the wall if you don't shut up."

"You're in the wrong house, you dumb bitch! I'm calling the cops!"

Laura leveled her gun at his head. "No you're not."

He looked her up and down. "Honestly, I don't think you've got the balls to shoot me dead in my own house. You look soft. I'm gonna take my chances." Smiling, he moved to the phone.

Laura knew he was right. Insane white supremacist Cthulhu cultist or not, she wasn't going to murder the guy. Fortunately, she wouldn't have to.

A swift kick to the groin sent William Castle to the floor before he could dial the second 1. Laura didn't want to get shot in the back, so she gave him quick disarming blows to the neck, stomach, knees, and, for good measure, the groin again.

"Krav Maga," she told the gasping William Castle. "Learned it from a Jew." She ran from the house and down the block to her car. She fired it up and drove away, feeling exhilarated. A part of her was alarmed at how good she felt. Just two days ago, when she was driving a desk, the idea that she'd ever use her Krav Maga training had seemed absurd. And now she'd just stolen some evidence and neutralized a man twice her weight.

"Yeah!" she shouted to the empty car. "That's some fucking law enforcement!" It was actually some law breaking, but she didn't care. She'd said she was willing to go to jail to save the world, and she'd much rather be in jail for crushing William Castle's steroid-shriveled nuts than for accidentally shooting a shopper in the Providence Towne Centre.

For all that, she had no idea whether the file she'd retrieved would be of any use at all, but her elation over cleaning William Castle's clock lasted until she got to the van. She tossed the flash drive to Killilea, who copied it onto the hard drive of his computer.

"Do I want to know where you got this?" Killilea asked.

"Pretty sure you don't," Laura said.

Killilea just smiled. "Okay then. We'll see if anybody can make anything of this and just make sure we wipe everything clean before the subpoenas start flying."

"Anything happening next door?" Laura asked.

"Zip," Killilea replied. "Haven't seen a single human enter or leave since they all ran out of there last night."

"So, I'm just wondering, if somebody were to go in there, might there be a chance that the equipment might malfunction and erase the portions of the tape that revealed their presence?"

"You are full of piss and vinegar, aren't you? But the answer is no—I mean, don't get me wrong. I like you and I think some extra-legal means might be called for in this case, but I've got three kids and a mortgage. I can't go destroying evidence and put my income and my pension and, for that matter, my freedom at risk. So if you're going to go in there, I have to tell you now that I will deny you were in here before or that I had any knowledge of what you were doing. But I can also tell you that given the official indifference to this location, at this point it's extraordinarily unlikely that anyone but me will ever look at this…"

"Good enough. Thank you." Laura grabbed an extra-large Maglite—handy as a bludgeon as well as a flashlight—and headed over to the temple. Traffic was sparse, and the second she saw no cars on the street, she slipped in through the hinged board over one of the temple windows. She shone her Maglite around the large, empty room she found herself in, holding her gun in her other hand. "Providence police!" she called out. "We had a call for trespassing in here? Anyone inside this building must show themselves now."

No one showed themselves.

Having established to her satisfaction that the temple was empty, Laura examined her surroundings more closely. She was in a large room with scraps of ancient linoleum clinging to an ancient wooden floor that was filthy where it wasn't rotten. Pillars covered in cracked tile lined the perimeter of the room. At one end of the room, a cracked slab of granite that had once been a bar slumped onto the floor. The ceiling had once featured some ornate mural, but it was so badly water stained that all Laura could make out was that there had once been something painted there.

There was a lot of peeling paint, rotting wood, and God knew what kind of animal droppings everywhere. She glanced up and let out a yelp of surprise. Bats. But they seemed to be snoozing. It smelled like scented candles in here, but not as much as it smelled like mold and shit. Despite her best efforts, Laura felt her shoes squishing in piles of bat droppings.

"Hey," she thought. "I mean, I knew these guys were

batshit, but this is ridiculous!" She imagined Ted rolling his eyes and laughing. "Thank you! I'll be here all week. Tip your waitresses…" A pang of sadness hit her in the side as she realized that she might never get to share this very Ted-esque line of humor with Ted himself, since he was probably cooling his heels in a Providence lockup by now.

She pushed thoughts of Ted away and got back to the job at hand. She was pretty sure that this place was empty of anything that could harm her, but it was still creepy to be in here in the artificial darkness among the rot and decay and filth. She realized how right Ted had been to reject her initial hypothesis about this place—nobody was perverted enough to want to bring a date in here.

In the center of the floor, she saw evidence of a new secret society—Ye Olde New England Candlery scented candles, still in their attractive glass jars, sat in a circle on the floor. Some symbols were drawn in chalk on the ancient, peeling linoleum floor, and there were metal folding chairs arranged in a circle around the symbols. This was where it all happened. Laura pulled out her phone and quickly snapped a few pictures of the graffiti on the floor. Mastering her fear that she'd be sucked into another dimension just by touching the chalk inscriptions, she stomped on the floor. She then ran her flashlight carefully over the linoleum, looking for seams, looking for hinges, and finding nothing. Whatever secrets this temple held, a trap door was not among them. There was nothing here but some linoleum even nastier than what Laura's grandma had in her kitchen, which was saying something. She took a few more pictures of the floor in question.

She returned to the van. Killilea looked up. "Find anything?"

"No."

"Well, I guess even if you had found something, we couldn't have used it anyway."

"But it's what I didn't find that's important! There's no trap door! Shouldn't that convince them of something?"

Killilea just looked at her. "It should. But I can tell you from my conversation with Nguyen that it won't."

Laura thought of arguments, thought about calling Nguyen herself, but she was new and inexperienced, and all telling him she'd broken the law would accomplish would be to get her suspended or fired, and then she'd really be no good to the investigation. Fuming, she sat down, put on her headphones, and clenched her teeth. She spent the day listening to nothing happening in the temple and poring over William Castle's cached web pages, pathetic job application letters, and angry racist letters to the editor. Necro.pdf opened as a bunch of unintelligible symbols—she checked against the pictures on her phone and found several that matched. She supposed she could spend a day calling various professors at Brown or Providence College until she found somebody who knew what the symbols meant, but even if she had the time to do that, she doubted that anybody practicing an ancient, depraved religion in an abandoned building would amount to anything more than a trespassing complaint in the eyes of her superiors. If Nguyen didn't believe a supernatural conspiracy was afoot, then the fact that a document she'd obtained in an illegal search matched some graffiti she'd found on an illegal search wouldn't really carry much weight, even though it seemed like rock-solid evidence to Laura.

Sitting in silence, Laura felt her bad mood infect her every thought. She started playing back memories of Ted that she still resented. Countless times in college when she'd helped him through drunken puking, acid freakouts, and weed-induced paranoia. That exam in her first year of law school that she'd gotten a B on because Ted called her after midnight crying about some girl who'd told him he was a scary delusional lunatic after he'd confided in her... sitting in the van, she just felt the weight of ten years of Ted on her shoulders. It might be kind of a relief if he did get arrested, a nasty little part of her pointed up, but her rational brain reminded her that this would mean losing the only other person on earth who believed in the seriousness of what was going on here. And as she tried to imagine life without Ted, it felt strangely empty.

Finally, after several silent, sullen hours in the dim humidity of the van, the silence was broken by the chirping of Laura's cell phone. Killilea looked disapproving, but said, "Well, might as well take the call—nothing happening here. But you really shouldn't have it turned on in the van..."

"I know, I had it in my pocket when I was breaking and entering, and I just forgot..." Laura looked at the phone and saw that it was, of course, Ted. She silenced the ringer and let it go to voice mail. She was still mad at him, she was annoyed with him for calling her in the van and embarrassing her, and if he'd made his one phone call from jail to her cell phone, she was going to have to answer some pretty uncomfortable questions about how it was that she and her friend the fugitive just happened to be on the same block fifty miles from Boston.

Agh. She held the thought of him in jail in her head for about thirty seconds before she decided she did have to pick up the voice mail, and she did have to bail him out, and even if he was just calling to make up, she had to do that too. She didn't know how much he was right about, but it was kind of weirdly admirable that he could still be so trusting after all this time, and it was one of the things she loved about him. She dialed the voice mail number. After entering her password and pressing one to listen to new messages, Laura heard Ted screaming.

"Laura, it's happening, they're in the mall! Help!"

She dropped the phone and ran out of the back of the van. She heard Killilea yelling behind her, but she ran full out, drawing her gun and hoping she wasn't too late.

THIRTEEN

Ted walked to the coffee shop, got a pint glass full of Organic Peru, grabbed a stool by the window, and stewed. Laura was such a jerk. What he really hated—geez, where on earth did he start—what he hated the most was that "wiped your nose" comment, her whole thing about how he was a little kid. It might have actually been true, but it was really unfair. She'd only seen him behead Bitsy—she hadn't seen any of the others he'd killed, she hadn't had her roommate staring at her, puncture wounds in his big, stupid neck and tears pouring down his face, going "Teddy, please, you have to fucking kill me! Don't make me end up like them, don't make me melt in the sun, please! Please, for Christ's sake, kill me before I turn! Kill me! Make it quick!"

Ted knew that he'd saved Steve from a fate worse than death, but that didn't make the memory of swinging the axe any easier to live with. And so, yeah, he was a mess. And he was coming to the conclusion that he'd always be a mess. And it was probably easy to look at him and say he was a baby if you hadn't seen what he'd seen and done what he'd done.

And it wasn't like he wanted to have Laura be the only person in his life. That's why he was always telling people, and last night, for the first time, it didn't feel like a terrible mistake.

Except—he drained the last of his coffee and started walking to the mall—Laura did make a pretty good point about how it might not have been the best time to tell somebody, and if Cayenne were smart, she would have googled the Queequeg's shooting immediately when she got home and probably found a picture of his long-haired. bearded former self. She would have found out that his name wasn't Jonathan and that he was wanted in connection with the Queequeg's killings. And, he supposed, after you'd found out that your own dad was a murderer, it wasn't too much of a stretch to believe that some guy you just met was a murderer, even if he seemed nice and told you he didn't do it. Yeah, probably only innocent people ever said that.

Shit. Laura was right. He really was an idiot. He hoped he didn't have to watch the end of the world through the windows of a jail cell.

Ted's heart was hammering as he turned the corner, and he had no idea if it was because he'd just pounded sixteen ounces of organic fair-trade coffee or because he was terrified that Cayenne was going to turn him in, Laura would be right, and Providence would soon have a really big, really ugly problem that he'd be powerless to stop.

He thought about that for a second. Despite what he'd said last night about how he was tired of it coming down to him, he found he really couldn't stand to be on the sidelines if the fate of the world was at stake. He wanted to help.

His phone gave four beeps, announcing a text message. Ted looked at the screen and saw it was from Cayenne. He had no memory of giving her his number, of going through the laborious key-presses necessary to enter her number in his phone. Well, they'd had a lot of margaritas.

He scrolled down and read the message: HUNGOVER & HORNY. U? Ted smiled. He actually thought of forwarding the message to Laura. "See?" he thought. "She does like me! I was right!"

Unfortunately, he'd known Laura so long that he could hear her voice quite clearly in his brain saying, "Of course she's sending you naughty messages. She's afraid you're spooked about spilling the beans, and she wants to make sure you walk into the trap waiting for you at the mall!"

Damn that Laura. "ME 2," Ted sent back. Well, in five minutes, he'd be inside the mall, and he'd either be leaving in cuffs or else on cloud nine, feeling like he finally had somebody else to trust, that he could stop being such a burden to Laura, that a new phase of his life was beginning. Maybe his new life would be Laura-free, maybe she was Teddy's friend, Ted's friend, and maybe Jonathan didn't need her anymore, didn't want her smug judgments anymore.

Of course, without Laura's help, Ted/Jonathan's new life might last all of about two days, or as long as it took for him to succumb to madness at the very sight of the indescribably awful Old Ones. And, as he tried to imagine his life without Laura, even if the Old Ones didn't materialize, it just felt wrong, somehow. Sure, it would be great to have Cayenne to trust, to really get close to someone else, but Laura had been there. They'd grown up together. Or, at least, he'd watched her grow up from the perch of his permanent adolescence. He didn't want to lose that.

Ted took a deep breath, grasped the brass handle, and pulled open the door of the mall. He scanned the mall feverishly. He saw a few old people, a few tired-looking mall employees, and a couple of security guards. He didn't see any cops, or even anybody who looked like they might be an undercover cop. He took the escalator up to his pushcart. Cayenne was already sitting at hers. She smiled and waved and pointed at her phone. Ted's phone beeped again, and the screen said: 2NITE LESS BOOZE MORE SEX.

Ted smiled broadly, sat down on his stool, and gave Cayenne the thumbs up. He felt a wave of relief and happiness wash over him. It felt good. He wondered if this was how happy people felt all the time. It was bizarre—for the first time in a decade, he wasn't speaking to his best and only friend, and there were angry white guys preparing a wake-up call for a thing of unimaginable horror, and Ted felt great—better than he could remember feeling in a really long time. Maybe ever.

He continued to feel great as he unpacked his cell phone skins and started stacking them on the shelves of his pushcart. He wanted to say something to Cayenne, but he found that he had no idea what to say, especially with her sending those sexy messages. His cell phone skins artfully arranged, Ted turned to walk over to Cayenne's cart when he spotted John Thomas, wearing what appeared to be the same rumpled suit he'd been wearing the first time Ted saw him, walking toward him with a serious look on his face.

"Good Morning!" Ted called out, goofy grin plastered to his face.

John Thomas did not return the smile. "Sorry, son," he said, his face and tone of voice still deadly serious, "I gotta shut you down."

"Wait—what? What do you mean?"

"I mean you have to cease operations here, or at least suspend operations." Ted scanned John Thomas' face closely, looking for any sign that this was some kind of joke, but he still looked like he was on his way to a funeral.

"Why? Nobody could complain about cell phone skins."

John Thomas took a deep breath, and his face changed to the "I'm so disappointed in you" face that Ted had seen from far too many employers over the last ten years. "Signage, son, signage." He took another deep breath and shook his head slightly. "I told you that you needed signage, you have no signage. The agreement your employer signed clearly states that signage is a condition of doing business here. No signage, no cart. I'm sorry, but I really can't make an exception here."

"Signage."

"Right. Get some signage, get back in business." John Thomas tried to smile, but the result was anything but warm and reassuring. He reached into his pocket, drew out a key ring, and padlocked the shutters on Ted's pushcart. Without another word, he walked away.

Ted stood there for a moment, looking and feeling stupid. "So," Cayenne called over, "looks like you're out of business."

"Uh, yeah, I guess so." How could he surveil the mall now? Unless he could just pretend he was a puppy dog wannabe boyfriend pathetically hanging around the hot body-jewelry clerk. Of course, that wouldn't really be pretending, but it would allow him to both hang out with Cayenne and keep watch on the mall. "Uh, hey, he didn't padlock my stool. Can I come and sit with you? I can be your assistant."

Cayenne smiled. "Well, I can't pay you. At least not in money…" and Ted was at her side atop his stool.

The first two hours of the day went slowly, and Ted and Cayenne talked about movies and music and other things that Ted couldn't really focus on, because he kept trying to look around the mall, but then he kept getting distracted by that stud in her tongue, and whenever there was a lull in the conversation, she pulled out her phone and sent him a pornographic text message.

Around lunchtime, a wave of shoppers arrived, and Ted turned to the atrium and tried to actively observe everyone and everything in the mall. He ran everybody he saw against his racial and behavioral profile, and he came up empty. He saw two white guys who looked like they could be suspects, but he recognized them as the probable FBI agents from yesterday. Today they were not even bothering to make a circuit anymore, just sitting on a bench by the ferris wheel, drinking coffee and eating Cinnabons,.

"Hey, Buffy, what are you doing? Are you really checking the mall for evildoers?"

"Yeah, I actually am. And do you think you could maybe call me Van Helsing or something? Does it have to be Buffy? I mean, it is slightly emasculating."

"Okay, Van Helsing. The last thing I want to do is emasculate you." She smiled. "I thought the undead only came out at night."

"These guys aren't undead—just white guys with a chip on their shoulder, and a really bad magic trick up their sleeves."

Cayenne looked quizzically at him, and Ted began, hesitantly, to test her ability to believe outrageous crap yet again, by launching into an explanation about the Angry White Guys and their Cthulhu Cult. He watched her face closely for signs of disbelief, but all he saw was a shock of recognition when he started talking about the Cthulhu part.

"Oh, yeah," she said, "I read all those stories! I had this

boyfriend in the ninth grade who was obsessed with Lovecraft, so I read pretty much everything he wrote. Weird shit."

"I can't believe that."

"You can't believe I read? Thanks a bunch!"

"No, I can't believe a kid who was really into Lovecraft actually had a girlfriend in the ninth grade. Especially... you know... you. It kind of goes against the profile."

"Oh my God, I was hideous in the ninth grade. Acne... well, I'll show you a picture sometime. But trust me when I tell you this guy actually did *me* a favor."

"I don't believe that for a second, but okay." Ted told her the rest of what he knew about the surveillance at the temple and about the cultists' plan to wake up Cthulhu.

When he'd finished, Cayenne looked at him for a long time. "You know, of all the crazy shit you've told me in the last twenty-four hours, for some reason the part about you having a friend who's a lesbian FBI agent is actually the hardest to swallow."

"So the part about eighty-year-old horror fiction being true and the guys planning to start some kind of supernatural race war..."

"Entirely credible. But why the hell is a lesbian FBI agent gonna hang around with you? Are you like... Is there a lesbian equivalent of a fag hag?"

"I... well, here we go again. I saved her life. She was there, in the sorority."

"A lesbian was in a sorority?"

"Well, she was still rushing, or whatever, but yeah..."

"You've gotta work on the real-world part of this stuff."

"I can't work on it! It's true!"

Cayenne looked at him. "Okay. But that part sounds made up. The vampires, the Old Ones, I'm right there with you. But the lesbian-sorority-girl-FBI-agent-friend-of-Jonathan part, that needs work. I mean, a lesbian in a vampire sorority? It sounds like a porno movie! Were there, like, naughty naked pillow fights or something?"

Ted paused. "I don't know. I mean, she never mentioned that. And…" Well, he had to tell her. If she hadn't turned him in yet, it would be safe from a law-enforcement perspective, but he wasn't sure how she was going to take the news that he'd lied to her about his name. "Ugh. Okay. She's not a friend of Jonathan. She's a friend of Ted. That's my real name. Ted."

Cayenne smiled. "Okay, Ted, you passed. I wasn't too hung over to work the computer this morning, and I found all the stuff about your former place of employment, and there was no Jonathan mentioned in connection with that. Just some devilishly handsome guy named Ted with long hair and a beard and an unfortunate piercing deficiency."

Ted stopped. He really had been stupid. Laura was right about that. He was just lucky enough to have opened his mouth to the right person.

"So," Cayenne continued, "what's it gonna look like, when these guys make their move?"

"No idea. I mean, I have no idea if it'll even be inside the mall. They might be outside, or on the roof, or something. I don't really know what summoning the Old Ones looks like. And worse yet, I have no idea what to do if I do recognize it happening."

A few more hours passed. Since Ted wasn't selling any cell phone skins, he couldn't afford lunch, and Cayenne very nicely offered to buy him a burrito. He minded the cart while she was gone and sold three rings but found that he had no idea how to operate the cash register.

They ate burritos, they talked, they held hands, and just as Ted was thinking that he wouldn't have to save the world today, that today, tonight, he could just concentrate on having fun, he saw Mr. Average again. He was standing here on level three looking out on the atrium.

Well, maybe he needed to resupply at Ye Olde New England Candlery. Ted looked around the mall atrium to see if there were anymore. He glanced down at the food court, and the FBI guys were nowhere to be seen. He looked around the whole mall.

The behemoth who'd bought a cell phone skin from Ted yesterday was standing about thirty feet away. He had a nasty bruise on his neck and looked even angrier than he had yesterday. Ted looked around, and he spotted angry white guys holding sheets of white copy paper standing right by the metal-and-glass barriers, facing the atrium on every level of the mall. The other shoppers just strolled by as if nothing interesting were happening, and Ted supposed that if he weren't looking for exactly this, he wouldn't have suspected anything unusual happening.

Ted panicked. He fumbled for his phone, pushed down on the 1 key to call Laura, and looked at Cayenne's face.

"What is it?" she said, obviously alarmed at the look on his face.

"It's happening, they're doing it, shit, I don't know what to do, I… shit! Voice mail! Laura, it's happening, they're in the mall! Help!" He hung up the phone. "Shit, Cayenne, we gotta take these guys out, I don't have… Jesus, if you believe me at all, please help me with this, I don't know what to do. How do I take as many of these guys down as quickly as possible?"

He looked and saw that the cultists were all looking at Mr.

Average, who held his palm up to his followers like some sort of demented pope.

"Okay, single woman who walks a lot. You want the Mace or the Taser?" Cayenne asked as she rooted through her bag.

"Taser. I'll go right, you go left. Take as many out as you can. If they have this many here, let's hope that means they need this many for it to work. Realistically, we'll never get the ones on the other levels, but we should be able to get all of the ones up here." Mr. Average was counting down with his fingers. Five… four… three…

"Thank you," Ted said to Cayenne.

"Hey, I often fantasize about macing random guys in the mall," Cayenne smiled. Ted kissed her quickly and hard and then ran, and, as Mr. Average got to one, Ted reached the cultist nearest him. He pressed the Taser into the guy's back and squeezed the trigger. He heard a buzz, a crack, and the guy dropped to the ground. Somebody at the Sunglass Hut saw him and screamed.

He continued to run. There were four on this level, so twelve total. How many did they need to get this thing off the ground? He looked across the atrium and saw Mr. Average with his hands over his eyes writhing in pain. A mall security guard was chasing Cayenne.

"*Yog-Sothoth!*" the next cultist was chanting, along with his co-religionists. "*Mesha'al… Yog-Sothoth… agggh!*" he was interrupted, mid-chant, as Ted took him down. More people were pointing and screaming. They really would never make it down the escalators to get the other guys. He just had to hope that four was enough. He looked across the atrium and saw Cayenne wrestling with the cell phone skin guy, who held her wrist in his massive hand, preventing her from pulling the Mace trigger. Ted ran to her, faking out an out-of-shape mall security guard chasing Ted on a Segway, in the process.

In the center of the mall, a rip appeared. Ted tried not to even look at it, because he didn't want to go completely insane, but it was definitely a rip—it looked like the center of the atrium was a sheet that somebody had sliced open in the middle. A sickly greenish-yellow light began to pour out of the rip. Ted was five steps from Cayenne, who was screaming, "OW! Help me, Ted, he's breaking my fucking arm! Ow!"

Ted reached the guy, but he picked Cayenne up and held her over the atrium. "Yog-Sothoth!" he chanted. "R'lyeh... Cthulhu." He stopped speaking and let Cayenne go.

"No!" Ted heard himself screaming. "No!" He watched, helpless, as Cayenne fell into the rip in the fabric of space and time, or at least the fabric of the mall, and disappeared.

Without thinking, without even bothering to tase the guy who did this, Ted vaulted the railing and jumped for the rip. He had a moment of panic when he realized that he might not make the rip, because it seemed to be shrinking, and he had just enough presence of mind to realize that if Lovecraft was right, he'd probably be better off flattened on the food court than making it through the rip. He was actually laughing as he was suddenly surrounded by cold and the mall around him disappeared, replaced with greenish-yellow light.

FOURTEEN

L aura sat alone in a booth at T. Q. Cholmondley's Pub and Eatery on level two of the mall. The walls were festooned with old tin signs and a bunch of other crap that was supposed to make this place feel jolly. It wasn't working. Laura held up a finger, and her striped-blouse-wearing waitress brought her another beer and another shot of tequila. She hadn't felt the first one at all. She wanted desperately to be drunk, to be able to forget everything, to be able to stop herself from remembering herself running into the mall too late, feeling confused and helpless as she saw only the top of Ted's bald head disappearing into some kind of rip in the fabric of reality. Again she asked herself whether she could have made a difference if she'd picked up the phone when Ted called. Again she remembered the last thing she said to Ted, who, despite everything, she did love. Now he was probably dead, and the last thing she'd said to the person who'd saved her from an eternity of damnation had been some shitty thing about him being a baby, about how hard it had been to be nice to him for ten years when he'd spent the same ten years trapped in a nightmare of blood and fire.

And, while she'd spent the early part of the day remembering every time Ted had pissed her off, she now found that she couldn't turn off the good memories—the movie nights, the disastrous double-date in DC, all the times he'd made her laugh. She tried to remember a time she'd laughed really hard without Ted there, and she couldn't. What the hell had she been so serious about? Jesus, Ted had seen so much worse, had done so much worse than her, and he still never lost that goofy grin, never stopped making the stupid jokes, even when he was sobbing, when he was puking, he'd never lost touch with his sense of humor. Where had hers gone? Right now she felt so bereft that she couldn't imagine ever laughing again.

She tossed back the tequila. It burned her throat, and she was glad to be able to punish herself at least that much, but it did nothing to quiet the chaos and horror surging through her brain.

She felt herself ready to cry, and she took a long slug of beer to try to hold back the tears. She slammed the mug down on the table a little too emphatically. Suddenly there was someone sitting across from her, and she was sure it was going to be the manager telling her that she was cut off, that she didn't have to go home, but she couldn't stay here, her obvious drunkenness was frightening the family diners.

Instead, it was an old white guy with glasses and disheveled white hair wearing a rumpled brown suit. He reminded Laura of a calculus professor she'd had once. "Agent Harker?"

"Sorry," Laura said. "I think you've mistaken me for somebody else."

"Oh, I don't think I have. I'm from the Pentagon—here's my DOD ID," he said. He slid over a laminated plastic card with a digital photo of himself wearing a sickly half-smile. Laura looked at it, then reached down to her bag, pulled out her .38, and aimed it at the guy under the booth.

"Funny—uh, Terry Marrs—but you don't have an up-to-date DOD ID that reflects all the post 9/11 changes. Here's what a *real* government ID looks like these days." She pulled out her ID and slapped it on the table. "So why don't you take your government agent impersonating ass out of here before I go Han Solo on you under the table and splatter your internal organs all over the Mainers Drink Moxie sign over there."

The guy looked bemused, which really pissed off Laura. "I don't really think you're going to shoot me in the middle of T. Q. Cholmondley's Pub and Eatery. You'd be all over the news, for one thing, and your effectiveness as a field agent would be compromised, and you'd probably have a hard time convincing even the most trigger-happy of your superiors that I constituted a threat you needed to counter with deadly force. So if you'll give me a minute, I can explain about the ID. You see, I work for a branch of the Department of Defense that doesn't technically exist, or hasn't since the current administration came to power."

Laura looked at him skeptically.

"Oh, yes, I'm sorry, how silly of me. Let me say first off that I know about how your friend Ted dragged you from a burning house full of vampires ten years ago, and about who really shot up the Queequeg's in Boston, and about what happened here earlier today."

Laura felt panicky and sweaty. Well, this was how her career ended. She decided to try to brazen it out.

"I really don't know what you're talking about. Vampires? Are you off your meds or something?"

"No," he said, still smiling that smile that, in Laura's current mood, really seemed to be inviting a backhand slap across the mouth, "I'm on my meds, and my prostate has shrunken to a manageable size. Thank you for the inquiry. And I do appreciate the fact that you wish to deny these essential facts about your life to a complete stranger—it shows that you're cautious and suspicious, both of which are assets in your profession. So let me tell you my story.

"When I was a child, my mother was murdered by a werewolf." He paused for a second and looked at Laura as if waiting for her reaction. She remained stony-faced. Did he really think she'd be surprised by this information after everything that had happened to her? "Insisting on this simple truth bought me many years of therapy. Like you, I was spurred by my tragedy into a law-enforcement career. I took a rather convoluted path, but the part of this that's relevant now is that back in the Carter Administration, I joined up with the Supernatural Defense section of the Department of Defense. We were well-funded, and we put out fires all over—vampires here, werewolves there, that outbreak of dog-eating fairies in the Smoky Mountains—the point is, we kept our country safe from all kinds of threats that it was important that the public never know about. And we were only hours away from taking out that nest of vampires when your friend Ted beat us to it. Which I'm sure is cold comfort to both of you, since you certainly wouldn't have lived to see our operation take place, at least not in human form, and Ted—well, on the one hand, he really didn't have to do all that killing and burning himself, but, on the other hand, if he hadn't, the rest of the campus would have been saved while all his friends were dead. All I can say in defense of our tardy response is that a certain senator's daughter was the person we really had to look out for—" Laura glared at him, and he shrugged semi-apologetically—"sorry, but politics is a reality of our work that's possibly even more hateful than all the supernatural realities. In any case, Ashley didn't attend that party, so we felt safe in delaying.

"Be that as it may, our funding got cut under Reagan, but we were still able to operate at a reasonable level, and when Clinton got in, I was appointed director, and we got a big boost. He personally asked me to look into whether there were succubi in the Ozark mountains."

Laura, in spite of her foul mood and her determination to be a hardass, gave a snort of amusement. She thought of it as a little tribute to Ted.

"I know—it has all the earmarks of a joke, but he was correct. What led him to suspect the presence of succubi in his home state is something we can only speculate about. But let me tell you, the demons who seduce wayward men and then steal their souls are just about the least dangerous things that live in the Ozarks. Well, of course, the people are the least scary—I'm speaking of the supernatural beings.

"In any case, once the conservatives took over the congress in '94, there were serious rumblings among several of the representatives and even a senator or two, who should have known better, that they were going to hold closed-door hearings and make sure we only got funded if we used, and I'm quoting here, Bible-Based Supernatural Defenses. Which are fine as far as they go, but when you've got a djinn running around Death Valley, as we did just recently, your bible-based defenses are going to prove completely ineffective. Take our current predicament, for example. Try telling the Old Ones to Get Thee Behind Me. Your best possible outcome in that scenario is being crushed quickly and completely.

"So we resisted, but these lunatics got more powerful, and they were threatening to take us public and tell our constituents that their tax dollars were funding Satanist Rituals or something. So while the outcome of the 2000 election was still in dispute, Clinton signed an executive order taking us off the books. He got some friendly Senators to hide a little trust fund for us in a gigantic appropriations bill, and we officially ceased to exist. I invested this money very wisely, but the fact is that we're stretched very thin, and it's extraordinarily difficult to recruit. Especially if you have to go through the tedious process of convincing people that supernatural threats to their security are real."

Laura took a large swig of beer. She didn't know what to think about this story. But at least he wasn't somebody from DC come to fire and/or imprison her. "Okay. It's an interesting story, but, I mean, so what? Why are you telling me this?"

"I'm telling you this so that you'll understand why you were even working on this operation in the first place. Though our offices are no longer in the Pentagon, I'm of course still plugged into the computer network with the absolute highest clearance—"

"Is that level Z?"

Marrs smiled. "Our programmers really are geniuses. Yes, level Z clearance. I'm the only one who has it. In addition to the other benefits, it allows me to change personnel files at will. So I got you transferred to counter-terrorism especially so you'd be able to work this investigation, and though your superiors have given up on it, it's obviously not over, and I'm going to need your help completing it. I think you'll do more good working for me than you would in the regular Bureau."

"You're the one who got me transferred?"

"As soon as I saw you looking up Cthulhu on the database.

We've been keeping tabs—to the extent that our ever-thinner resources have allowed, of course—on you and Ted for the last ten years. Mostly through credit card records, student loan applications, things like that. I was delighted to see that you'd joined the Bureau."

"Yeah. Well, I was pretty psyched at first, too, but it hasn't really worked out that well."

"Ah yes. First the fruitless hunt for Mr. Bulger, and now this. When I saw you trying to access my *Necronomicon* file, I knew it was time to act. We need your help, Laura."

"And you want to catch the fuckers who took my friend?"

"Yes. I can say without hesitation that this operation is our top priority at the moment. So, do you want to work for me?"

Laura thought for a moment, then decided that the guy knew enough already for her to throw caution to the wind. "Okay. I really feel like I owe these guys a lot of pain. And can we get Ted back?"

"Ah. Well. I think it's probably unlikely that... well, you see, what we need to do... I mean, obviously we need to permanently seal up the rift, not open it again. I'm afraid Ted is..."

"Consigned to an eternity of madness and horror?" Laura took another drink, trying not to think about what her words really meant.

"Oh, no. He's almost certainly dead."

FIFTEEN

Ted wasn't dead. At least, he was fairly certain that he wasn't dead. He was still solid, he hadn't floated toward a light, he couldn't hear the sounds of the Ramones playing with Keith Moon sitting in on drums that he was sure awaited all righteous souls when they died, and he couldn't hear Cherrified's greatest misses, which was a fate he was sure awaited the damned.

He could look down at himself and see a body there. All this argued strongly against his being dead. And yet.

He'd just come through what felt like an eternity of mind-rending despair. As soon as he'd jumped into the rip, he'd spent what felt like weeks in the most profound, unendurable despair he'd ever felt—the worst of his post-traumatic depression was a day at Disneyland compared to what he'd felt—the sense of utter hopelessness, of loss, of dread, the complete certainty that everything was hopeless forever. Not only was Cayenne lost, he, Ted, was lost, Laura was lost, everyone living and dead would spend eternity in unendurable pain.

He suspected that this was the part of glimpsing the Old Ones that drove people barking mad in the Lovecraft stories. He had felt his mind straining under the certainty that all that awaited him and everyone forever was endless torment. And then, it had ended, and he'd found himself face down on some foul-smelling flagstones.

Lovecraft was certainly right about the geometry. It was all wrong—looking around, Ted couldn't get a fix on what was up, what was down, and even whether he was looking at a sidewalk or a wall. He seemed to be in a city, in that there were streets and buildings, but it was like being trapped in that Escher drawing he'd hung on his dorm wall freshman year. Except that it smelled horrific, as though the contents of the Queequeg's dumpster he'd sat in just a few days, or possibly several hundred thousand years ago, had been pureed with a thousand decaying corpses and four tons of dogshit, and spread everywhere.

Actually, Ted's freshman room had also smelled horrific, due to his roommate's aversion to doing laundry as well as a jar of kimchi, which some kid from down the hall had left sitting in the sun on their windowsill one hot afternoon and which had exploded all over. If you magnified the stale crotch-sweat and fermented cabbage smell of his freshman room a thousand times, it might come close to the smell of what he assumed was R'lyeh, the city that, somewhere, held the sleeping Cthulhu.

And, hopefully, Cayenne. Uneasily, Ted stood up . He found that he was on a sidewalk, or possibly a roof. "Cayenne!" he called. "CAYENNE!" he screamed again. He wondered if his screaming might possibly wake the sleeping Cthulhu, which couldn't possibly be a good thing. But as he called Cayenne again, he realized that there was something else funny about this place. Despite the fact that he was standing on a flat expanse of stone with other flat expanses of stone all around—he wanted to think of it as a plaza, but then it kept looking spherical from certain angles—his voice wasn't echoing at all. In fact, it sounded much quieter than it should have in his ears. It seemed that sound waves weren't propagating properly here either.

Ted wandered aimlessly for a period of time through the streets, sewers, hallways, plazas, walls and rooftops of R'lyeh. He had no idea how long a period this happened to be. His feet did not get tired. He did not feel like sleeping. He was not hungry. He didn't have to pee. The light in and around R'lyeh—a sick greenish-yellow glow that emanated from the sky, or possibly the ceiling, or, then again, maybe the floor, did not vary at all.

All of which seemed to argue only that Ted hadn't been walking for very long. Yet it felt like at least three hours. Then again, he'd been to ninety-minute movies that felt like three hour movies simply because they were dull, and dull was certainly a good way to describe R'lyeh. Oh, sure, the city was dotted with statues of what he assumed to be Cthulhu—a big, octopus-headed creature—but these didn't live up to Lovecraft's billing of mind-destroying wrongness—they were a little weird, but Ted had seen weirder at Goth dance clubs, and they were not weird enough to distract Ted for long from the monotony of his surroundings and the feeling of dread and despair that was welling up inside him.

He called for Cayenne again, got no response, and started to run. When he found himself suddenly on a wall that used to be a sidewalk, he shouted at the top of his lungs that he was "Your Friendly Neighborhood Spider-Man." This remained entertaining and funny for a period of time, and then, suddenly, the dam burst on his despair, and he began to cry.

He'd been a fool to hope, to believe even for a second that

he wasn't doomed to live a shitty life, that everything hadn't been ruined that night in the sorority. He'd only known Cayenne for a few days, but he felt a connection with her that he hadn't ever felt with anyone. He had dared to hope that he was going to get a third act—the one where he got to be happy and live some sort of approximation of a normal life and possibly end up as the patriarch of some large happy family instead of just being a ghost that haunted Laura.

Well, that's what he got for hoping. It seemed God, or whoever ran things, was pretty pissed at Ted and had His own special plans to make Ted suffer. Even this place, with its boredom and horrible smell and bad geometry, might be endurable if he and Cayenne were together. He'd given up everything for her—the hope of ever setting foot in his own reality with its comforting, Euclidean geometry again—and it turned out to have been a sucker bet. He couldn't help her, he couldn't help himself.

And maybe, he thought, he was actually dead. Maybe this was hell—this terrible solitude, the boredom, and the sense that everything you'd done was ultimately for nothing. Maybe the cruelest part was that when he'd first found himself here, he'd been allowed to feel some hope.

He curled up and cried for a period of time. Or maybe, he thought, for a period of no-time. Did no-time even have periods? Or was it menopausal? Ted made himself smile with that, and then thought that showed he was desperate for a laugh. Ted went to wipe his eyes and found that they were dry. So maybe he hadn't been crying. Except he remembered crying. Maybe this was the part that drove people crazy—this inability to be sure of anything, ever.

More no-time did or did not pass. Ted wandered. None of the structures he passed looked familiar, but since he might be seeing them from different angles, he couldn't be sure if he was just walking through the same area over and over and over again. "Hey," he said aloud in his strangely too-quiet voice. "Where the hell's Cthulhu anyway? I mean, the guy's supposed to be friggin' huge—how could I possibly keep missing him?"

Armed with a purpose, Ted went wandering again. He alternated calling for Cayenne and calling for Cthulhu. Neither answered. He had three more dry-eyed crying fits as he sank into a pit of despair. He emerged from the pit of despair and walked. Eventually, or else immediately, he came upon a long wooden box. It was definitely a rectangular solid with right angles at the corners, and so was unlike anything else he'd seen in R'lyeh—it was definitely an object from his own dimension. He spent some time trying to figure out how to open it and eventually pried the top off. The smell of vomit and decay rose from the box, and, inside, he saw a corpse with blistered red burns all over it.

"Ah, Half-caf, we meet again," he said. Half-caf said nothing. Ted briefly imagined the horror of enduring the trip here sealed in a dark box, mind already straining at the seams from the pain of the untreated burns. He felt a swell of pity for Half-caf, and a pang of regret about burning him so badly. Then he remembered the young couple with their brains all over the Queequeg's wall, and he remembered Cayenne and the whole city of Providence, the whole earth that this guy had been trying to destroy, or at least transform into a facsimile of this stinking, unchanging shithole. "Tough luck, buddy," he said to Half-caf. He replaced the lid to the box and walked on.

He thought about Half-caf for several days while he walked in circles, or arcs, or intersecting parallel lines or something.

He decided that he would try to mark time by singing some of his favorite albums over and over again. This broke down when he couldn't remember some of the lyrics from Matthew Sweet's "Girlfriend." Then he couldn't remember which song he'd been singing. He tried to sing every Ramones song he knew, but then felt like he'd been singing "The KKK Took My Baby Away" for a year and a half. Perhaps he had. It occurred to him that he could think of eighteen-month periods he had spent in far worse ways. This made him smile. He was happy.

He was sad. He walked. The wall he'd been walking on suddenly became a ceiling. This made him laugh out loud. "What a feeling," he sang. "Dancin' on the Ceiling." This was funny, but the ceiling he was dancing on suddenly turned out to be a floor.

He decided that trying to play both ends of a chess game in his mind might help pass the time, or at least keep him sane, but then he found himself cackling rather alarmingly as he yelled out, "Yes! Feel the sting of my fianchettoed bishop! Put that in your Nimzo-Indian and smoke it!" This struck him as even funnier, and he started calling out chess openings that never existed outside of this greenish, strangely constructed zone outside of time and space. "Ah, yes, Townsend's hard drive! But black counters with the Queen's knickers! Fantastic move. Ah, White has reached Gilligan's Island by transposition! Now, if this were Gilligan's Island, which I guess it is, who am I? Am I Gilligan? Or am I the Professor? Or possibly Mary Ann?" He wondered why no one had ever made a pornographic version of *Gilligan's Island*, then realized that someone almost certainly had. "Great idea for a porno movie," he said, and then began to cry as he realized he would never ever see it.

Except in his mind, where Ginger and Mary Ann frolicked enthusiastically for quite some time. Or no time at all. Or something.

Finally, or, then again, initially, Ted rounded a corner, or cornered a round, or fianchettoed the bishop, and was knocked out of his pornographic reverie by the sight of the gargantuan Cthulhu, sleeping.

Sixteen

I n books, people were always suddenly sobered up by hearing something surprising, but Agent Marrs, if that was his real name, with his absurd tale of werewolves and Bible-based supernatural defenses and Ted being dead, did not sober up Laura one bit. Indeed, her encounter with Agent Marrs made her, feel, if anything, more drunk, like hearing about secret government anti-supernatural fighters was something that just happened when your brain was fogged, kind of like calling your ex at one in the morning. Perhaps it was just the tequila hitting bottom, but she suddenly felt that all the alcohol she'd consumed that hadn't had any effect on her at all had suddenly kicked in.

"Bullshit," she said. "I mean, it's all bullshit, probably, but Ted being dead is definitely bullshit. The guy—I mean, a sorority full of vampires and a mass killing in a Queequeg's and the guy walks away without a scratch. There's no way that something like being sucked into another dimension of unimaginable horror could possibly kill him. The guy is immortal."

Marrs gave Laura a look that she recognized as, "You poor dear, you're in denial, but I'm not going to burst your bubble right now."

"Well," he said, "be that as it may, I would really like to put a stop to this whole Cthulhu Cult business, and I'd love your help if you're willing to work for me."

"Let me just ask you this, Mr. Marrs—" Laura killed her beer and signaled the waitress for a refill, and then suddenly started to giggle as she imagined what Ted would do if faced with somebody named Marrs. "Are you related to the M.A.R.R.S. who did 'Pump Up the Volume'?"

For the first time in this conversation, Marrs looked unbalanced. "I'm sorry," he said, "I'm afraid I don't…"

"I'm kidding, I'm kidding. But that would be pretty funny, though, if that was like a fund-raiser for your department or something."

Marrs looked at her blankly, and she tried to make her brain serious for a moment. "Okay, listen—you know about the Omega house, you were just about to stop it, you know about this, you have the power to get me transferred, but why the hell can't you do anything about it? I mean, these losers were digging up the *Necronomicon* on a public street! You couldn't do that?"

"Oh, we've had the *Necronomicon* for years. The great majority of it is completely useless. Largely the insane rantings of someone who'd been hitting the hashish a bit too hard."

"Hence the 'Mad Arab' thing, huh?"

"Right. But there are approximately thirty pages of incantations in the *Necronomicon* with all kinds of deadly implications. But they're coded. You can't do anything with them without a key to the code."

"Which these guys obviously have."

"Right. We don't even know what book contains the code, what it looks like, what language it's in, anything. Frankly, we didn't believe there were any extant copies."

Laura smiled. "Say that word again."

"*Necronomicon?*"

"Hee! That's a funny one too, but I mean 'extant.' It sounds funny, you know? Like, something that used to be tant. Whatever *tant* is."

"Well," and Marrs shifted uncomfortably in his seat, "I think perhaps we should continue our conversation in the morning—"

"But, I mean, why couldn't you just kill all these guys, or at least arrest them or something? Why'd you let them dig up the *Necronomicon* in the first place? Why didn't you kill the vampires? If you know about all this shit, why don't you fix it?"

Marrs sighed heavily, removed his glasses, rubbed his eyes, and put his glasses back on. "Right now," he said. "I mean at this very instant, my branch consists of me and five other people in the office. We spend a lot of time monitoring information on computers, we piggyback on the surveillance whenever the FBI is investigating anything that we think might be supernatural—we work very hard, I want you to understand this—we all work seventy, eighty-hour weeks, and through anonymous tips and selective use of arson, sunlight, crosses, silver, and numerous magical spells, we've actually been able to prevent probably thousands of deaths.

"But this is a very very big country, Laura. I should probably have one agent assigned to Sasquatch duty full time. Especially during mating season. They grow rather irascible then. But we simply don't have the personnel. When I flew out to Death Valley to perform the simple matter of the Anti-Djinn incantations, some people dug up a *Necronomicon*.

I don't know how long our money has to last, so we can't spend like we'd like to, and, as I said before, it's damn hard to recruit when your pool of qualified applicants includes only those people who believe in the reality of vampires. I can't tell you the number of pale-skinned, black-attired Anne Rice devotees I've turned away—no law enforcement background, and most of them want to play bass for Lestat instead of wanting to rid the earth of bloodthirsty murderers."

Laura's next shot and beer arrived. She shot the tequila and suddenly had the presence of mind to wonder when she'd had this much to drink in this short a time before. Probably ten years ago at a party that this hot girl's sorority was having… And she was suddenly annoyed with herself. Time might be of the essence here, and she'd just taken herself out of the investigation for at least a few hours.

She thought, "I investigate better when I'm drunk," and then found herself laughing. She'd laughed a lot in the last few minutes—not too bad, when she'd thought she would never laugh again just a few minutes ago. Maybe she should get shitfaced more often. Marrs looked slightly annoyed.

"Listen, Ms. Harker, you're obviously not in any condition to make a decision right now, but I'm going to give you my card—" he pressed a card into her hand—"and if you'll give me your cell phone number, we can have a conversation in a few—"

"Don't need to think about it. I wanna do it." The words spilled out of Laura's mouth before she had a chance to consider what she was saying. But then she thought about it. This was what she wanted to do all along—to work on this kind of case. And if she stayed with the regular FBI, she'd have to look for Ted on her own time, and every time something obviously supernatural came up, some jackass would tell her it was a magic trick and she couldn't have any resources. It didn't seem like Marrs had much in the way of resources either, but at least he'd let her use her time the way she wanted.

Marrs smiled. "Delightful. Well, I can't obviously take you as seriously as I'd like given your condition."

"Being a lesbian is not a condition, okay? And I don't know why it should prevent you from..."

Marrs looked uncomfortable, and his face turned red. "Well, no, I was actually referring... I mean, obviously who you choose to... that is..."

Laura let loose a flood of giggles. "Gotcha!" she said. Marrs didn't look amused. "So when do we start, and where?"

"I really don't think we should discuss this right now. I will call you first thing in the morning. So I suggest you cut off your consumption at this point so as to be in suitable investigating condition. I find that water, in addition to a supplement containing a rich B-vitamin complex does a wonderful job of helping one avoid some of the worst symptoms of the hangover."

"B vitamins?"

"Consumption of alcohol depletes your supply of B vitamins. This adds tremendously to the complications of a hangover. A spoonful of brewer's yeast, or possibly—"

"Yeah, what's that shit Ted drinks? Some kind of fizzy vitamin shake..."

"Just the ticket. I'll call at six." He extended his hand. "We're happy to have you on board. I believe you're the first rug-chewing lush we've ever had in the department."

Laura looked blankly at Marrs' extended hand and debated whether to smack him. Then he laughed a hearty laugh and said, "I believe I owed you one!" and Laura wasn't sure whether to smile or deck him. Finally she shook his hand.

"Do we get to take 'em out?"

"Who?"

"The guys who… who did this to Ted. Do we take 'em out?"

"Well, if they were supernatural creatures, certainly—pile of ashes, puff of smoke, what have you, problem solved. But these cretins aren't supernatural, so not only do they tend to have next of kin, they also leave behind remains that are far more difficult to dispose of, and we simply—"

"I know. Resources."

"Exactly."

"Well. Till tomorrow, then."

"Fine," Marrs said, smiling. He walked out of the restaurant. Laura pondered the beer that sat in front of her and decided not to drink it. She called for her check and paid it. She walked unsteadily down the street toward the panel van—though she hardly knew Killilea, he'd been better through this whole thing than he had to be, and she thought he deserved a goodbye. But the van was gone and Laura was officially transferred. She walked toward the unfurnished apartment that Ted would never set foot in again, stopping at a convenience store a few blocks from Ted's apartment (No, you told him it was your apartment, remember, when he tried to kick you out of it for calling him a baby, a really annoying voice in her brain reminded her.) and bought a packet of what she hoped was the same fizzy vitamin thing Ted always drank as well as a liter of water. She poured the powder into the water and began to drink it.

The phone woke Laura up at six a.m. Her first, half-awake thought was "Leave it to Goddamn Ted to call at six in the morning when I'm trying to sleep off…" And then she realized that Ted wasn't calling, that Ted might never call again, and she was wide awake and felt like crying.

She felt extraordinarily tired, as she'd been up at least three times to pee in the night, but her head didn't hurt, her muscles didn't ache, and her stomach felt only slightly sour. She punched the green button on her phone.

"Harker."

"Marrs. Ready to get started?"

"I think I should shower first."

"By all means. Meet me at the coffee shop catty-corner from the mall in half an hour."

"Okay." Laura hung up the phone and reflected that she always said "kitty-corner."

Half an hour later, she was catty-corner, or maybe kitty-corner (Pussy-corner? she asked herself, and then allowed herself two and a half seconds to think that it had been way too long since she'd gotten laid.) from the mall, looking at an enormous latte and Marrs, who sipped from a small tea.

"Tannins," he said, "You know, even the black teas have fantastic antioxidant—"

"I'm sure they do, but can we talk about how we're going to get Ted back?"

Marrs looked down at his tea, and then back up to Laura. "I need to be really clear with you now that you're sober. While we'd love to have Ted and the young woman who disappeared back—"

"There was a woman?"

"Yes—mid-twenties, ran a pushcart at the mall—"

"Too many piercings?"

"Judging by witness accounts, yes. She fell or was thrown into the rift first, and Ted jumped in after her."

Laura fell silent. So Ted had done it again. He'd gone after somebody he cared about. She'd chided him for being this brainless puppy that followed people home, but she had to hand it to him—he also had the best qualities of a dog, in that he loved unconditionally and with complete loyalty. If he liked you, there was really no limit to what he would do for you, whether it was beheading Bitsy or jumping into another dimension that would likely kill him or drive him hopelessly insane.

The self-loathing came bubbling up from her midsection again. Why the hell hadn't she appreciated him more? There probably weren't many people in the whole world who'd be as selfless as Ted when the chips were down. He was a puppy, but she was a heartless, ungrateful bitch who kicked puppies in the teeth. Ugh.

"In any case, Laura, I need to be very clear here. The goal of our investigation is to shut this Cthulhu operation down, permanently if we can. Getting Ted back would involve either allowing them to open the rift again, or opening it ourselves. Now, Lovecraft has given us some idea of what's on the other side, but we have no idea how reliable his descriptions are, or, even if he's accurate about the Old Ones, what else we might be inviting into our world if we throw a window open like that."

"So we just let Ted and… and this girl—"

"Jennifer. Apparently she went by Cayenne."

"Like the pepper?"

"Right."

"Of course she did. Anyway, so we leave them to whatever horrible fate they're suffering now—I know, I know you think they're dead, you don't have to give me that look."

"Listen. Let's assume that the only place we were putting at risk by opening the rift again was Providence. One hundred and seventy-three thousand people live in Providence. We can't put them all at risk to save two people."

We can when one of them is Ted, Laura thought. She knew Marrs was right, and yet.... "Is that the kind of fact you just know off the top of your head? The population of Providence?"

He gave a small smile. "I looked it up. I anticipated having this argument with you."

"Okay. So if I have to be satisfied with just taking this operation down, that's what I'll do." In her mind, Laura crossed her fingers behind her back. "So how do we do it?"

"Well, you have one address—oh, by the way, you've now officially been transferred out of the Boston office, and nobody knows exactly to where, and everyone thinks someone else is responsible—exploiting the natural confusion attendant on any bureaucracy is a specialty of mine."

"Fantastic."

"At any rate, you have one address from the man you followed. We have all the surveillance video, and I've been able to pull some decent photos out of them that we can show around. The New England League of Illusionists, an organization I invented, has claimed responsibility for what they call "An act of magical guerilla theatre." The newspapers are fulminating about the need for better mall security, which could only help us, and fortunately for us, an attractive young white woman has disappeared in the New York area, so the cable news networks are running with that story and essentially ignoring this one.

"So. We could continue to watch the mall. We could also tail the person you know about, whose name is—"

"William Castle."

"Yes. Those are pretty much the options I see, unless you have something else."

"Well," Laura produced her flash drive, "I copied the documents off that guy—William Castle's hard drive. And, uh… let's see. Oh yeah—Ted told me the guys who dug up Lovecraft's street had an Ocean State Power truck. So maybe one of them works there."

"That's certainly worth investigating. Why don't you head over to the maintenance lot at Ocean State Power—here." Marrs reached below the table into a giant leather man-purse and pulled out a sheet of paper with a bunch of digital photos which he handed to Laura. "Here are the images we grabbed off the security videos, so you can ask after your guy. I'll take your flash drive and see if I can come up with anything interesting or worthwhile."

They stood. "Uh, I have a question," Laura said.

"Yes?"

"Is there any—I mean, I know about the resources, but, you know, I drive a Corolla. I think I need a town car or something to look like I'm actually an agent. You know what I mean?"

"I do. You can take my car—it's a large American rental, no idea what make or model. Here's the key," and he handed her a key on a rental car company chain.

Laura headed for the Ocean State Power maintenance yard closest to College Hill, where they'd presumably dug up the *Necronomicon.*

The lot was surrounded by eight-foot-tall chainlink and was full of idling trucks and panel vans and men in jeans and khaki work boots and blue Ocean State Power jackets drinking from large Styrofoam cups from Dunkin' Donuts.

Laura walked across the lot to the office, stifling the urge to pull her badge and gun on the group that was loudly speculating about what her ass might look like in a nicer outfit. She realized she was still in her two-day-old surveillance clothes, and that a change of clothes might have been better for being taken seriously than a big American rental car. She turned her head and covertly sniffed her pit. Not great, but not horribly offensive.

In the office, she talked to someone named Frank, who sat beneath an insurance agency calendar with a photo of a typical New England lighthouse above the month. He appeared to be in his forties, wore a blue jacket, jeans, and khaki work boots and drank from a Dunkin' Donuts cup.

"We're just following up on the incident at the mall yesterday, trying to get some more witness statements, see if anybody saw anything that might be at all helpful, you know sometimes people think they don't have anything worth telling us about and it turns out that they've got that final piece of the puzzle. Anyway, another witness said she thought she remembered some people in OSP jackets. Any of these men look familiar to you?"

"Sure. That's Dick there on the left. And Tracy is the other one. I don't recognize the rest."

"Wonderful. And are either of these gentlemen in today?"

"Well, they both clocked in, but they're not here. Let me just check—yeah, they're on the same crew. Leak near McCoy Stadium up in Pawtucket."

"Okay—can you give me their home addresses, just in case we miss each other when I'm driving up there?"

"Sure."

Back in the car, she called Marrs. "I got two," she said.

"Fantastic!" Marrs answered. He sounded genuinely thrilled, the first time he'd sounded anything but professorial.

"Anything on the flash drive?"

"A really shocking amount of foot fetish pornography—if you can call it pornography. I assume close-up photos of feet tied lovingly with silk cords count as pornography?"

"I don't know, but you're making me hot just talking about it." There was a pause. "I'm kidding, I'm kidding. Anything else?

"Yes. There's a file that suggests this group may possess a copy of the book that provides the key to the dangerous parts of the *Necronomicon*. I cross-referenced Mr. Castle's files with our copy of the *Necronomicon*, and though I personally lack the expertise to do the correlation, my resident cryptologist is very excited by what we've got thus far."

"Glad to hear it. The supervisor at the power company told me these guys are out on a job, so I'm going to go see what I can find at their houses.

"All right. But please try to avoid any kind of confrontation. Satisfying as it is to employ your hand-to-hand training, if two of these men are assaulted by you in their home, they will be clear that we're on to them."

"Got it."

A few moments later, Laura arrived at the closest address, which was the home of one Richard Johnson. "Dick Johnson," she thought to herself. "No wonder he turned evil." She felt a sudden pang as she imagined what kind of riff Ted would have done at finding the home of Dick Johnson.

Dick Johnson lived in a small, beige ranch house in a middle-class neighborhood of Providence. A small yellow sign on his neatly trimmed lawn announced that he had an alarm system, and a small white sign on his lawn announced

"A Pit Bull Lives Here!" Fantastic.

She called Marrs. He asked her a series of questions about what she was seeing, and then told her which wire to cut to disarm the alarm. Of course, she had nothing to cut it with, so she asked him for directions to the nearest hardware store for wire cutters. Once she had the proper tools and had cut the alarm, she asked Marrs, "What about the dog?"

"Well, I can direct you to a supermarket if you want to buy him a steak," Marrs said. "Otherwise, I'm afraid I can't be much help. While my expertise in subduing supernatural creatures is considerable, my mastery of the more mundane inhabitants of our planet is far more limited."

"Don't you have any sleeping spells or anything I could use?"

"You really don't want to attempt to perform any magic unless you are a hundred percent sure you know what you're doing." Laura had rolled her eyes and made the "blah blah" gesture with her left hand as Marrs had said that into her right ear.

This left the dog as the only problem to be overcome. Laura couldn't shoot it without bringing Providence police around. She'd just have to hope that they were slower to respond to barking dog complaints than they were to gunshots.

She approached the back door. She heard the dog barking and scratching at the door. She took a deep breath. She hoped that everything she'd learned about dealing with a human attacker would be applicable to a dog. She picked the back door lock quickly, then turned the door knob slowly, without actually opening the door. The dog was growling and barking uncontrollably, losing its mind in its desperation to get to her. Laura crouched five feet from the door and pushed it open with the rake.

The dog reacted exactly as she'd hoped he would. As he sprang for her, barking and snarling, Laura caught him in the chest with her foot and used his momentum to flip him over her head. There was a whine of pain as the dog struck the sidewalk, but Laura was already running for the door. She had it closed and locked before the dog had managed to get up.

She had no idea if any of the neighbors were home or if any of them had seen or heard anything. She decided she had to proceed quickly.

Laura began to search the house, and the dog scratched at the back door, barking like mad.

SEVENTEEN

T ed was tap dancing on Cthulhu's forehead. "Wake up, you dirty fucker! Wake the fuck up! You'll be late for school!"

Cthulhu did not respond, did not stir. It had been this way through all of Ted's attempts to wake Cthulhu, which had been going on for at least two hours and at most several thousand years. When Ted had first caught sight of Cthulhu—supine, but large as a skyscraper, with a hideous ovoid head from which emanated hundreds of tentacles, each the thickness of a telephone pole, each covered in something viscous and green that occasionally dripped off and landed with a wet squelching sound—he'd screamed.

When he'd finished screaming, he cried, and then he laughed, and this cycle repeated itself until Ted was thoroughly bored with himself. He was incapable of any new responses, he was just thinking and feeling the same things over and over, and he could feel his mind beginning to strain. Finally he decided he'd had enough. Ted was bored of playing word games trying to describe the passage of whatever passed here, was bored of trying to describe the geometry—once he'd come up with the perfect description, who would ever hear it? Who would ever appreciate how funny it was? Cayenne?

Perhaps, but Ted had no way of knowing whether she'd actually made it through alive, whether she was even here. Certainly the first few hundred years he'd spent searching for her hadn't borne any fruit.

Whatever this existence was, it seemed to be close enough to hell that Ted wanted out. So he'd kicked Cthulhu in the tentacle. And then he'd broken a stone off the roof of a nearby plaza and chucked it at Cthulhu's eye. It remained closed. "Wake up and kill me!" he implored the Old One. But, like many Old Ones, Cthulhu was apparently difficult to wake from his nap.

Ted kicked, stomped, screamed, bludgeoned, did everything he could think of to awaken Cthulhu. But the quiet, wet breathing continued, a tentacle would sometimes twitch involuntarily, and Cthulhu slept on. At some point the quality of the sounds emanating from Cthulhu changed. Ted decided that he was snoring.

He eventually grew bored of trying to wake Cthulhu and tried in vain to think of something else to do. He tried to stop himself thinking, because he could feel his thoughts spiraling downward into the abyss of depression he'd visited on his way here. Once he reached the bottom of the pit of despair, what would bring him out, since everything was apparently hopeless? No way, he couldn't allow himself to start thinking like that, or at all.

In the past, when he'd wanted to stop himself from thinking, he'd tried drugs, none of which were available here; pornography, ditto; and, of course, television. Which of course did not exist here but which existed, blessedly, in his memory.

"Okay," he said to Cthulhu, "now, the most recent thing I can remember watching was this reality show called

Massachusetts Marriage. So I'll take all the parts—what's that?—no, you can't have the part of the slutty girl who makes out with everyone, that's the best part!"

And Ted told the entire story of *Massachusetts Marriage* to Cthulhu, who was unmoved. From there, Ted began working backwards, assembling entire episodes of *Law & Order*, *Seinfeld*, anything he'd ever watched, which, he found, was an enormous storehouse of material. How many hours had he spent in front of TV Land, watching, for example, a *Munsters* marathon? How many days after school had he swallowed the delicious cocktail of *The Brady Bunch/Gilligan's Island* back-to-back episodes?

"Ah, Sherwood Schwartz," he said aloud, "bard of the blended family, chronicler of the castaways, how do I revere thee on this day!" He then proceeded to tell Cthulhu about how Mom always said don't play ball in the house, and how Gilligan's last-minute blundering had turned the burning S.O.S. into a greeting for an astronaut named Sol.

"And Laura used to give me that tut-tut thing about the TV—you know, 'you could at least read a book for God's sake, even those pathetic comic books you read are better than this crap!' But look at me now! Hanging with a celebrity and saving my sanity, such as it is, only because I wasted so much time! Ha!"

Bringing up Laura's name brought a pang of sadness to Ted, and he fought not to think about how he'd never see her again, about how he might perhaps have leaned on her a little too hard over the last ten years, about how he didn't do enough to show her how much she meant to him. He could feel tears forming when he could swear he heard Cthulhu say something in a tiny, high voice.

His head whipped around. "Whatchutalkinbout, Cthulhu?"

he asked. There was silence for a moment, and then he heard it again. Somewhere, someone was saying, "Wake up!"

Ted ran to the top of Cthulhu's head and looked down the other side, where he saw what had to be a hallucination. It was obviously a hallucination, because he was cursed, doomed to live a thousand thousand lifetimes of loneliness and despair, and that simply didn't square with the sight of Cayenne kicking Cthulhu in the tentacle. His heart leapt, and he began running down Cthulhu's slimy head, screaming, "Cayenne!" but, as before, his voice wasn't carrying, and Cayenne appeared to be lost in a reverie of rage and despair, so Ted actually got quite close before she could hear him.

"Oh my God, it's you!" she called, and she immediately began to sob. He ran to her and put his arms around her and felt her body heave up and down and she gave great, gulping sobs. "I thought… I thought… Oh, my God I was going crazy, I was going so crazy, how many decades have I been here, how long have I been wishing… Oh my God, you can't be real, I must just be completely insane, and I don't care."

Ted thought about insisting that he was real, but he just didn't feel all that sure of things after however many lifetimes in R'lyeh. Maybe, after all, he was Cayenne's hallucination, and it just took a while to find her. That would explain the absence of hunger or thirst or fatigue, though not how he'd known so much about television, or even Laura's name.

He said none of this. He simply held Cayenne in his arms, thrilled at her presence, her aliveness, her separateness from him. They stayed like that, embracing and feeling the solidness of each other's presence, for what might have been a year. Then Ted pulled away and kissed her face, and then her mouth, and soon she broke away and said, "Let's find some place away from prying eyes and tentacles."

They walked, hand-in-hand, for a while, and Ted didn't dare to let go of her hand for fear she'd disappear and he'd never find her again, or that one of them would simply stop existing without the other one there to perceive them. Finally they found an opening in a wall or floor and crawled into a pyramidal or possibly spherical space and were alone together.

To say it was the best sex either of them had ever had was akin to saying that a chocolate truffle is mildly preferable to a shit sandwich. Which is to say that what passed between Ted and Cayenne appeared to be an eternity of bliss, an extra-temporal festival of the flesh that had every nerve in Ted's body singing for joy for what must have been days. Each of them had orgasms that lasted centuries, and what transpired between them for those eons they spent in R'lyeh was simply the Platonic ideal of sex, the sex that all sex on earth, in real time, strove to be and could never be because of the regular passage of time. Ted had occasion to think at one point that he'd thought himself in hell earlier, and now he felt he must surely be in heaven, that if he were to die right now, he'd feel that his life, despite the killing and the blood and the eternities of despair wandering the streets of R'lyeh, had been an embarrassingly lucky one, that the good far outweighed the bad, and that he was glad he'd been alive.

EIGHTEEN

Trying to shut out the sounds of the pit bull's insistent barking and her own heart beating, Laura searched Dick Johnson's house as methodically as she could. The living room revealed nothing but the obligatory large television, the sectional sofa, the complete works of Lovecraft, white supremacist pamphlets, video games, and pornography. (Laura paused when she uncovered DVDs labeled as volumes one through six of *My Big Fat Black Cock,* realizing that she'd probably just uncovered something pretty significant about the psychology of the white supremacist, but she went immediately back to her search that could never be as thorough as she wanted it to be.)

The kitchen looked unused, and the fridge, though clean, was in all other respects a stereotypical bachelor fridge. One half-eaten jar of mayonnaise, a package of hot dogs, a bottle of ketchup and three bottles of beer sat on otherwise empty shelves. The freezer held only three inches of frost and a half-empty ice cube tray.

Dick Johnson's bedroom, like every other room in the house, had plain white walls uncluttered by art work or photographs. It featured a king-sized bed with plain white sheets, a dresser full of white undershirts, white briefs, and white polo shirts. "I get it, I get it, you like white," Laura said to Dick Johnson. His closet held one suit, one white dress shirt, one tie and a pair of dress shoes with a layer of dust that suggested they hadn't been worn in years.

A laptop sat atop the dresser, and Laura opened it and waited what seemed like ages for it to boot up. Meanwhile, the dog barked and scratched, and Laura thought she heard a car door slam outside. "Come on, come on," she coaxed the computer, but it was booting up in its own sweet time. Finally it seemed that whoever had gotten out of the car had not decided to come and ring the bell. Perhaps it was Providence police surrounding the house, though. Finally the computer was ready for business, and Laura inserted her flash drive and copied the documents file.

She looked at her watch. Eighteen minutes had elapsed since she'd walked into the house. The police should be here soon. Assuming they'd been called. But she hadn't found anything interesting, and she still had to check the basement.

She'd just opened the door to the basement when she heard yelling outside. "Johnson!" a voice said. At the sound of this voice, the dog barking got further and further away from the back door and now seemed to be coming from the front. "Goddammit, shut your fucking dog up!"

Laura descended to the basement and peeked out of the basement window. She saw a fortyish black man standing outside the gate yelling at the house while the dog barked at the gate in front of him. "I work all night! Sleep deprivation can make a man do crazy shit, Johnson! Don't be surprised if something happens to this dog! Police won't do shit, so don't be surprised if somebody comes over here and does the neighborhood a favor one day!"

The man looked at the dog. "Shut the fuck up, ugly." He walked away, disgusted, and Laura began to search the basement. She wondered how exactly she was going to get out of here.

The basement was surprisingly clean. An immaculate furnace and water heater sat on unfinished concrete. There were no cobwebs, no piles of musty cardboard boxes, no old bicycles, nothing that looked basement-like at all. Except, of course, for the coffin freezer behind the furnace.

Given what Dick Johnson had done to his buddy in the temple, Laura thought it was a distinct possibility that there was actually a body in the coffin freezer. She threw the lid open and found only boxes and boxes of frozen dinners. She rooted through these. "Hmmm… Turkey… Meatloaf… Salisbury steak… what's this?" Amidst all the "Big Eater" frozen dinners was one "Light 'n' Active" frozen dinner. It felt significantly lighter than the others, but Laura supposed that was to be expected. Upon closer examination, though, she found that one end of the "Light n' Active" frozen dinner featuring grilled chicken and brown rice pilaf had been opened and retaped. Throwing caution to the wind, Laura ripped the box open.

A thin, leather-bound book tumbled out.

The green leather of the outside was completely blank. Inside, the title page bore handwritten cursive script that said: *Ye Keye To The Spirit Worlde, as Shown in Ye Anciente Necronomicon.*

So this must be the key to the dangerous parts of the *Necronomicon* that Marrs had talked about. Now they wouldn't need some cryptologist to crack the code. Once Marrs had his hands on it, they might find a way to bring Ted back! Laura felt a thrill of triumph and tucked the book under her other arm and headed upstairs. Now she just had to get past the dog again. She went and opened the back door a crack, and Fido came limping toward the door, barking. She closed the door and listened as Fido barked and scratched at it. Well, it appeared that he wasn't running as fast as he used to, which should help her plan.

Laura peeked out the front door. She stretched out her legs and hoped some part of her body remembered all those gymnastic meets back in middle school.

Throwing the door open, she ran for the front gate. She had only gotten a few strides up the front walk when the front door slammed closed. This brought Fido limping around the front. Without breaking stride, Laura ran to the white fence at the front, placed her right hand on the wooden ball atop the gate and swung her legs over the gate. A perfect vault, and she stuck the dismount. Fido barked on the other side of the gate while Laura pointed her arms skyward. "Ten-point-oh!" she shouted.

Book in hand, she ran back to Marrs' rental car, feeling exhilarated and relieved. She'd gotten something very important, she hadn't been injured, and she was going to get Ted back.

She started the car, then pulled out her phone to call Marrs. Her hands were all sweaty from being nervous, and the phone slipped out of her hand and onto the floor of the car. She bent down to retrieve the phone and heard a fantastically loud BOOM! She was showered with glass that she gauged had come from the back window, and she heard a man yelling, "Race traitor! Thief! If that shot did not dispatch you, I shall make you beg for the sweet mercy of death!"

Christ. It was Ted's Mr. Average, who must, she thought, be Dick Johnson. Without raising her head, Laura threw the car into reverse and hit the gas. She felt a thump as she hit something she hoped was Dick Johnson and not his justifiably aggrieved neighbor. Peeking up, she threw the car into drive and hit the gas.

She heard another boom and felt a sharp pain in her shoulder. She glanced down and saw a tiny spot of blood. It must have been a shotgun.

Laura looked back and saw a man limping toward an Ocean State Power van. She began to panic. She had no idea where she was or what was the best way to lose this guy. She had imagined a thousand car-chase scenarios in Boston, but she knew the streets of Boston. She knew nothing about Providence. Heart pounding, she called Marrs.

"I've got something!" she yelled into the phone, "but I'm being pursued!"

"This is your idea of avoiding confrontation?"

"Yes! I am fleeing! Get it?"

"All right. Do not discharge your weapon," Marrs said. "It's still your FBI gun, and the ballistics will be on file."

Laura spun the car around a corner and heard another shot.

"So what am I supposed to do?"

"Lose them. Hang on, I can track you here... Okay, got it. You're two blocks from 95. Once you're on the highway, you've got eight cylinders of American engine under the hood. They should have a difficult time pursuing you."

"I see it!" Laura said as she spotted the sign for 95 North. She allowed herself to feel relief. She exhaled and felt her shoulders relax when a shock went through the car and she found herself spinning out of control.

"Fuck!" she screamed. When the car came to a stop, she looked around and saw that she'd just been rammed in the driver's side by a big Dodge pickup. The driver's side window was shattered, and William Castle was getting out of the Dodge and walking toward the car with something in his hand. Laura could feel the beginnings of a powerful headache starting behind her eyes, and now her left shoulder had an ache to match the sharp pain of the shotgun pellet lodged in her right shoulder.

"Please keep working," she begged the car. She hit the gas and felt the car move forward with a definite shimmy. She gunned it and headed for the highway. With a great deal of effort, the car got up to seventy miles per hour, but the steering wheel was shaking in Laura's hand and the car felt like it might break apart. Another bump from behind, and Laura saw that another white guy in another pickup truck was ramming her from behind.

She had no idea how many of them there were, but they seemed confident that she was not part of a bigger force, because they were not shy about ramming the shit out of her.

Remembering Marrs, Laura held up the phone. "Marrs, are you still there?" she said.

"I am. And yourself?"

"Just barely. Listen, what the... I don't know what the fuck to do here. This car has had it."

"Don't worry. The credit card I used to rent it bills directly to the blind trust that holds all the assets of the Vice President of the United States. Kind of a clever bit of computer chicanery, if I do say so myself. I liked it so much I rented a Dodge Viper after you took the Lincoln—"

"I'm more worried about my life than how you're going to pay for the goddamn car," she yelled. "I know what to do in Boston, but not here! I don't know how to lose them!"

"Then go to Boston. Do you think the car will survive another hour?"

"Well, nothing's on fire yet."

"Good. Go to Boston. Keep your phone with you. I can track you and hopefully use something less traceable than your service weapon to help you. I'm leaving now, and I will assist you as best I can."

"Okay. Thanks."

She spun into the next lane in time to avoid another tap from the pickup.

After five minutes, she was able to coax the car up to eighty. Traffic got heavier, and the pickup did not try to ram her again. As she glanced back through what used to be the windshield, though, she saw that the pickup had been joined by an Ocean State Power truck and a slightly dented red Dodge pickup. So if they'd given up on trying to kill her on the road, they were just going to wait until she stopped. Well, they were in for a surprise.

After what felt like hours, she finally came to the exit for 138. This would be the hardest part—taking this two-lane road into Boston. She cut across three lanes of traffic and pulled off the exit. She hoped that would buy her some time. She made it through the intersection just as the light turned. Behind her, the red Dodge had taken the lead and continued to follow her.

Through Mattapan Square and onto Blue Hill Ave, she spun the car onto Morton Street. It crossed her mind to stop here and get out of the car in the middle of an almost completely black neighborhood, just to see if these guys would dare to follow her. But she figured it wouldn't be responsible law enforcement to expose the good people of Mattapan to armed racists full of homicidal rage. She sped down Morton Street with Franklin Park on her right. She took a sharp right as though she were going to drive under the road that bisects the park and come out on Forest Hills Street. Instead, just as she got to the underpass, she stopped the car and sprinted up the crumbling staircase, dodging the nip bottles and used condoms, and ran into the park. Once she reached the top, splinters of granite flew into her arm. They were down on the road, shooting at her. Well, they'd have to do better than that.

She crossed the street and quickly found the path that led to the hundred steps that went up the hill through the woods. Powered by adrenaline, she took the hundred granite steps two at a time. Once she reached the top, she found the metal 55-gallon drum with the plastic garbage bag inside. "Don't Trash Your Park!" a sticker on the side of the drum implored, "Park Your Trash!" She looked down and saw William Castle wheezing his way up the steps. She rolled the drum down and watched with delight as it took him out at the knees. He went sprawling and struck his head on one of the granite steps. He lay on a landing bleeding profusely from his head, with his leg splayed out at an angle no unbroken leg could manage. One down.

"Who else wants some?" she shouted. No one answered. Cutting to the left, Laura took to the woods, picked up a substantial stick, and crouched to wait. Only thirty seconds later, a white man she didn't recognize emerged at the top of the stairs. He had gone around to cut her off. Or else he was just a white guy out for a walk in the park.

"Brother William!" she heard him yell as he saw the prone form of his fellow cultist down the steps. Without waiting for further confirmation, Laura threw the stick as hard as she could. It struck her would-be attacker on top of the head, and by the time he had turned around to see where the blow had come from, Laura was already leaping toward him. She delivered a kick to the sternum that sent this guy falling down the stairs as well. He screamed as he fell, and there were two horrible cracks as his limbs broke against the granite steps. Adrenaline won out over nausea, and Laura ran back into the woods trying not to think about what she'd just done to two fellow human beings.

It wasn't long before she heard the voice of Mr. Average, Dick Johnson. "Surrender the book, and I will kill you quickly," he called into the woods.

"Are you afraid, Dick?" Laura called out. "Is your Johnson shriveling up?"

"Oh, it is you who should be afraid. Do you think your efforts can stop us? Our victory is inevitable! Emerge from the wilderness and I will put a bullet in your brain, thus sparing you the torment of enslavement once the Old Ones come back to rule."

"Come and get me," Laura called out. Her mind worked feverishly. Dick Johnson had a gun and she didn't. She knew the woods and he didn't. She wanted him alive. She came to a clearing where she found the remains of a campfire, an empty half-pint bottle of gin, a tiny plastic bag that had once held crack and, of course, a used condom. Good old Franklin Park. Hovering over the campfire was a seven-foot-tall puddingstone boulder. Laura went to the back of it and climbed up, hiding herself from the path where she heard Dick Johnson approaching.

When she was sure Dick Johnson was in the clearing, Laura leapt from the boulder, hoping to drop on him. Unfortunately, he was a few feet behind where she thought he would be, so she ended up leaping onto the hard dirt and found herself looking up at the barrel of Dick Johnson's gun.

"The book, young lady, and your death shall be far more merciful than you deserve."

She had practiced disarming from this position in Krav Maga class, but nothing prepared her for what happened. She reached up and pulled Dick Johnson forward by the gun. As she did so, Dick Johnson squeezed the trigger, and the gun went off, shooting a bullet into the ground between her knees, showering her with dirt, and nearly deafening her in the process.

As Dick Johnson fell forward, Laura brought a knee into his neck, and he fell, gasping to the ground. Laura grabbed his gun and stood up, out of range of any kicks or blows Dick Johnson might deliver.

She was holding a gun that would never be traced to her over the man responsible for sending Ted to another dimension. "How do I get Ted back?" she said to Dick Johnson.

He started laughing. "Ted? That bumbling idiot? Great Cthulhu is feasting upon his soul."

"Bullshit. How do I get him back?"

"You don't! Your only hope of ever seeing your friend again is setting me free to bring Cthulhu back. Then perhaps you will recognize your lover Ted as a stain on Great Cthulhu's foot. Ha! You are defeated, and your love is gone forever!"

Vastly amused at his own joke, Dick Johnson laughed, clutching his stomach. Without thinking, Laura approached and kicked him squarely under his jaw. She watched with satisfaction as half a tooth shot out of his mouth. "Laugh at me again," she said. "Laugh at my grief. Laugh at my friendship." The gun shook in her hand, and Dick Johnson apparently sensed that Laura had gone over the line to irrationality, into that place where anything is possible.

She moved the gun down from his head to his groin. "Maybe they'll have to start calling you Dickless Johnson," she said. "Maybe every time you look at the void between your legs you'll think about the time you laughed at my pain. Would you like that? Does that seem just to you?" It was so tempting. He'd made her suffer; he needed to suffer. There was no other way to punish him.

She noticed with some satisfaction that Dick Johnson had begun to cry and beg for his genitals, but his cries weren't penetrating all the way to Laura's brain. "Kiss your Johnson goodbye, Dick," she said. Just then, something shot past her head and into Dick Johnson. There was a crack, and he convulsed at the end of the wires Marrs had fired at him.

"You really can't maim him," Marrs said. "Believe me, I understand why it's tempting, but you simply can't do it." He flicked a switch and Dick Johnson stopped twitching. "Come now," Marrs said. "Hand me your weapon and let us leave this park as soon as possible."

Reluctantly, Laura handed her gun to Marrs. She followed him silently through the woods and to a red Dodge Viper parked by the stadium. They got into the car and drove back to Providence as fast as possible, which was very fast indeed.

As they drove, Laura began to feel nauseous. She thought back on the violence she'd committed, the lives she'd very likely taken, and the worst part was not the memory of the sounds, or the sight of the blood and broken limbs. The worst part was the memory of how much she had enjoyed it. It wasn't just a fight for survival; it was one of the biggest thrills of her life, and she was still high from it. And that was the disgusting part. She wondered if that was what kept

Ted up at night—not what he'd seen in the Omega house, but what he'd seen in himself. That he was not only capable of committing violence, but he was capable of liking it. Or maybe that was just her.

She still had the book in her pocket. It occurred to her that she could refuse to hand it over to Marrs, that she could use it to try to get Ted back. That was a dumb idea, but still, once she handed the book to Marrs, the door to wherever Ted was trapped was closed forever.

Still, she didn't want to be in charge of something that had the power to destroy the world. If she had it instead of Marrs, then it would be her fault if somebody stole it and did this again. The hell with that. Who the hell wanted that responsibility? She couldn't even keep a cat, much less the key to the *Necronomicon*.

No, Ted was gone, and she had to suck it back.

Back at Marrs' hotel, he tapped away on his computer, removing her prints from the national database while Laura showered. She tried to wash away the killer instinct, the joy she'd felt at being able to strike back at the men who'd taken Ted from her, but all of that seemed to cling to her.

When Laura emerged from the shower, she reached into her pocket, pulled out the book, and gave it to Marrs.

His face lit up like this was the best present he'd ever received. "This is really remarkable! Fantastic!" He thumbed through it. "It looks to be early eighteenth, possibly late-seventeenth-century. If we only had the resources, we could really find something out about this—you know, I wouldn't be at all surprised if this particular copy weren't related to that business in Salem…"

"You mean the witch trials?"

"Right." He continued to page through the book.

"But I thought those were a power grab, an expression of the misogyny of puritan society, a—"

"Yes, absolutely. They were all of those things. But there were real witches, too." Laura stood awkwardly for another five minutes watching Marrs turn pages, and finally cleared her throat.

Marrs looked up like he was surprised she was still standing there. "Yes? Oh, right."

"So what's next?"

"Well, we've got some chupacabras outbreaks in Puerto Rico—of course, I always prefer it when those happen in January—nothing like chupacabras duty when there's snow on the ground… or, Cambridge, Ohio, has seen two killings that could be vampiric—I suppose you should take that one, as you're the expert. Perhaps you could pass for a grad student…"

"Uh, but what about Cthulhu?" And what about Ted?

"Well, Cthulhu is about as done as we can manage. We have the book. We have to assume that they've made copies, but I have to believe you've thrown a scare into Dick Johnson and his fellows, and I suspect they'll be lying low for a while—"

"Are they dead? His fellows?"

"One is. The other is just seriously injured."

"They were going to kill me."

"I haven't said otherwise, and the good thing about our limited resources is that we do not have any internal affairs department to pester you with questions. You trusted me by signing on to my shoestring operation. I trust you that you will not wantonly kill."

He said nothing for a moment, then said, "Though I did wonder there at the end. You really are much tougher than you look, aren't you?"

Laura smiled. "I'm tough as an old boot. But should we go after the other guys? I mean, what if they have copies of the book?"

"Oh, they almost certainly do. At least, we have to assume it. We found a fragment on William Castle's hard drive, and I'm going to assume that there's something on Dick Johnson's as well—we can wipe the hard drives of everyone who accesses their online meeting places with a fantastically devious worm that one of our colleagues designed. And they have no idea how under-resourced we are. We'll do a little more—post some cryptic threats in their chat rooms, stuff like that. Unless they're incredibly stupid as well as evil they'll lay low for a while."

"But they killed—God, they killed those people at Queequeg's, they killed Ted and his girlfriend… they're just going to get to walk around free?" Suddenly she wished she had emasculated Dick Johnson while she had the chance.

Marrs closed the book and looked up at her. "Look. We can't go after them—the shooter is languishing in another dimension, we have no proof that they were involved. The immediate threat has passed, and if they get themselves organized again, well, we'll come back to deal with it, and this time—" he held the book up—"it will be far easier to deal with. We could probably do it with an incantation instead of a Taser and a can of Mace."

"What?"

"That's what Ted and Jennifer used. They took out four cultists. Might have been enough to prevent the rift from growing to Cthulhu size. They really did a tremendous thing."

Laura paused. She hadn't known that. "Can I… could I…

do you have a copy of the tape I can look at? I'd just like to see Ted..." She couldn't finish her sentence because she was crying, and she hated that, because it made her look like a weak, emotional woman, though Marrs didn't seem like the kind of employer who'd hold it against her.

He stood and placed a hand on her shoulder. "I know. I know. I spent my first three years on this job tracking the werewolf who killed my mother. I finally found he'd grown old and died wealthy. I'd love to be able to offer you closure, or justice, or anything, and sometimes we do get that—if it's really a vampire we've got in Cambridge, you can stake the bastard yourself—it's a remarkable rush—but in this case, I can't offer that. The bad guys—well, most of them, anyway—are going to get away, but at least they haven't won—if they had, it would be Cthulhu's world, and we would just be living in it. But today most of our fellow citizens woke up and went about the business of their daily lives without worrying about the Old Ones. We won. Remember that. It's important."

Laura found that her tears wouldn't stop. "I know it's important, it's why I got into this, it's just... It's not enough."

"I know," Marrs said. "I know."

NINETEEN

A funny thing happened after several eons of sweating, grunting, and writhing, with every neuron firing super shots to the pleasure center. Ted found himself growing bored. He couldn't imagine why—he felt better than he'd ever felt, and there was no indication that he ever needed to feel bad ever again. Surely this was what he'd been chasing for the last decade, what every drug, every second of television, every minute of McJob monotony had been aiming at—just take the pain away, I just want to feel good, I've felt bad enough for a lifetime, now I just want to feel good forever, is that so much to ask?

And yet, now he'd achieved that and never needed to feel bad ever again, it was somehow lacking. It wasn't just that he was craving some afterglow—though he was, and he wondered briefly if this made him a chick—it was just that even nonstop pleasure could, it seemed, get monotonous. Maybe, he thought, he needed a little of both—some pain to balance out the pleasure, some misery to make him appreciate happiness, some—he was thinking too much, and he untangled himself from Cayenne.

"Oh my God, I'm so glad you did that," she said. "I was starting to… I don't know…."

"I know," Ted replied. "It was… I mean, don't get me wrong, it was fantastic, amazing, wonderful, but…"

"Well, speaking for myself, the idea of doing that forever was starting to freak me out. Actually, the idea of forever has always freaked me out."

Ted felt a sour feeling in his stomach all the sudden. "Yeah. Me too. And now it looks like we may have to get pretty well acquainted with forever."

There was a pause, and Ted ran his fingertips over Cayenne's stomach. She curled up next to him, and Ted thought it really was strange—there was something about being scared that made curling up with her better. It just made it sweeter.

They didn't talk for a long time. Though he wasn't cold, Ted wanted his clothes. He reached around for them absentmindedly, then really began to look. Eventually he saw that his clothes had drifted to the opposite surface from where he and Cayenne were—either they were floating on the ceiling, and their clothes had dropped, or they were on the ground, and the clothes had floated. Whichever the case, their clothes were inaccessible.

"How long do you think we've been here?" Cayenne asked.

"You mean in this room?"

"No, in this city."

"Oh, God, I have no idea. I really can't even imagine—I honestly… I mean, it couldn't be less than ten years. I really believe that." Ted was lowballing his estimate—he feared it had already been at least a hundred years. He thought about all the time since he'd found himself face down on the stinking flagstones and felt very, very old.

"I was going to say fifteen. I'm glad it's not just me."

"I wonder why Cthulhu can sleep, and we can't."

"You know what I think? I think it's an act of mercy. I think Cthulhu was a very bad boy, and this place is his jail—I thought about this a lot, probably for a year at least—and as they were closing the door, he was begging for death, and they gave him sleep instead. Because it would just be too horrible to be trapped here awake forever."

And Ted's stomach went sour again. "Like us."

Cayenne looked troubled. "Yeah. Like us."

They sat in silence for a very long time. Ted tried to count seconds, but somewhere around two hundred Mississippi his brain wandered off into a recitation of "Fifty Nifty United States," and he had no idea how long that went on, but it led to every song he'd learned in elementary school, and every *Schoolhouse Rock!*, and he...

"Do you think we're dead?" Cayenne asked. "I mean, we could actually be dead, right? From what I remember of my Buddhist phase, they believe that you eventually reach this unchanging state of enlightenment, that all the changes of the wheel of existence finally stop, and you are free."

"I don't feel enlightened. I've been thinking about TV a lot. And, I mean, call me a gerbil, but I want back on the wheel. I mean, it's not just the stench, or the gross light, or the fact that I can't tell walls from ceilings from floors—because I'm almost sure we're on a ceiling right now, but it was definitely a floor when we came in here—it's that I just.... I want something to happen. I mean, finding you was the only thing that's happened in ten years or more. And I love being with you, but what are we going to talk about if we don't have any experiences?"

"Well," Cayenne said, smiling, "we can do it all the time."

Ted wanted to protest that he needed a break, that it would be better if they waited a while, but, then again, they'd already had a break that lasted at least a few days, and if it was monotonous to be in a state of constant ecstasy, it was far preferable to contemplating eternity in this filthy shithole.

The next few years were very, very good ones.

TWENTY

L aura sat in an airplane. She was flying to the Cincinnati airport, which was apparently not even in the same state as Cincinnati, and then driving about sixty miles to Cambridge, Ohio, where one undergraduate and one town resident had been murdered, drained of all their blood. Marrs was of the opinion that she wouldn't get the sharpened stakes through the airport x-ray, so he was FedExing them to her motel in Cambridge.

Marrs had the book, but Laura now had the clearance to access the department's documents and files, and once they had decoded everything, Laura had every intention of getting that information and using it to get Ted back. It was difficult to wait, but the only way she could make sure she continued to have the access she needed was to keep working for Marrs, which meant, for now, flying to Ohio.

She was next to the window, and two seats away was another professional-looking woman in a suit. Laura barely noticed her or anyone else on the half-empty flight. As soon as she was permitted to use electronic devices, she booted up her laptop and watched the security video again. The angry white guys walked to the atrium railing, and began to chant, quietly at first, then louder and louder. Then she could hear

Ted's voice screaming, "Laura, it's happening, they're in the mall! Help!" into the phone. It was the exact same words she heard on her voice mail every day. She began to cry, again. How was it possible that Ted's voice existed on this hard drive and on the hard drive of the voice-mail server as a bunch of zeroes and ones that computers were able to translate into his voice? How could it be that the zeroes and ones lived on while Ted was gone? It just didn't make any sense.

Laura wiped her face and watched as Ted and his girlfriend raced around the mall atrium, Cayenne pumping her fist every time one of the cultists went down. Laura marveled at Ted's agility—he faked out and dodged the security guards ably—but, more than that, she marveled at his decisiveness. She watched him move and couldn't understand how this guy who had been so lost in real life, so unable to choose a direction that he'd attached himself to her like a remora, could suddenly transform into this dynamo of purpose in a crisis. He wasn't hesitating, he wasn't stopping to think, he was just doing what needed to be done. Laura had been able to do that, finally in Franklin Park, but by then it was already too late.

Laura had to pause the video to cry as Ted completed his final decisive act on earth, vaulting the railing to the atrium and doing a cannonball into the rift in time and space that was in the middle of the mall. She cried for two minutes, then held back the tears just so she could punish herself. She unpaused the video and made herself watch the horrible, cringe-inducing part—as people ran around and screamed, a female FBI agent came in with gun drawn. You could see it in the way she moved—she was terrified and confused—she had no plan, she looked tentative. She walked to the railing, saw the rift knit itself up, and looked completely lost, completely befuddled. Big, strong, cool, Agent Harker was panic-stricken and ineffectual. After watching this video more times than she could count, she decided that this particular part was the worst—one of the cultists walked right past the stunned agent. She could have grabbed him, she could have at least beaten the crap out of him, and every time she watched it, even though she knew it was crazy, she willed the little figure on the screen to reach out, to take a swing with the butt of the pistol, to do something to stop the guy who was walking right past her... and, for the millionth time, her little avatar on the screen did nothing. She was a total waste, and the fact that she'd later dealt out some rather severe punishment to three of these guys did nothing to lessen her contempt for the idiot on the screen with the perpetrators walking past her.

Laura turned the laptop off and hung her head.

She breathed deeply and tried not to think about Ted and how much she missed him. She thought about her current mission, about killing vampires, about how she was going to be the scourge of the undead for decades to come, and every time she sent one of those bastards screaming to hell, she'd get right in their foul, unclean faces and say, "That's for Ted, bitch!"

Her reverie of violence and death had nearly flushed the sadness from her system when a voice from two seats away said, "Sad movie?"

Oh, great. She turned to glare at her interlocutor and saw that it was the woman sitting two seats away. She was a very attractive woman about five years older than Laura with shoulder-length chestnut hair and an expensive suit. Laura decided not to bite the woman's head off, but instead said, "Yeah. It's... I just lost my best friend."

"Oh my God, I'm so sorry," the woman said. "And it's

probably really annoying to have somebody in your face when—I'm sorry, I just... I felt bad because you looked so sad, and I know I should have just kept my mouth shut, but, I mean, I know about sadness, which is why I wanted to say something but which is also why I should've known enough to keep my mouth shut and mind my own business. Listen, I'm really really sorry. I'm going to shut up and leave you alone now."

"No, that's okay. It's kind of nice to get outside of my own head. I actually need to stop watching that. So my best friend—" she paused briefly as she said this, wondering when she'd ever told Ted that he was her best friend—"anyway, my best friend just died. What's your story?"

"Sole survivor of a car accident on prom night. They still show the footage in drivers' ed classes. I was as drunk and stupid as everybody else, but I was hanging out the window vomiting, and so I got thrown and got away with a broken clavicle and a concussion. Everybody else was in pieces."

Laura was silent for a moment. "Jesus. That's horrible. I... I mean, I know what that's like—" and she felt sudden empathy with Ted's desire to tell everybody everything, because she wanted to say, yeah, I know about carnage, but instead she said, "I survived a fire unhurt in college. Twelve people died."

The other woman looked at her, shook her head, and didn't say anything. Laura reflected that this was pretty weird for air travel small talk. She realized, briefly, that grief must still be screwing her up.

Laura spent the next hour talking with Elaine, who worked for Gillette and was going to Procter & Gamble headquarters in Cincinnati to try to save her job after the merger, or to try to convince her new bosses that she was indispensable, or something. Laura just volunteered that she had a new job in law enforcement.

When they parted at the rental car counter, Laura had Elaine's card with her cell phone number on the back and the information that Elaine was staying at the Westin.

Laura drove up the highway to Cambridge, Ohio, which was lined with little crosses marking car crash fatalities, wondering if Elaine had been hitting on her or was just looking for a friend. She decided that Elaine had definitely been hitting on her. She pondered this—Ted would have told her to go for it, and she might simply have to honor Ted's memory in this way. Of course, this led her to thinking about Ted, which led her to another crying jag. She just couldn't stand the fact that Ted was either dead or trapped in an eternity of torment, and she was doing nothing—well, she might get to kill a vampire and she might have sex with a stranger, both of which were activities that Ted would have approved of mightily, but she wasn't doing anything to help him, if he could even be helped at this point. He'd faced down an eternity of damnation for her, and she'd done nothing for him, at least not when it counted, not when it might have mattered. She'd even given back the book that held the key to opening the rift again, so there was no way she could even hop through to check to see if he was dead....

Laura was just driving through the campus of Cambridge University of Ohio when she slapped her forehead. Really, how could she possibly be so incredibly stupid? What the hell did she get that Summa Cum Laude for, anyway? She didn't need the book! She didn't need to wait for Marrs to upload anything onto the department servers! She could try to get Ted back as soon as tonight!

Laura spent the day wandering around the campus, not

really finding anything out. She kept looking at her watch, wishing the day away so that she could go to Cincinnati and get her job done.

That is to say, her job getting Ted back, or at least checking to see if he was still alive. Her job of investigating the killings in Cambridge would, she supposed, have to wait.

But what if somebody died (or worse) here while she was in Cincinnati on what amounted to personal business? Oh hell, it was worse than personal business, because she'd be putting the entire population of the Cincinnati metro area at risk, and she didn't know the figures, but she imagined Marrs would tell her that Cincinnati was even more populous than Providence, so she was actually being several times more irresponsible.

She tried to stop thinking about trans-dimensional search and rescue and start thinking about the undead killers right here. She felt torn, and she had no idea where to start in finding out if this killer was actually a vampire. Well, according to Marrs, the slayings had been two weeks apart, and it had only been five days since the last one. So maybe Drac Junior would hold off for another nine days, in which case, Laura's desertion wouldn't be such a big deal.

But would she? Despite the fact that Marrs labeled her an expert, she knew nothing about vampires, really, except that they existed and how to kill them. She supposed this gave her two significant advantages over most people.

She flashed her badge and asked random students if they had seen anything scary, if they felt threatened, if there was anybody acting suspicious. The only thing she was able to conclude from this was that the students in Cambridge University's honors program considered the rest of the campus a bunch of meathead alcoholic date-rapists, and those not in the honors program considered the honors students to be whiny, superior pains in the ass.

This might be interesting from an anthropological standpoint, but it was pretty much a dead end from a vampire-hunting perspective. The sun was sinking in the sky, and short of arming herself and walking around hoping to be vampire bait (and she hadn't been to the motel to check on the stakes yet), Laura felt like there was very little she could possibly do to help.

She trudged up Cambridge's main drag, past the bars and pizza places, and as she approached her rental car, parked outside of the Suds & Suds bar/Laundromat, she saw a familiar face going into Tower of Pizza.

She thought that must be Becky Barnham, the teen star who was always smiling that heavy-lidded drunken smile from the tabloid covers in the supermarket. Did she go to Cambridge University of Ohio? Why hadn't Marrs told her? She remembered the Senator's daughter detail from years ago and thought she might have just come across a crucial lead, though she didn't really understand exactly what it meant. Once before the vampires had been targeting a high-profile young woman, or else had just happened to be in the same place as one. If that wasn't just a coincidence, then maybe they were after Becky Barnham too. She had one more thing to do before she could go look for Ted—she hoped that if Ted were still alive, her delay didn't cost him his life.

She turned and walked into Tower of Pizza, a loud, bright place with red formica booths and fluorescent lights. As she walked over to Becky Barnham's table, two large, burly men in black t-shirts, one white, one black, suddenly appeared in her path.

They didn't speak. They just looked at Laura.

"Okay, fellas, I've got a badge here, which I am going to reach into my bag to ge—" She saw the white guy get kind of twitchy and immediately said, "No no, you know what, here, you reach into my bag and get the ID." She handed the bag to the white guy, leaving the black guy, obviously the calmer one, to look at her. The guy dug Laura's ID out of the bag, showed it to his partner, and then they nodded at Laura.

"Thanks," she said, and walked over to Becky's table.

"Ms. Barnham—Laura Harker, FBI; I wonder if I can ask you a few questions."

Becky Barnham looked up at Laura with annoyance all over her face. "I don't know—can you?"

"Heh-heh. Yeah, look, I'm investigating the murders here, and I'm just—I wonder if you can tell me if you've joined a sorority."

Becky looked at her like she was the single stupidest person on earth. "Bids go out at the end of freshman year," she said. "I couldn't join one yet."

"Okay, great. Uh, are you expecting any bids?"

Becky gave Laura a long look that communicated clearly that she had thought it was impossible for Laura to get any stupider, but she'd just proved her wrong. "Uh, yeah? Like twenty?"

"Okay—is anybody—I mean, I understand that you're being recruited pretty aggressively, but is there anybody that you think is going to extraordinary lengths to recruit you?"

Becky took a bite of pizza, chewed, and looked at Laura. "I mean, not to be too conceited, but I am famous. They all want me. But I guess maybe the Omegas want me even more than the other ones."

Laura's heart jumped. It couldn't be—could it? Even if the

same person, or vampire, or whatever were masterminding things, they would have chosen a different sorority this time—wouldn't they?

"Okay—just one more question, and then I'll get out of your substantial hair." Becky looked at Laura blankly, and Laura was glad to see that Becky was, in fact, too stupid to know she was being made fun of. "Have you been to any afternoon teas at the Omega house? Or pancake breakfasts for charity? Anything at all that's taken place during the day?"

Becky bit a slice of pizza and chewed. "Not that I can remember. But, I mean, I don't really like to go to the daytime events anyway—it's like a lot easier for people to get pictures of me from far away during the day. You know?"

"Not a phenomenon I'm personally familiar with, but I do understand what you mean. Well, thanks for your time!" Laura extended a hand, and Becky just looked at it like it might have just been used to pick up feces, and Laura walked away.

"Nice kid," she said to the bodyguards as she passed their booth, "real sweetheart."

The black guy shook his head just slightly and said under his breath, "You should see her when she's mad."

"I hope to never have to see her again," Laura said, and kept walking.

Behind her, she heard the white guy squeak out, "Take us with you!" in a falsetto.

The sun was beginning to set. Laura had basically no evidence, but she was sure in her heart that the Omega house was a vampire's nest. She called Marrs, who told her to wait until daylight and then get into the house and look around.

If she was right, she could just open up some shades and dispose of them all without the stakes, and if she was wrong, well, hopefully she wouldn't get caught, and if she did, he'd have very little difficulty getting her out of a breaking-and-entering charge.

So tomorrow was her day for vampire slaying. Fantastic. Ted went in at night, armed only with a can of gas, a Zippo, and an axe, Laura's mind reminded herself, and she considered again the incredible courage he'd shown. Well, it was time for Laura to show some courage herself. She was going to get Ted back dead or alive, or die trying.

As she drove to Cincinnati from Cambridge, Laura wondered if she were doing the right thing. She knew what Marrs would say about putting the population at risk, about how her responsibility to the public had to outweigh her loyalty to Ted.

Except it didn't. Laura didn't know if there was a God—it seemed kind of hard to believe, given all the evil shit that seemed to be wandering the earth. But, then again, maybe things did happen for a reason. Though it might have cost him his life, would anybody but Ted have been able to crack the whole Cthulhu Cult thing? Would anyone else have been able to stop it? So maybe God, or whoever, had put Ted in the path of the Queequeg's shooter. In which case She would understand that Laura owed it to him to get him back. And if She did exist, and She was working in the world, would She let Cincinnati be destroyed because of Laura's love for her friend? Well, then, She was probably just looking for an excuse to wreak destruction anyway, and if Laura didn't open the door, She would probably find some other way to destroy the Earth.

Laura decided she needed to find a place of power. The

cultists had had twelve chanters trying to open a Cthulhu-sized hole—she hoped she could open a Laura-sized hole by herself, or maybe with somebody's help. She called Elaine on her cell phone. After some nice preliminaries, Laura said, "Uh, I have something really strange to ask you."

"Oh my God," Elaine said, "please tell me this isn't the 'I'm straight but curious' conversation. I've really done that enough."

"No, I'm not—I mean, I am curious, but not straight—I mean, I'm curious about—anyway, no, I mean, you've been to Cincinnati before, right?"

"This is my third trip."

"So what are the big important places? I mean, places where there are important buildings, places where people congregate, stuff like that."

"Well, there are the stadiums down by the river, and there's a big park there too...." Water. Was that important for a place of power? She couldn't remember what those new agey websites had said about that. "Let me see... I mean, I really don't know much outside of downtown... there's the fountain right outside the hotel here. It's kind of like the center of downtown. I guess they have like lunchtime concerts there and stuff. People eat lunch there in the daytime."

Laura wondered—riverfront or fountain? Well, there was water in both places, and if the fountain was the center of downtown, it might be a place of power. Well, she could always try the riverfront if the fountain didn't work. "Okay. I'll try the fountain. Where is it?"

"Fifth Street, between Walnut and Race."

"Great. Can you meet me there in half an hour?"

"Uh... I suppose so. Why?"

"I—I really have to—I can tell you in person."

"Okayyyyy. See you then, I guess."

"Thanks!"

Well. So now Laura was throwing her trust at some random woman, just like Ted would've done. It wasn't really her, but she needed an assistant, and Elaine was pretty much her only choice. It wasn't like she could call Marrs for backup on this one.

Once she reached Downtown Cincinnati, Laura parked in a public garage and booted up her laptop. She played the video of Ted's Last Stand again, listening closely to the audio. She tried to block out the sound of Ted screaming and just focus on what the cultists were chanting. She played it through three times until she was sure she had it. She wrote a phonetic transcription of the incantation on her arm in permanent marker. She was pretty sure she remembered it, but she had no idea what a trip through a rip in space-time might do to her memory.

Even still, the incantation might not work from the other side. It might be Earth-specific. In which case, assuming they were even alive, she'd be stuck there with Ted and his girlfriend forever, which sounded kind of suspiciously like something Jean-Paul Sartre would have dreamed up. From the unspeakable horror of the Old Ones to the nauseating horror of the meaninglessness of existence in one short trip! Or would it be a short trip? Laura found she was as nervous as she had ever been. It occurred to her that she might just die. It would be safer, and better, and more practical for her to stay alive and kill vampires and hunt down evil and mourn the death of her friend. Unless, of course, he wasn't dead, in which case she'd never really sleep again, wondering if she could have done more. No. The hell with it. She was going to do the best she could. And maybe if there was a God watching over everything, She would help Laura find her friend.

She walked to Fountain Square and wondered if she would find Elaine there. She put her chances at about fifty-fifty. Why was she even doing this? She didn't really need any help, did she? But then, if Elaine did help, and Laura ever made it back, Elaine would have to believe, and then… Well, that was a stupid way to think about somebody you talked to for an hour on an airplane.

The fountain was a large, greenish sculpture with what looked like a woman on top with water pouring out of the downward-facing palms of her hands. Spotlights illuminated other figures with water pouring over them, and there, standing in front of the fountain, was Elaine.

"Hi! Thank you so much for showing up! I really had no idea if you would or not!"

"Yeah," Elaine smiled. "It was about fifty-fifty, but I've already seen everything on HBO tonight, and I figured if you turn out not to be completely insane, you might be like spontaneous and fun or something."

Laura couldn't help laughing. She looked back on her entire life and wondered if anyone had ever considered her spontaneous or fun. Maybe before the fire, a little bit, but that was a different person, a different life. Well, maybe this was too.

"Well, what I'm going to say here is not really going to convince you that I'm not nuts. I'm going to stand here and say some strange words, and if you could say them along with me, that would probably help. I'm also going to be playing a video of people chanting the same thing. If all goes well, I'm going to… okay, here's where you write me off as a complete nut, but anyway, if all goes well, I'm going to disappear."

She could read the "Oh, shit, she really is a whack job" look on Elaine's face and just hoped she could get her to play along.

"I know, I know how insane that sounds, especially because I mean really disappear, not in a like David Copperfield way. Anyway, in the event that something goes wrong, I'm gonna need you to just take my phone and press and hold the one button. A guy will answer, and if you just tell him what's happened, he'll hopefully fix it. Also, I've downloaded a worm that's going to wipe my hard drive about five minutes after I leave. If you can just double check and make sure that happens, I'd really appreciate it."

"Uh, okay, sure…." *You complete freakin' psycho* was left unsaid, but it was fairly clear.

"Okay… Ah, you're not gonna do the chant with me, are you?"

"I don't really see that happening."

"Okay then." Laura's heart was pounding. Thoughts were trying to bubble up from somewhere deep in her brain. Is this the last thing I'll ever see? If I die, will this be enough to redeem my betrayal of Ted? What about all the people….

With great effort, Laura silenced all her fears, all her regrets. She was not going to die. She was just going to do a quick disappearing act, and then she'd be right back after these messages. Right. It crossed her mind to give Elaine a quick kiss, but this would almost certainly send her running back to the Westin, and she really did hope Elaine would be able to call Marrs and fix things if she accidentally opened a Cthulhu-sized hole in space and time and caused the return of the Old Ones. Well, he had the book, right?

Instead of a kiss, she said, "You really seem like something special, and I hope we can get to know each other better when I get back."

Elaine said nothing. Laura handed her the cell phone and turned away. She put the volume up as high as it would go on her pathetic, tinny little speakers and started the video. Along with the cultists, she chanted, *"Yog-Sothoth, flshrauv, Yog-Sothoth, sil'iah, menduru, Yog-sothoth, r'laugggggg... Yog-Sothoth, R'lyeh mesha'al... Cthulhu."*

Nothing happened. On the video, a rift was opening. Maybe Laura had been wrong—maybe this wasn't a place of power, or maybe one person chanting wouldn't get it. The cultists restarted their chant, now interrupted by the occasional scream as shoppers noticed the rift or Ted and Cayenne taking cultists down.

Laura was disappointed, but at least now she could tell herself that she'd done the most she could do, and she'd obviously messed up her chances with Elaine, but she'd done right by Ted at least. Nobody could say she hadn't done everything she could have possibly done for him; she'd disobeyed orders, put a mid-sized city at risk, she'd made an attractive stranger think she was nuts—now she could sleep easy and...

Five feet in front of her, something glowed with a sickly greenish-yellow light. As Laura watched, the rift opened. It grew to about the size of a ten-year-old child, then stabilized. All of Laura's relief drained away and was replaced by panic. She forced herself to walk forward and tossed this in Elaine's direction: "It's just never easy to do the right thing, is it?" she said.

"Uh, I guess not," a stunned Elaine said quietly. Without looking back, Laura stepped into the rift.

TWENTY-ONE

Ted and Cayenne had disentangled, and they had been lying in place for several years. They'd talked about being bored, they'd exchanged detailed life stories, and Ted was contemplating whether it was time for sex again when he heard a sound.

It sounded like vomiting. He sat up and looked at Cayenne, who was sitting up and looking at him.

"Who's puking?"

"I don't know. Cthulhu?"

Ted pondered this for a moment. "I think… It sounds too small to be Cthulhu."

"Where's it coming from?"

"Aw, who the hell can tell. Let's go outside, or maybe inside, up, down, whatever, let's walk!" Ted heard the inappropriate enthusiasm in his voice. Something was happening! It might well be something bad—but there was such a flood of relief in Ted's guts that he didn't even care. He wanted back on the wheel, and if things were changing, the wheel was turning, and maybe, after all these centuries, he could get back on.

"Hold my hand," Cayenne said. "I don't want to lose you again." Ted grabbed her hand. The thought of being all alone, of never finding Cayenne again, of spending decades more walking through the streets, canals, skyways, or possibly sewers of R'lyeh looking for her was too awful to contemplate.

Hand in hand, Ted and Cayenne strode through the doorway. Whatever it was, it had to be close, because although it sounded faint, they simply wouldn't have heard anything at all if it had been far away. But he saw nothing.

They heard another retch, and then sobbing. Ted looked up, or, anyway, in a direction other than straight ahead, and saw her. Laura was hunched over in a pool of vomit, crying.

Without thinking, Ted ran down the wall, or up the ceiling, dragging Cayenne with him. "Laura!" he called. "Laura! What are you doing here?"

Laura raised her head. Her eyes were red and puffy, and there was puke in the ends of her hair. "Ted!" she screamed. She rose to her feet and ran to him. Ted dropped Cayenne's hand and hugged Laura as hard as he could.

"Oh my God, Ted, it was so awful, so fucking awful, everything was lost, everything was useless, everything… Oh, God, I thought it would never end, it… oh, God, it made me insane!" and she cried and cried, and Ted held her, and he felt good about being able to comfort her for a change.

"Oh, God, Ted, I'm sorry I was such a bitch, I'm sorry, I…"

"Shh. That was at least two lifetimes ago for me. I'm not mad. I'm sorry too."

Laura looked over Ted's shoulder and said, "Oh! Hi there!" to the naked Cayenne. "Wow, I didn't know you could pierce that!"

"Hey." Cayenne answered. She sounded pissed. Well, Ted had told her Laura was a lesbian, but he guessed if Cayenne had just dropped his hand like a hot potato and run naked to embrace her gay male friend, he might be feeling a twinge of jealousy. He pulled away from Laura.

"Jesus! You're naked!" Laura said.

Ted's chest felt wet and cold. "And you're covered in puke." He said.

All three of them looked at each other for a minute.

"Well," Laura said. "This looks like a charming little love nest, but what do you say we get out of here?"

"Oh my God, really?" Cayenne said. Ted saw the tears in her eyes and felt the tears in his own. It was really way too good to be true.

Laura was rolling up her sleeve, and there was writing on her arm.

"Cheater!" Ted couldn't help saying. "You'll get a zero on the exam, Ms. Harker."

"Ted, shut up. You guys ready? We have to read this a couple times through, and hopefully it'll take us back. And if not... well, we're fucked." She paused. "Or at least you guys are. Ready? One... two..."

Ted started, with "Cthulhu," while Laura said, "three."

Laura and Cayenne looked annoyed at him. "You didn't let me get to three, Ted."

"I thought it would be *on* three, like one, two, Cthulhu, not one, two, three, Cthulhu."

"Jesus!" Cayenne said. "It's one, two, three, Cthulhu, okay?"

"Okay, okay." Once again Laura counted, and this time the three of them began the chant. They chanted through once, twice, three times, four times. It wasn't working. Nothing was happening. Except then the ground beneath, or possibly above them, began to shake.

"It's not working!" Laura said. She sounded panicked.

"We're going to be stuck here!"

Suddenly Ted had a brainstorm. "Wait! I've got it! We're saying the chant with R'lyeh in it!"

Laura looked at him like he was a complete idiot. "Well, that's the chant, Ted."

"No! We're *in* R'lyeh! That must be the chant to get here! Maybe we just have to say Providence instead of R'lyeh to get to Providence!"

Laura looked at him. "Well, it's worth a try. But it's not Providence. It's Cincinnati."

"Cincinnati? Why?"

Cayenne interrupted. "Who gives a shit? Can we just get out of here?"

Ted looked around. Behind them, buildings, or whatever those forms were, appeared to be collapsing. And then they heard it.

It was the loudest thing Ted had ever heard. This was saying something, given the sound-deadening qualities of this place. The closest Ted could come to describing it was a roar, but it was a roar like a tornado was a breeze. And suddenly, Ted felt something he hadn't felt in a long time. He was afraid.

"Oh shit, " Cayenne said. "He's awake."

"What?" Laura said. She looked scared.

"Cthulhu," Ted said. "He sounds pissed. We must have woken him up."

"What the hell are we going to do?" Cayenne yelled.

"Keep chanting," Laura said. "On three!" She looked at Ted.

Ted, Cayenne, and Laura chanted, making sure to substitute "Cincinnati" for "R'lyeh". Ted didn't see a rift, but it looked like the air in front of them might be shimmering a little bit. He was finding it hard to stand up because whatever was under him was shaking so hard. They said the chant again, and again, and the roaring continued, and Cthulhu must have exhaled, or farted, or something, because if it was at all possible, it suddenly smelled worse here than it ever had. Everything was swimming in front of Ted's eyes, but he didn't know if that was because they were rending reality or just because Cthulhu's breath had that effect.

Ted felt his stomach clenching, felt the bile rising, and knew he was not going to be able to hold it for very long. Cayenne and Laura looked similarly green. "Cthulhu!" Ted shouted, and projectile vomited. He saw puke shooting out of Laura's and Cayenne's mouths at the same time, and the noise was splitting his head wide open, or that's how it felt, and he looked back and saw Cthulhu rising up over, under, between, and around the structures of R'lyeh, and he knew he was going to die, the noise and the stench, the wrongness of the place had just increased to mind-destroying levels, and his brain was going to liquefy in his skull and leak out his ears and that would be the end of him, he was sure of it, and it seemed to be happening already.

He looked back at Laura and Cayenne, hoping he could say something before they all died, hoping he could tell them something about how much he loved them both, how they had made his twenty-nine years on earth and four score and twenty or whatever in R'lyeh worth living, how—and then he saw the rift.

Laura was pointing, and Ted saw it—a doorway-sized rift. Hands clasped tight, the three of them jumped headlong into the rift.

A microsecond later, Ted was face-down on flagstones again, still puking. But it was quiet, at least. Ted figured that it was because his eardrums had been destroyed.

But then sounds started to leak in. A waterfall? A honking car horn? A female voice yelling, "Holy shit, holy shit, you really did it! That's completely impossible!"

Ted looked up briefly and saw Laura and Cayenne, and there was some tall lady standing over them. He had enough time to smile at Laura and Cayenne. "Thank you!" he shouted at Laura. "Thank you!"

Cayenne was grinning and saying, "We did it! We did it!" and Laura was laughing—a deep, hearty laugh that was a happier sound than anything he'd heard out of her mouth in a long time.

The lady was still screaming, and Ted started to laugh. "I love you!" he shouted at Laura and Cayenne and Cincinnati and the screaming lady. "I love you!"

And suddenly, Ted's head felt far too heavy to hold up. He set it gently onto the cool flagstones, and, for the first time in at least a century, he slept.

EPILOGUE

L aura stood on the front porch. It felt good to be outside in the warm spring sunshine after five days inside the Westin. The doctor told them their eardrums would heal in a couple of weeks, though they might have permanent hearing loss of between five and twenty percent. Laura had actually been glad for her near-total deafness as Marrs read her the riot act about her irresponsibility, how she had put over three hundred thousand residents of Cincinnati, not to mention hundreds of thousands more in the metro area, at risk, blah blah blah. He had gone on at length about how, in the good old days, when he had the resources, he would have simply had her taken out, but now he didn't have the wherewithal to dispose of her body, and anyway she was obviously a talented agent, and he still needed her, so she was lucky, but she still had a job.

Elaine had flown back to Boston. Laura had her phone number. She had no idea if the fact that Elaine had witnessed something so bizarre would make them bonded forever or just make Elaine want to avoid her forever. Ted told her she couldn't call until they got back to Boston. Easy for him to say—he had Cayenne waiting back at the Westin, probably sitting next to Marrs with a new laptop, searching cyberspace

233

for supernatural fires for them to put out.

She looked over at Ted, standing beside her on the porch, and felt a surge of affection. He looked completely ridiculous, but happier and healthier than she could remember seeing him in ten years. He was wearing steel-toed boots and criss-crossed ammunition belts holding rows of wooden stakes and vials of holy water.

She really hadn't expected him to take Marrs up on his employment offer. She thought he'd say he'd done his part, he was done for life, and now he was going to settle down and live the boring, normal life he'd always pined for. But when she talked it over with him, she found that, deep down, he wasn't all that interested in a normal life. "I know too much for that," he'd said. "I couldn't… now that I know this stuff is out there, I can't just go get a house in the suburbs and sit on my hands and let somebody else take care of it. I mean, I really couldn't stand that."

So, after thinking it over for a day, Ted had told Marrs that fighting supernatural threats to homeland security was the only thing he'd ever really been good at, except for making lattes, and that, based on his experience, both careers were fairly equal in terms of the danger he would be exposed to, so he'd like to keep saving the world.

Back on the porch, Ted was nervously flicking the Zippo, with the engraved portrait of Elvis on the side, in his left hand and looking at Laura, waiting for the okay. Laura felt the stakes strapped to her sides, unstoppered the sport bottle of holy water in her left hand, and felt the reassuring weight of the gigantic silver cross on her chest.

"On three," she said to Ted, probably too loudly.

"Does that mean on three, or one, two, three, Cthulhu?" Ted asked, smiling.

Laura smiled. "One, two, three, Cthulhu," she said.

"Got it," Ted said.

Laura felt the adrenaline tide come in. Her heart pounded, and she felt like a coiled spring. "One… two… three…"

"Cthulhu!" Ted yelled. He raised his steel-toed boot and kicked hard. The door of the Omega house cracked and splintered, and Laura and Ted ran inside.

BEYOND GOOD... BEYOND EVIL... LIGHTBREAKER.

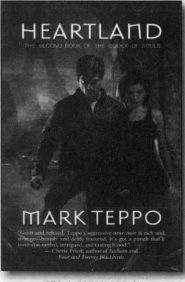

978-1-59780-138-6
Mass Market / $7.99

978-1-59780-155-3
Mass Market / $7.99

Markham has returned to Seattle, searching for Katarina, the girl who, a decade ago, touched his soul, literally tearing it from his body. But what he discovers upon arriving is dark magick... of a most ancient and destructive kind.

An encounter with a desperate spirit, leaping destructively from host to host, sets Markham on the trail of secretive cabal of magicians seeking to punch a hole through heaven, extinguishing forever the divine spark. Armed with the Chorus, a phantasmal chain of human souls he wields as a weapon of will, Markham must engage in a magickal battle with earth-shattering stakes.

Markham must delve deep into his past, calling on every aspect of his occult training for there to be any hope of a future. But delve he must, for Markham is a veneficus, a spirit thief, the Lightbreaker...

From newcomer Mark Teppo comes Lightbreaker, an explosive, action-packed occult thriller combining Western magick, Hermetic traditions, and shamanism.

And Don't Miss The Second Book of the Codex of Souls, *Heartland*, coming soon.

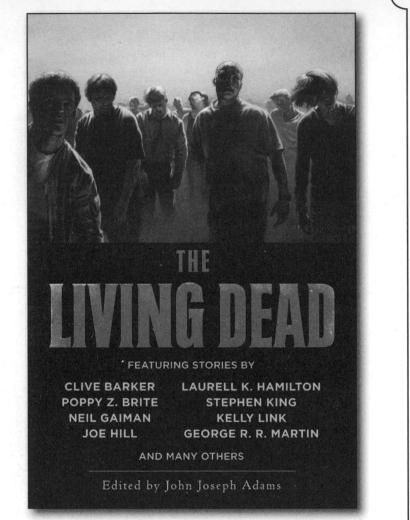

THE
LIVING DEAD

FEATURING STORIES BY

CLIVE BARKER   LAURELL K. HAMILTON
POPPY Z. BRITE   STEPHEN KING
NEIL GAIMAN   KELLY LINK
JOE HILL   GEORGE R. R. MARTIN

AND MANY OTHERS

Edited by John Joseph Adams

ISBN 978-1-59780-143-0 , Trade Paperback; $15.95

"When there's no more room in hell, the dead will walk the earth."
From *White Zombie* to *Dawn of the Dead*; from *Resident Evil* to *World War Z*, zombies have invaded popular culture, becoming the monsters that best express the fears and anxieties of the modern west. The ultimate consumers, zombies rise from the dead and feed upon the living, their teeming masses ever hungry, ever seeking to devour or convert, like mindless, faceless eating machines. Zombies have been depicted as mind-controlled minions, the shambling infected, the disintegrating dead, the ultimate lumpenproletariat, but in all cases, they reflect us, mere mortals afraid of death in a society on the verge of collapse.

Find this and other Night Shade titles online at
http://www.nightshadebooks.com or wherever books are sold.

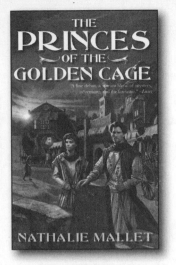
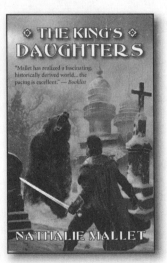

Follow the Continuing Adventures of Inspector Chen, Singapore Three's Premier Supernatural Investigator

978-1-59780-107-2
Mass Market / $7.99

John Constantine meets Chow Yun-Fat in *Snake Agent*, a near-future occult thriller. Detective Inspector Chen is the Singapore Three police department's snake agent – that is – the detective in charge of supernatural and mystical investigations.

Chen has several problems: In addition to colleagues who don't trust him and his mystical ways, a patron goddess whom he has offended, and a demonic wife who's tired of staying home alone, he's been paired with one of Hell's own vice officers, Seneschal Zhu Irzh, to investigate the illegal trade in souls.

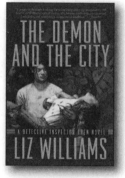

978-1-59780-111-9
Mass Market / $7.99

In *The Demon and the City*, when Detective Inspector Chen leaves Singapore Three on long-deserved vacation, Hell's vice-deceive-on-loan, Zhu Irzh finds himself restless and bored. An investigating into the brutal, and seemingly-demonic murder of a beautiful young woman promises to be an interesting distraction.

The trail leads to one of Sigapore Three's most powerful industrialists, Jhai Tserai, the ruthless heiress of the Paugeng Corporation. While Zhu Irzh isn't normally attracted to human woman, Jah Tserai seems to have an unnatural effect on Zhu Irzh's natural appetites. Inspector Chen returns to Singapore Three to find Zhu Irzh's erratic behavior has placed the demon under suspicion. Tensions flair and the entire city find's itself under siege from otherworldly forces both Heavenly and Hellish in nature.

978-1-59780-084-6
Mass Market / $7.99

In *Precious Dragon*, Chen and Zhu Irzh are assigned as diplomatic escorts for an angelic emissary to hell, just as the endless cold war between opposing realms starts to get hot. A mysterious young boy born in hell but raised on earth seems to be at the center of it all.

Find these Night Shade titles and many others online at http://www.nightshadebooks.com or wherever books are sold.

Seamus Cooper's work in a major coffee/lifestyle chain leaves him plenty of time to pursue his occult research and occasional forays into fiction. Lacking both the charisma and the multiple wives necessary to be the charismatic founder of a polygamist cult, Seamus lives alone. His home in Providence, Rhode Island is a stone's throw from the H.P. Lovecraft house, provided the stone is thrown by someone (or something) possessed of superhuman strength.